THE DISTANCE
FROM ME
TO YOU

THE DISTANCE FROM ME TO YOU

Marina Gessner

G. P. Putnam's Sons
An Imprint of Penguin Group (USA)

G. P. PUTNAM'S SONS
Published by the Penguin Group
Penguin Group (USA) LLC
375 Hudson Street
New York, NY 10014

USA | Canada | UK | Ireland | Australia
New Zealand | India | South Africa | China
penguin.com
A Penguin Random House Company

Library of Congress Cataloging-in-Publication Data is available upon request.

Printed in the United States of America.
ISBN 978-0-399-17323-3
1 3 5 7 9 10 8 6 4 2

Design by Annie Ericsson.
Text set in Maxime Std.

For Athena Woodward

*May your trails be crooked, winding, lonesome,
dangerous, leading to the most amazing view.*

May your mountains rise into and above the clouds.

—Edward Abbey

1

McKenna couldn't believe it. Maybe her ears were malfunctioning. Or her brain was playing tricks on her. Either option—deafness or insanity—seemed better than believing the words coming out of her best friend's mouth.

"I'm sorry," Courtney said. She started to cry and put her head down on the table.

McKenna knew this was the moment to reach over and pat Courtney's head, say something comforting. But she couldn't. Not yet. Because not only was Courtney getting back together with *Jay*, she was also backing out of their trip.

McKenna and Courtney had been planning this trip for over a year—a two-thousand-mile hike down the Appalachian Trail—and they were supposed to leave in less than a week. They'd deferred their college acceptances. They'd spent their life savings on camping gear and trail guides—McKenna had, anyway; Courtney's father had footed the bill for hers. Hardest of all, they'd talked their parents into agreeing to the plan: two girls hiking the entire length of the Appalachian Trail, from Maine to Georgia.

And now Courtney was changing her mind. For the lamest possible reason: a guy. And not just any guy, but a guy they'd spent the last four months ripping to shreds. Honestly, McKenna was so sick of talking about him, she could barely get his name out.

All around them, the Whitworth College Student Union buzzed with conversations and clanking silverware. McKenna's parents were both professors here, and she had been eating lunch in this cafeteria since before she could remember, the surrounding tables as familiar as her own living room. It was a bright day in early June, sunlight pouring in through the atrium windows, and McKenna knew that Courtney *must* feel the same urge she did, to get away from the places they'd seen a million times, to go out in the world and live under that sun.

"But Courtney," McKenna said, keeping both hands firmly in her lap. *"Jay?"*

"I know," Courtney mumbled, her face still buried in her arms.

This trip, this plan, had been McKenna's dream for as long as she could remember. And now, so close to when they should have been leaving, Courtney was bringing the whole thing crashing down.

"Courtney," McKenna said again. Even if it weren't for the hike, this would be terrible news. She couldn't stand the thought of Jay breaking her friend's heart. Again.

"Don't say it," Courtney said, finally sitting up. "I know, I know all of it. And I forgive him. I love him, McKenna."

What could McKenna say to that?

"I'm sorry," Courtney said again, her voice calmer after the declaration of love. "I know how much you wanted to do this."

"I thought you wanted to do it, too."

"I do. I mean I did. But it's just too long to be away from him right now. You know?"

McKenna didn't know, not at all. Even with her eyes red and her face puffy, Courtney looked beautiful. She was the last person who needed to change her life for a guy, let alone *Jay*. Courtney had shiny blond hair that McKenna—being the only brunette in her family—envied. Both girls were on the track team, but Courtney was the star, running the mile in under six minutes. Both girls took riding lessons, but Courtney was the one who usually won ribbons when they showed. Most important, Courtney was a loyal friend. In other words, she was worth a thousand Jays, ten thousand Jays, a million.

"Courtney," McKenna said, fighting to keep her voice steady. "Jay will still be here when we get back. You can text or call him from the trail, send him postcards. It's only a few months."

"Not a few. Five months, maybe even six. Things are fragile right now, McKenna, we're only just back together. I can't march off into the woods and leave him. Not right now." She sounded like she'd practiced her argument, as if she'd anticipated everything McKenna would say.

Because he'd probably spend the whole six months hooking up with other girls, McKenna thought.

"You'll be leaving him if you go to Wesleyan," McKenna

3

pointed out. Jay was going to Whitworth, here in Abelard, the most boring and predictable of all choices. What was the point of even going to college if you weren't going to leave your hometown?

"Wesleyan is barely an hour away," Courtney said. "And anyway, I'm not going till next year. I deferred, remember?"

"You deferred to go on our trip," McKenna said, finally letting herself sound as petulant as she felt. "Not to date Jay."

"I know," Courtney admitted.

"Well, what are you going to do next year, then? Bag your first-choice college for a guy? Stay here and go to *Whitworth*?" McKenna glanced around the Student Union meaningfully. Going to Whitworth would be like going to college in her own house.

"Jay is not just 'a guy.' And a camping trip isn't college, either."

"A *camping trip*?" How could she reduce their plan to those two words, make them sound so trivial? McKenna drew in a strengthening breath and said, "Maybe being apart will make your relationship stronger. Like with Brendan and me . . ."

"You can't compare you and Brendan to me and Jay."

Well, *that* was true. Brendan would never cheat on McKenna. He just wasn't that kind of person, not a player, but sweet and honest and serious. They'd been together three months, and Brendan was headed to Harvard in the fall. Would McKenna ever try to stop him from going to the school of his dreams so they could be together? Of course not—not any more than he would stop her from hiking the Appalachian Trail. They had a mature relationship and they supported each other. McKenna said as much to Courtney, who rolled her eyes.

"McKenna," Courtney said, "you guys are about as romantic as a trail map."

McKenna ripped her chopsticks apart with a splintery crinkle. Their sushi sat untouched between them. McKenna poked at the spicy tuna roll but didn't pick it up. If romance meant giving up your dreams for some undeserving guy, Courtney was welcome to it.

"There are different ways to be romantic," McKenna countered. "Maybe to you romance is a candlelight dinner. But to me—" She broke off, afraid she might cry if she said it aloud.

To McKenna, romance was a night under the stars. She didn't need a boyfriend with her to make it romantic. She just needed clean air, the scent of pine. No sounds except crickets and spring peepers and the wind in the trees.

Courtney reached out and touched McKenna's hand. "I know how much this trip meant to you," she said. "And I'm sorry. I don't know how many times I can say it to make you understand that I really am."

A hundred arguments still swirled in McKenna's head. Forget Jay. She could remind Courtney of the forms for the two-thousand-miler certificate they'd pinned on their bulletin boards next to their badges from Ridgefield Prep hiking club. They'd also ordered AT Passports—green booklets to have stamped at hostels and landmarks along the way to document their journey. They'd planned their itinerary so they could bring Norton, Courtney's huge, snarly shepherd mix, tracking all the campgrounds that allowed dogs. They'd spent hours poring over maps and guidebooks. They'd climbed Bear Mountain with full packs, training with heavy weight on their backs. They were ready to go.

But instead of reminding Courtney of all this, McKenna kept quiet, because something in Courtney's voice was telling her that no matter how she begged, the answer would be the same.

"Well," McKenna said, finally popping the spicy tuna into her mouth, "if you can't come, I'll just go by myself."

Courtney's eyes widened. Then she laughed.

"No, really," McKenna said. She sat up a little straighter. Saying it again would strengthen her resolve. "I'll go by myself."

"You can't spend six months in the woods by yourself," Courtney said.

"Why not?"

Six months in the woods by herself. A minute ago, McKenna had felt deflated. Now, under every inch of her skin, excitement was gathering, tingling.

"Well," Courtney said, "it's not safe, for one thing."

"I'm not going on this trip to be *safe.*"

She bit off the last word with distaste. *Safe* was doing what was expected of you. *Safe* was following the rules, getting good grades, going to college. *Safe*, in other words, was everything McKenna had done every minute of her whole entire life.

"Seriously, McKenna," Courtney said, her face scrunching into worry. "You can't do it alone."

Of course Courtney didn't think she should do it alone—nobody would. But the images were already forming in McKenna's mind: all those miles of fabulous solitude, her body getting stronger, her mind growing wider. In preparation for this hike she'd read a mountain of books—wilderness guides, memoirs, novels. One of her favorites was by a woman who'd hiked the Pacific Crest Trail alone without even a debit card, and before iPhones and GPS. If she could do it, why not McKenna?

"Your parents will never let you," Courtney pointed out.

McKenna threw down her chopsticks. "That's why we're not going to tell them," she said.

Crossing the campus quad, McKenna bounced in her hiking boots, which she wore even though everyone around her was in flip-flops and canvas sneakers. She had worn her boots every day for two months, determined that they be perfectly broken in by the time she hit the trail. She was so used to the heavy shoes that she had no problem jumping out of the way as a skateboarder nearly crashed into the student beside her, his nose buried in his phone. McKenna rolled her eyes. On this perfect day, the breeze tinged with the scent of honeysuckle, the sun shining steadily, almost every single student walked across campus with eyes glued to a phone.

At home, McKenna's stack of trail reading material was

heavily populated by Thoreau, and she thought of one of her favorite quotes. In fact she'd used it as the epigraph to her college entrance essay: *We must learn to reawaken and keep ourselves awake, not by mechanical aids, but by an infinite expectation of the dawn, which does not forsake us in our soundest sleep.*

Every day, McKenna saw people who'd given up real life for Instagram and Facebook. If she had her way, she wouldn't be bringing her phone at all. Now that she was going alone, though, she knew it would be crazy to give up that lifeline. But McKenna was determined to keep it in her pack and only use it in case of emergency. She wouldn't talk or text, not to her parents or Brendan or even her little sister, Lucy.

That would be harder, of course, now that she was going to be on her own.

On her own. She knew the phrase should scare her, but instead it brought on a smile. After finally convincing Courtney that her mind was made up, they had worked out the details of their ruse. For one thing, Whitworth would be off-limits, Courtney could *not* risk running into McKenna's parents while she was supposed to be on the trail. Courtney offered Norton, but McKenna decided against it. She wanted as few reasons as possible for Courtney's parents to try to get in touch with hers. Everything had to look like it was going according to their original plan, the one McKenna's parents had agreed to, albeit reluctantly.

She unlocked the car door with an electronic *beep.* Soon

her life would be gloriously free from such noises, nothing but birds and bugs and rustling leaves.

It couldn't come soon enough.

Her boyfriend, Brendan, was only slightly more enthusiastic about the solo plan than her parents would have been.

"It's not like some amusement park where all the danger is pretend," Brendan said. "It's the wilderness. With bears and bobcats. And guys named Cletus who keep stills in the woods."

"Lions and tigers and bears, oh my," McKenna said.

They were driving to the movies after burgers at the Abelard Diner. In this last week of civilization, McKenna was determined to indulge as much as possible—hot baths, TV binge-watching, and especially food. Despite the huge meal, she fully intended to get a tub of popcorn, dripping with fake butter.

"I'm serious, McKenna," he said.

Even in the darkish car, she could tell his face looked very concerned. Brendan was not an obviously handsome guy, like Jay. He wasn't much taller than McKenna, with unruly dark hair. But McKenna loved his face, which was brown-eyed and dimpled and crazy intelligent. Brendan was very practical. One of only two Ridgefield Prep graduates to get into Harvard this year, he had his whole future mapped out. Harvard undergrad to Harvard Law School to lobbying in Washington, DC, to eventually starting his own firm. No doubt there was a wife and 2.3 children somewhere in those plans, but he and

McKenna had never talked about that. He wasn't the kind of guy to marry his high school girlfriend. *Practical.*

Now, as Brendan listed reasons why she shouldn't go on the hike alone, McKenna reminded herself that he was only being discouraging because he cared about her.

"It's called the *wild* for a reason," he said. "There aren't any safety nets. It's not a joke. There are a thousand ways a person could die out there."

"Not a person who knows what she's doing," McKenna said.

"Accidents happen all the time. I'm not saying you're not prepared, but especially for a girl—"

"Why 'especially for a girl'?" Nothing he said could have made her more determined to go ahead with her plan. Brendan should've known better. His mom had raised him on her own, and was also one of the best surgeons in Connecticut.

"McKenna," he said, his eyes barely flitting away from the road. "I don't think you need me to spell it out for you."

"Look," she said. "It's not like college is the safest place in the world. Statistically, I'll be safer on the trail than I would be at Reed. No cars. No keg parties. No date-raping college boys."

They passed under a streetlight, and McKenna could see he was frowning.

"I'm a smart person," she went on. "I'm not going to take unnecessary risks. I'm going to camp in designated spots, stay on the trail. I won't camp within a mile of any road crossings. I know what I'm doing, Brendan."

Brendan reached out and took her hand. "I wish you'd let

me call you, though," he said. "It's going to be so weird, not talking to you."

"Just think how happy you'll be to see me at Christmas break," McKenna said, "when all that absence has made your heart grow fonder." He looked dubious, but McKenna pressed on. "So you'll help? You won't tell my parents?"

"I won't tell your parents," Brendan said. "But that doesn't mean I like this. That doesn't mean I think it's a good idea."

She picked up his hand and kissed it. Maybe he wasn't in total agreement. But she knew he wouldn't do anything to stop her. For now that was all she needed.

The next day, McKenna got home from her last day of work for the summer. For three years, she'd been waiting tables at the Yankee Clipper, a breakfast and lunch place. During the school year she just worked weekends, but summers she worked six days a week, and this summer she worked right up to three days before her big departure. Not many Ridgefield Prep students had a job like this. Most of them had parents who were hotshot lawyers, or hotshot stockbrokers, or hotshot surgeons. The Burneys could afford Ridgefield thanks to Whitworth's tuition reciprocity program. Because Whitworth would pay McKenna's tuition at any participating university, her parents didn't have to save money for college, but could use the money for Ridgefield instead. Not that the Burneys were poor—far from it. Her mother picked up extra money consulting for an architectural firm, her father wrote a blog for a national political magazine

("Just the Facts," by Jerry Burney), and both of them pulled in decent salaries as tenured professors. McKenna knew she was lucky. She didn't envy her classmates, at least not much, for their trips to Europe or their Marc Jacobs handbags. For one thing, she liked working. And material things didn't particularly matter to her. At home, her ancient, thumbed-over copy of *Walden* was underlined and asterisked to the point where the pages were bloated, warped from overuse. Like Thoreau, she knew possessions were only "pretty toys." McKenna was interested in the deeper things life had to offer.

She had been hiking most afternoons to get in shape, and today her dad was going to try to make it home in time to join her. He was her original inspiration for hiking the AT. Her whole life, she'd heard the story of how he and his best friend, Krosky, hiked the Pacific Northwest Trail the summer after they graduated high school. Of course, that was part of the reason he'd agreed to let her go. How could he say no after he'd always told her it was the greatest experience he'd ever had?

"Dad?" McKenna called, opening the front door.

Her sister, Lucy, would be at day camp, but at 3:30 both her parents should be home—one of the perks of their jobs as professors was having summers off. Plenty of time to spend with your eldest child before she embarked on a long journey.

"Mom?" McKenna called, making her way upstairs.

She already knew there wouldn't be a response. Mom was probably at the architectural firm, giving her opinion on the latest blueprints.

Dad probably got held up at his office meeting with an ambitious poli-sci student. Even in summer, he kept office hours, holding court with adoring students, often bringing gaggles of them home for dinner. Sometimes McKenna wished he was still just an assistant professor with plenty of time to go hiking.

McKenna banged into her bedroom and flopped across her bed, staring at the ceiling. She heard a jangling sound and pushed up on one elbow to see Buddy, the family's arthritic chocolate Lab, amble into the room. He walked over to where she was lying, licked her face, and put his two front paws on her bed. These days he could only climb up if McKenna gave him a boost.

"Don't tell anyone," she whispered, "but I'm going to hike the Appalachian Trail all by myself." She stroked his head. "I'm going to miss you, Buddy."

Later that evening after hiking Flat Rock Brook by herself, McKenna found her dad in the kitchen, opening a beer.

"Hey, kiddo," he said. "Back from a hike?"

"Yeah," McKenna said. "Remember you were maybe going to go with me?"

A shadow passed over his face, but he quickly recovered. "Sorry about that," he said. "An incoming grad student came by my office and I couldn't get away."

It annoyed McKenna that he wasn't admitting what she could tell from his face—he had totally forgotten.

"It's okay," she said, pouring herself a glass of ice water.

"I spoke to Al Hill this morning," her dad said. "He's getting his research organized and is really excited that he'll have your help."

As part of the bargaining to go on her hike, McKenna had agreed to work for her father's friend, cataloging his bird research up at Cornell. McKenna's Yankee Clipper money had covered all the gear for her trip. But while out hiking, she'd be using her parents' credit card, and this job would be a way, at least in part, of paying them back. It was also something McKenna was truly excited about, working with one of the top ornithologists in the country.

"Great," McKenna said. "Are you home for dinner tonight?"

"No, your mom and I are having dinner with a new lecturer. You can get something together for you and Lucy, right?"

"You bet," McKenna said, and gave him an encouraging little smile, as if nothing he'd done—or not done—had ever bothered her.

2

The night before McKenna was supposed to leave, Buddy lay on the floor in a forlorn heap. McKenna's bed was covered with everything she planned to pile into her pack, plus Lucy, who sat on the pillows, her scrawny ten-year-old legs crossed as she examined the equipment.

"I don't think it's going to fit," she said.

A couple weeks ago Lucy had chopped off her long white-blond hair, and McKenna was still getting used to it. The cut was shaggy and uneven, which somehow made her look like even more of a wild child than when it hung halfway down her back.

"It'll fit," McKenna called from her bathroom, where she was washing her face. For the next several months it would be nothing but Dr. Bronner's peppermint soap, so she was doing her best to luxuriate in the warm water and take full advantage of the mirror.

Their mom poked her head into the bedroom. "Dad has a couple students coming to dinner," she told them.

"Mom," McKenna objected, coming out of the bathroom, her face still soapy. "It's my last night. I was really hoping it could just be us."

"Sorry, honey, one's a new TA. He's going to be helping out with research and this was the only night we could make it work."

McKenna walked back into the bathroom and splashed her face, giving up her last hopes of having her family to herself for a real good-bye. It was just as well, she thought, grabbing a towel. With guests at the table, there'd be less of a chance for her to let something slip about hiking the trail alone, since there'd be no chance for her to speak at all.

Her mom stood in the bathroom doorway. "I know it's short notice, but do you want to invite Courtney?"

"No," McKenna said. "Her parents are having a special good-bye dinner for her, with her favorite meal. Just the family."

"Well," her mom said, apology creeping into her voice, "I did make enchiladas."

"Thanks, Mom."

After their mom left, Lucy picked up the giant, collapsible water jug. "This is going to take up half your pack when it's full," she said. "How much do you think it'll weigh?"

They filled it to the brim in McKenna's bathroom and saw that Lucy was right. It was so heavy, McKenna could barely haul it out of the sink by its plastic handle.

"I don't think that's going to work," Lucy said.

According to McKenna's thru hiker's guide, there were enough shelters on the AT, spaced close enough together, that some people didn't even bother carrying a tent. McKenna had no interest in that—she wanted the choice of camping on her own rather than bunking with strangers. But generally there were freshwater sources wherever there were shelters. And if not, McKenna also had a water filter, plus an impressive supply of iodine tablets in case the filter broke.

"Forget the jug, then," McKenna said. "The smaller water bottles should be fine."

Lucy picked up the two thirty-four-ounce bottles and slid them into their holders on the exterior of McKenna's pack.

"Sporty," Lucy said, shaking a shock of hair out of her eyes.

"Sporty," McKenna agreed.

The doorbell rang and the sound of their father's enthusiastic voice carried up the stairs. He was ready to hold court.

Lucy sighed and said, "I'm really going to miss you."

McKenna sat down on the bed. She was dying to tell Lucy that Courtney wasn't coming with her, that she'd be going the trail alone. But she couldn't risk it, and anyway it wouldn't be fair to make a ten-year-old shoulder that kind of secret. Both girls were rule followers, and Lucy had always been more of a worrier than McKenna.

"Hey," McKenna said. "Maybe you can do the same hike after you graduate. We could do it together."

"You mean it?" Lucy asked, her blue eyes widening.

"Of course I mean it," McKenna said. "By then I'll know all the tricks."

Lucy picked up the key ring lying next to McKenna's collapsible pot and cookstove, and blew the whistle. The ring also had a small canister of pepper spray attached. "Is this one of the tricks?" she asked. "To keep away murderers?"

"Well, I got it in case of bears," McKenna said. "But I'm guessing it would work on murderers, too."

Lucy nodded. McKenna thought she looked like she might be fighting tears.

"I'll be fine," McKenna told her. "And I'll be back before you know it."

"I know," Lucy said quickly. "I'm just going to miss you. That's all."

McKenna pulled her sister into her arms, all sixty-three pounds of her. Lucy felt lighter than air and twice as bony.

Their mother's voice traveled up the stairs, calling them down to their guests, but McKenna ignored her, at least for a minute. She hoped her parents would remember to pay plenty of attention to Lucy while she was gone. It could get lonely in this house with everyone so busy, everyone always on the way to somewhere else.

Her dad's new TA, a skinny guy who had a two-year-old daughter, couldn't believe McKenna's parents were letting her and a friend hike all alone. If he only knew, McKenna thought, smiling to herself.

"The summer I was eighteen I hiked the Pacific Northwest Trail," her dad said. "Now, *that's* wilderness. We barely saw another soul all summer. Packed in every bite of food we ate. Krosky and I lost sixty pounds between us."

Both grad students nodded. McKenna had seen a million of them, all hanging on her dad's every word.

"Compared to the PNT," her dad said, "the Appalachian Trail will be like a parking lot."

McKenna frowned and speared a piece of lettuce. "Maybe we should drive out West tomorrow," she said. "Do the PNT instead."

"No, no, no," her mom said. "The Appalachian Trail is plenty wilderness enough." She turned to the TA. "McKenna's always been like that. Don't ever challenge or dare her. Ridiculously brave, even when she was little. Never had a single nightmare. She watched every episode of *Buffy the Vampire Slayer* when she was ten."

Across the table, Lucy, who was prone to nightmares and couldn't stand to watch anything scary, shifted uncomfortably. Her mother took another sip of wine and launched into stories they'd all heard a hundred times about McKenna's childhood.

Listening to her mom, McKenna smiled at Lucy in a way she hoped told her she didn't have to be as brave as she was. At the same time, she had to admit, now that her mind was on the trail, she liked hearing about her own fearlessness, her own resourcefulness.

McKenna had no doubts at all; she would be just fine on the trail.

The next morning, McKenna stood in the driveway with her parents and Lucy, waiting for Courtney and Brendan. Originally, Brendan was going to drive the girls up to Maine and drop them off at Baxter State Park, so they had to make it look like that was still the plan.

"You sure you have everything?" McKenna's dad asked. "Did you use your checklist when you packed?"

McKenna nodded, not meeting his eye. All she had to do was get in the car and drive away, and she'd have made it. She'd be free.

"Listen," her mom said. "I was thinking you could text us every morning. Just to let us know you're all right. You know, just, 'Good morning, I'm alive.' Something like that. Before nine?"

"Mom," McKenna said, "I'm only bringing the phone in case of emergency. I don't want to be texting every day, or looking to see what time it is. And please remember not to call me, because I won't answer, and I won't check voice mail. I want this experience to be authentic."

"I can appreciate that," her dad said, in the hyper-reasonable tone that usually preceded a contradiction. "But you need to appreciate, your mother will be worried." Her mom shot him a look that demanded solidarity, and he added, "I will be, too.

How about twice a week? Let's say Wednesday and Friday you'll send us a text by ten a.m."

"I really don't want to be looking at the time. Didn't you always say that was one of the best parts of your hike, never knowing what time it was?" McKenna argued.

"Before dark, then," her mom conceded. "Text us Wednesday and Friday before dark, telling us where you are. That's just safety, right, to let someone know where you are?"

She sounded so pleading, McKenna felt guilty. "Fine," she said.

And then, *finally*, there it was, Brendan's mom's minivan, rounding the corner. McKenna stood on her toes and waved furiously, as if they might drive past if she didn't flag them down.

Her dad picked up her pack. "Sheesh," he said, hoisting it onto his shoulder. "Are you going to be able to carry this thing?"

"Dad," McKenna said, reaching for the pack. The last thing she needed was for him to see the back of the van empty where Courtney's camping gear should be. "I can do it."

"No, no," he insisted. He headed to the back door of the van and opened it while McKenna battled a heart attack. But there lay Courtney's backpack, bulging almost as much as McKenna's. Any anger McKenna felt toward Courtney evaporated in a moment of pure love.

"You ready?" her mom asked Courtney.

"I'm ready," Courtney said. Her voice sounded high and nervous.

McKenna hugged her dad, and Lucy. Her mom hugged her a little too long, and whispered in her ear, "Be safe out there. Be careful."

"I will, Mom," McKenna said, and kissed her cheek.

Then she climbed into the backseat and didn't turn around to see her mom and dad standing in the driveway, waving good-bye.

McKenna would have been surprised to know just how long her parents stood there after the minivan pulled away.

"I can't believe it," McKenna's mom said when the van was completely out of sight. "I can't believe we're letting her do this."

"Don't worry," her dad said. "They'll be back in a week."

Her mom nodded, still waving, clinging to the sight of McKenna until the van rounded the corner.

"I hope you're right," she said, hugging herself and rubbing her arms as if she were cold, though the outside thermometer read eighty-eight degrees. "I really do."

3

McKenna leaned forward from the backseat, placing one hand on Courtney's shoulder and one hand on Brendan's. "I almost died when my dad opened the hatch. You were so smart to put your pack there! Thank you."

"Yeah, well, I have a dad, too," Courtney said.

McKenna sat back as Brendan drove down Broad Avenue. She let out a long breath of relief. All this past week, and especially last night, she'd had trouble sleeping because she'd been so worried about her parents putting a stop to her solo trip. So she'd barely had a chance to worry about the solo hike itself. Finally on the road now, Courtney dressed convincingly in hiking boots, she could almost believe they were going together as originally planned. But then Brendan pulled into the parking lot at Flat Rock Brook, where Jay sat waiting, and McKenna had to face the reality. Courtney was staying here in Abelard.

McKenna's stomach did an uncomfortable roll, full of jittery air, and she reminded herself that anxiety and exhilaration were close cousins. It was up to you what you wanted to call it.

. . .

It took seven hours to drive from Abelard, Connecticut, to Pis-
cataquis County, Maine. As she and Brendan made their way,
McKenna kept her eyes on the woods by the highway, thinking about how long it would take to walk this same distance.
By the time McKenna's hike brought her back to Connecticut,
she'd wouldn't even be halfway done with the trail.

As they drove along the coastal route in southern Maine, Mc-
Kenna buzzed down the window so the sea air could waft in.

"Hey," Brendan said. "I forgot to tell you, I booked a hotel."

"You did?" McKenna's hair escaped its ponytail and fluttered in her face.

They'd never worked out what the structure of their good-
bye would be. McKenna had assumed they'd spend the night
together, but figured it would be in sleeping bags in the back
of his mom's van. Brendan's dad was head of neurology at a
hospital in New Haven, and he had six children from two different marriages. Lots of resources, but they were spread thin.
It wasn't like Brendan to splurge on a hotel.

"I thought you'd want one more night in a bed before you
hit the trail," he said.

"Sounds great," McKenna said. In the three months she and
Brendan had been together, they'd never slept in the same bed,
and both were still virgins, although they'd come pretty close
to changing that a couple times.

When they got to the Katahdin Inn and Suites, McKenna
let Brendan hoist her pack out of the back of the van.

"Wow," he said. "You're sure you can carry this thing?"

"I can," she told him, trying not to sound defensive.

They checked in and headed to the room. There it was, one queen-sized bed. McKenna had never spent the night with a guy.

Brendan reached out and clasped her hand. "Hungry?" he asked.

"Definitely," she said.

River Driver's Restaurant was full of outdoorsy-looking people in various degrees of un-wash. Some still had wet hair after what might have been their first shower in days or even weeks. Others looked like they'd just come directly from the trail to the table. McKenna wondered if there were any thru hikers about to embark on the journey south. Most likely not, as thru hikers made up a small percentage of AT hikers, and most of the ones headed to Georgia would have started, wisely, at the beginning of June.

Brendan ordered a steak and McKenna ordered the summer-vegetable pasta.

"Carbo load," Brendan noted when her plate of pasta arrived, but McKenna had ordered it mostly because it would be a while before she saw fresh vegetables again. She'd packed her stove, but she wasn't much of a cook. Originally they'd decided Courtney would be the one in charge of cooking, but since she'd be eating alone, McKenna figured she could sustain herself on minimal trail meals and then splurge when she got to a town. Along with freeze-dried camping meals of various sorts of noodles, she'd packed a hefty supply of turkey jerky, dried fruit, and granola bars.

About halfway through dinner, the waiter stopped by to ask if everything was okay.

"Great," Brendan said. "Could I get a Molson?"

"Sure. Got an ID on you?"

"Oh." Brendan fumbled a little. "I think I left it in the hotel room."

"Sorry, bud," the waiter said, and retreated.

McKenna looked at him suspiciously. Usually Brendan said no to beer even at parties. She wondered again if he was planning something momentous for tonight.

Brendan shrugged, just embarrassed enough that it was endearing. She watched him dig back into his steak, his dark hair flopping across his forehead, his cheeks still pink from the waiter's rejection. It was so sweet and considerate of Brendan to drive her up here, stay with her, keep her secret. Really, he was the perfect boyfriend. Maybe tonight *should* be the night, whether Brendan had planned it or not. She was almost eighteen. Maybe it was time.

She reached across the table and touched his forearm. "I'm really glad you're here with me," she said.

Brendan looked up. "Me, too." He nodded toward her half-eaten meal. "You better finish that. Might be the last hot meal you see for a while."

Just then two college-aged guys of the just-off-the-trail

variety slid into their booth, one beside McKenna and one beside Brendan. Before McKenna could open her mouth, the one next to her held up a silver flask.

"We heard the waiter turn you down," he said, grinning through many days' worth of stubble. He carried the distinct odor of accumulated sweat and camp smoke, but both guys looked so friendly that McKenna couldn't help smiling. He hovered the flask over her Coke and she found herself nodding.

"Rum?" she asked, a little too late, after a liberal amount had been added to her soda.

"Bourbon," he said, doing the same to Brendan's drink. "I'm Stewart and this is Jackson. We just rolled in from Georgia."

"No way!" McKenna said. "You're thru hikers? And you just finished?"

"Yep," Jackson said. "Started in February. Did some serious winter camping."

"Wow," McKenna said. "Congratulations. And you made great time."

Brendan sipped his drink, looking grateful for the alcohol but ready for their new friends to get lost.

"Oh, that's nothing," Stewart said. "The record is forty-six days."

"I know!" McKenna said. "Jennifer Pharr Davis. I read her book."

She looked over at Brendan triumphantly, wondering if she'd remembered to tell him that the speed record for the AT was held by a woman.

"Of course, she had a team meeting her at intervals," Stewart said, "so she didn't have to carry much. Not like us."

"Or me," McKenna said. "I'm starting my thru hike tomorrow."

"Yeah. We are," Brendan added quickly. McKenna started to flash him an indignant look, but had to admit he was probably right to chime in. No sense advertising that she was heading out on her own.

"Wow." Jackson whistled, low and impressed. "Southbound. That's hard-core. Hope you have cold-weather gear for the last legs. Trust us, it gets cold in those southern mountains."

"I do," McKenna said. "I mean, we do."

"Katahdin's the hardest stretch of the whole trail. You better not have too much more of this," Stewart said, adding just the smallest bit more bourbon to each of their glasses. "Consider it your first dose of trail magic."

"Trail magic?" Brendan asked.

McKenna answered before Stewart or Jackson had a chance. "When hikers do things for each other, little surprises and kindnesses along the way."

"Good thing you brought this one with you," Stewart said to Brendan, putting his arm around McKenna in a brotherly way. "Sounds like she did all your research." And then he and Jackson launched into stories of home-cooked meals delivered to shelters by nearby residents, and ice-cold bottles of Coca-Cola waiting in streams.

McKenna smiled at Brendan over the rim of her glass. *See?*

she hoped her eyes said to him. *I won't really be alone at all.* There would be people every step of the way, looking out for her and keeping her company. Trail magic.

By the time they got back to the room, McKenna's belly was so bloated she had to unbutton her shorts before collapsing onto the bed, the bourbon throbbing dully behind her eyes. Last night she'd hardly slept at all, and today in the car she'd still been too excited and nervous to so much as close her eyes. Now the heavy food, the many hours without rest, and the alcohol started to take their toll. She willed herself to stay awake, but the sound of rushing water from the bathroom as Brendan got ready for bed made her eyelids close as effectively as a sleeping pill.

"Hey."

McKenna started. Brendan was leaning over her, shaking her shoulders gently. "Don't you want to brush your teeth?" he asked, his eyes slightly imploring, his voice just the tiniest bit slurred.

That particular look, full of questions, made McKenna feel surer than ever of his plan for how to say good-bye. Well, what the hell. She was no prude. As long as he had protection—something McKenna had certainly not thought to pack with her compass, trowel shovel, and camping rope. She slipped off the bed and grabbed her toiletry kit.

After brushing her teeth, she splashed water on her face and studied her reflection in the mirror: the smattering of freckles across her nose, the blue eyes. She searched for any trace of innocence that would be gone the next time she looked, but couldn't find any.

When she came out of the bathroom Brendan was already in bed. He was bare from the waist up, but knowing him, she was sure he wore something underneath that coverlet. McKenna had packed a pair of sweats for sleeping, nothing at all suited to this activity. As another wave of exhaustion came over her, she decided to leave the sweats in her pack.

She flopped onto her back next to Brendan, above the covers, her head on the spongy hotel pillow. Brendan propped himself up on one elbow, looking down at her.

"McKenna," he said. "I've been thinking. We're going to be apart so long. And you know I love you. And here we are. And I was thinking . . ."

"I know," McKenna said. "I could tell."

"Is it all right with you? Because if it's not—"

"It is," she said. "It's totally all right. But let's not talk about it."

She waited a minute, and when Brendan did not kiss her, she pulled his face down to hers and kissed him. Brendan was a good kisser, gentle and tender, and they kissed for a while. Finally, he moved his hand from her neck to her waist, and closed it around the hem of her T-shirt.

"Is this okay?" he asked, tugging it with more question than purpose. It wasn't like he'd never taken her shirt off before. It must have been nerves over what they were about to do that made him keep asking.

"Yes," McKenna said. She half sat up, to help him get it over her head. Both shirtless now, they kissed a while longer, until Brendan moved his hands to the buttons on her shorts.

"Is this okay?"

"Yes, it's fine, it's all fine, you don't have to ask."

McKenna appreciated the sentiment behind asking. She also liked the bourbon taste in his mouth when he kissed her. And for a while her breathing was appropriately heavy, and her sighs shuddery and involved. At the same time, her stomach was so bloated that it was a little uncomfortable when he leaned into her, and her head was foggy with the need for sleep. The litany of that question, "Is this okay? Is this okay?" became more lulling than seductive.

As if his voice were coming from another room, McKenna barely heard his last "Is this okay?" She couldn't hold on a second longer and answered with a light snore. Just vaguely, she heard him move away, his head hitting the pillow in frustration. She meant to apologize but couldn't manage it before falling into a deep, dead sleep.

4

The *first thing* McKenna saw when her eyes fluttered open was the white ceiling of the hotel room. She felt the tiniest flash of embarrassment over the night before, the barest remnant of bourbon left on her tongue, but it all disappeared in a second as she remembered: today was the day she would start her trek. She jumped out of bed. Lao-tzu said, "A journey of a thousand miles must begin with a single step." Well, so must a journey of two thousand miles, and McKenna couldn't wait to take that first step.

Then she realized she was almost completely naked. She scooped her T-shirt off the floor and pulled it over her head.

Light hadn't yet made its way through the curtains. She looked back toward the bed. Poor Brendan. He still lay sleeping, and she realized she had forgone her opportunity to wake up in his arms, to make up for last night.

She considered this for a minute. After all, Brendan didn't know she had bounded out of bed immediately. She could take off her shirt and crawl back under the covers, wake him with a kiss, and see where things progressed from there.

Outside the window, birds had started their predawn racket, all different songs mingling together. Whatever desire she felt for Brendan was eclipsed by the desire to start her adventure.

Maybe it was ridiculous to take a shower before heading off on a grueling day of hiking the most difficult stretch of the trail. But who knew when she'd have the chance to linger under a stream of hot water, and emerge from a steaming bathroom smelling of shampoo and lilac-scented hotel soap?

When she did emerge: *awkward*. Brendan sat on the edge of the bed, pulling on his jeans. McKenna averted her eyes, and then thought that doing so only drew attention to everything that hadn't happened last night.

McKenna pointed to her backpack. "I'm just going to grab my stuff," she said.

"Sure. Yeah. Of course."

She dragged the whole pack into the bathroom before deciding to put on the same shorts and T-shirt she'd worn the day before. What counted for dirty laundry in the real world probably represented the cleanest clothes she'd see on the trail. Her favorite outfit—her pink Johnny Cash T-shirt and skort—she could save for later. She braided her wet hair and zipped her pack, then filled her two water bottles at the bathroom sink.

McKenna lowered her eyes as she stepped past Brendan, who was waiting just outside the bathroom door. He closed the door with a private *click*, and she felt a flurry of annoyance. As much as she cared about Brendan, and as much as she was grateful to him for driving her all the way up here—and now that she thought about it, he had paid for dinner and she hadn't even thanked him—this wasn't supposed to be a day spent worrying about other people's feelings. Today was the beginning of total independence, selfishly focused on her own well-being. She would need all her strength for this first ascent and her first night alone on the trail.

Still, when Brendan emerged from the bathroom, his hair boyishly combed and his expression extremely uncomfortable, McKenna felt sad and responsible.

"Listen," she said. "About last night—"

Brendan cut her off, putting his hands on her shoulders. He pressed his forehead against hers, looking relieved that she'd finally brought it up. "No," he said. "You don't have to say anything. I understand. You weren't ready. I shouldn't have pushed you."

"You didn't push me," McKenna said. She could also have added that she *was* ready, or at least she thought she might be. But since his version let her off the hook, and also saved his pride, she just said, "Thank you for understanding."

He kissed her. "Should we get breakfast?"

Truthfully she still felt full from the night before and she was anxious to hit the trail. But here was Brendan with his puppy dog eyes, needing to do something for her, needing closeness. Besides, she knew she could get the first passport stamp of her journey, Katahdin, at the AT café, which was known for its huge, cheap, and awesome breakfasts.

"Sure," she said. "Something light."

After breakfast, Brendan drove her to Abol Campground in Baxter State Park. The cool New England morning was starting to give way to mugginess. Most days on the trail, she would need to start earlier. Already she could feel a gathering sense of purpose, the need to start covering miles.

Brendan lifted the hatch at the back of the van and pulled out McKenna's pack, staggering a tiny bit under its weight again. Then he looked up at the sky. "We should have checked the weather," he said, reaching into his pocket for his phone.

"No, don't," McKenna said, touching his wrist. "It doesn't matter. I'm going to hike every day rain or shine."

"Don't you want to know? Whether you need to put your raincoat on or whatever?"

McKenna looked up at the sky, than toward the road as an SUV drove past, filled with a family, a little girl pressing her face to the window to stare at her and Brendan. McKenna smiled and waved at the girl. The park was bustling with people on vacation. She wondered how many of them had brought along their electronic devices—watching Netflix at night instead of the stars, checking weather.com instead of looking at the sky.

"There's going to be a lot of places on the trail where I won't even get reception," she said to Brendan. "The last thing I want is to be dependent on my phone. Plus, I have to save the batteries in case of emergency."

Brendan nodded and put his hands in his pockets. In another eight weeks he would be headed to Harvard. McKenna imagined what that would be like for him. Lots of new friends, new ideas, new everything, including plenty of new girls. She was struck with one of those rare moments of absolute awareness: the next time they saw each other, they would be different people.

"Good luck at school," McKenna said. "I know you'll do great."

"Thanks," Brendan said. "Be safe out there. Okay?"

"You know I will be."

They kissed. McKenna tried to revel in the hug the way she'd reveled in her last hot meals and showers. But mostly she was just antsy to get on the trail.

"Do you want me to stay until you're on your way?" he asked.

She fought to keep from rolling her eyes. This was not like waiting in the car until she was safely inside her front door. This front door would lead her into the wild world, headed up a mountain. There was no getting safely inside. With every passing second, McKenna became more eager to shed everything about her old life and embark on this new one.

Her first step onto the trail seemed momentous, and strangely private. Thoreau had climbed Katahdin in 1846 and you can bet he didn't set off with anyone waving from a minivan.

"I'll be okay," McKenna said.

Brendan kissed her again. Then he got into his mom's minivan and drove away.

McKenna stood watching the cloud of dust rising from its wheels, until she was alone on the curb, just within sight of the trailhead.

Two thousand miles. All she had to do was put on her backpack and take that first step. She reached down and closed her hand around one shoulder strap, and hoisted the whole enormous thing onto her back. McKenna had practiced hiking with this weight. It didn't matter that it was crammed full to capacity, with enough food to last her till she got to the first outpost, plus her tent, her sleeping bag, her compass . . . everything on her necessities checklist, plus a few books. She had splurged on her pack, which was ergonomically designed to be carried on the back comfortably, no matter how many extras she'd crammed into it.

As she put a foot onto the trail, excitement made her light on her feet despite the thick straps cutting into her shoulders. She had planned, she had trained. She had prepared as much as she possibly could, both mentally and physically.

She was ready.

5

Hubris. That was the word that came to mind a few hours into McKenna's first day on the trail. Why in the world had she chosen the most strenuous route up Katahdin? For the first hour or so, the Abol Trail was not particularly formidable, just a gradual incline on an easy wooded trail, lovely canopy above her, gurgling stream beside her. A section of this stream was actually known as Thoreau's stream, so of course she stopped beside it for a little communion. She couldn't kneel down and splash water on her face because her pack was so heavy, but as far as the walking: piece of cake!

And then that hour was over and McKenna remembered that while Thoreau had waxed poetic about his time in the wilderness, at least one biographer claimed that the climb up Katahdin had brought him to the brink of hysteria. McKenna wasn't *quite* hysterical, not yet, though she was a lot more tired than she'd planned. Although she and Courtney had gone on a few overnights, most of the hikes she'd taken at home, in the afternoon after working, had been a couple hours. Out here, a couple hours was just the beginning of her day.

About a mile in, the grade of the trail changed from rambling and gradual to steep. Seriously steep. McKenna had to stop to catch her breath and take sips of water way more often than she'd anticipated. Her plan had been to hike five miles today—per her guidebook, she knew that the campgrounds could get crowded in the summer, so she'd made a reservation at the Katahdin Stream Campground. In her mind it had been a modest plan, even though she knew it was a dramatic uphill. She was young! She was in great shape! She might not be a star on the track team, but she was a solid runner, and she'd earned badges for more peaks in Connecticut than anyone else in her high school's hiking club. By starting her hike with the most difficult route, she would prove to herself that she was capable of doing this Herculean task she'd set for herself.

There weren't many other hikers on the trail, but the ones she saw quickly overtook her. At the Great Outdoor Provision Co., the guy who'd helped her pick out her gear spent a long time telling McKenna what she should pack and what she should leave behind. She knew weight would be important, but how much difference could it make, bringing four T-shirts instead of two, and her two favorite sweatshirts, and three pairs of shorts, plus the really cute Patagonia skort?

"You should bring a Kindle instead of books," the guy at the store had said when she'd shown him her list. "You can always charge it off the trail."

McKenna had nodded, not wanting to contradict him, but inwardly she thought that a Kindle would be sacrilege. Now, as the Abol Trail became ever steeper, she catalogued the copy of *Walden*, the two new novels, and the songbird guide she'd wanted to check several times but hadn't been able to because that would have meant taking the pack off and then putting it back on. And she had thought she'd been so clever, bringing just paperbacks. As a kid, when she hiked with her father, he used to talk about trail rhythm, that great moment when your feet start moving in time with your arms, and each step covers the same amount of ground. But how was she supposed to establish trail rhythm when, three hours in, she could barely stand upright?

Finally, as noon approached—or close to it, McKenna guessed, as the sun seemed to be directly overhead and was beating down with impressive strength—she knew she'd have to stop and rest. She chose a little outcropping with an inviting flat rock and shrugged the pack to the ground. It landed with a loud *thump*, the sound itself chiding McKenna for overestimating herself. She took a big chug of water and thought that if she'd gotten anywhere near as far as she'd planned, she would now be admiring an impressive vista instead of just the thickly wooded forest.

A blackfly buzzed her head, and she swatted at it, only to have another swoop down on her neck. When she unzipped her pack to dig for bug spray, it erupted with clothing, showing off the inexpert job she'd done at the hotel this morning. She made a note that from now on, she'd pack everything she might need during the day at the top and in the outside pockets.

She ate two granola bars and an apple and drank some more water. When she was ready to go, she hoisted the pack onto her back and immediately stumbled forward, scraping her shin. The shock of that sharp scrape made her push herself upright again. She could see blood dribbling down toward her foot, but with the heavy pack on her back, she couldn't really bend down to inspect it, so she decided to tough it out instead.

And tough it out she did, as the path only got steeper and more rocky. Sweat poured off her forehead and into her eyes. Her back was soaked. Above, the sky started to darken, rain clouds obscuring the strong sun, which would have been a welcome relief from the heat if McKenna had thought to zip the waterproof cover over her pack. As thunder crashed in the distance, she had no choice but to stop and dig out the rain cover—of course packed toward the bottom—jam everything back in, and hoist the pack onto her shoulders again.

She slogged on through light rain, not minding getting wet as long as the contents of her pack stayed dry. All the clothes McKenna had packed for the trip, including underwear, were quick-drying, except for her two favorite T-shirts, one of which she was wearing. It became sodden in no time, chilling her through to the skin.

The rain made it impossible to guess what time it was, and she started to worry she wouldn't make it to her campground before dark. She soon came to a steep wall of rocks that she would actually have to *climb*—finding footholds and handholds. She racked her brain, trying to remember her guidebook's description of the trail. Maybe this meant she was close to the end.

McKenna braced herself against the rocks. For a day hike with something light on her back, this might be doable. Hard, but doable. As it was, the weight of the pack pulled her dangerously backward as she tried to keep her balance. She took one careful step and then another. The rain came down like a mist, making everything that much slicker; she lost her grip as a mossy rock came loose and scraped both legs as she slid, before she managed to right herself.

A surge of adrenaline overtook her. She felt strong and determined and eager to get to her goal. On the other hand, she felt unsteady, and the drop-off to the east was steep and perilous. She remembered what Brendan had said back in Abelard: *It's not a joke. There are a thousand ways a person could die out there.*

She pushed his voice out of her head, instead riding a second surge of adrenaline, pulling herself up precariously. All it would take was one slide in the wrong direction. There was nothing to catch her if she slid off that drop, just an unforgiving ravine. *A thousand ways a person could die.*

"I could die," McKenna said out loud.

The words startled her. Despite all the warnings over these last months of planning, this thought had honestly never occurred to her in any kind of real way: what she was doing was actually dangerous. She could die. As much as McKenna didn't want to die before she turned eighteen, she especially didn't want to die on the very first day of her hike. Certainly that would make her go down in history as the most pathetic thru hiker ever.

Maybe if her pack weren't *quite* so heavy. Maybe if this were the last day of her hike, instead of the very first. Maybe if it weren't raining.

McKenna had to admit. She was already beaten.

This feeling came over her. A fount of determination. All she wanted to do in the world was ride that surge and keep climbing, finish what she'd started.

But if she did that, she would risk tumbling off the mountain. So very carefully, she crab-walked back down the small stretch of rocks she'd managed to traverse, and made the decision, for now, to turn around.

As she headed down the Abol Trail back toward Baxter State Park, the sky opened up and dumped in earnest. McKenna couldn't decide whether this was a sign that she'd made a wise decision or proved herself a total wimp. At least the rainwater would clean out her scrapes.

It only took her a few minutes of walking to remember: going downhill on a trail marked MOST STRENUOUS, carrying a pack that's far too heavy, is even harder than going uphill. By the time she returned to the first, early section of trail, the rain had let up, but her shoulders and back ached in ways she hadn't anticipated feeling until she was well into her forties—or at least well into her thru hike. The scrapes on her legs stung, she had guzzled every last drop of water. The thought of walking for another full hour made her throat fill up with tears. All she wanted to do was throw down her pack, lie on the ground, and give up. She took two steps off the trail and leaned back against a tree, looking up at the slants of after-rain light filtering through the dense northern canopy.

Something rustled just behind her. It couldn't be a person, it was coming from the wrong direction, off the trail. Heavy footsteps, cracking branches. Something big.

McKenna frantically cataloged the various animals it could be, and in her discouraged state arrived on the scariest possibility: *bear*.

Seriously? On my first day?

Just that phrase, *first day*, perked McKenna up a little. It was her first day. She hadn't given up. She would find a way to do this walk, one way or another.

The animal lurched into view. It was a moose. Larger than McKenna could have ever imagined, and twice as beautiful. Probably female, since it didn't have antlers. Her eyes were huge and dark and totally indifferent to McKenna. She bowed her head and scooped up some leaves, chewing thoughtfully as McKenna stared.

"Hi," McKenna said once she'd recovered. She wanted to reach out and touch it, but of course knew better. Instead she said again, "Hi, Moose."

The moose did not reply, but McKenna felt heartened all the same.

Back at Baxter State Park, McKenna walked around the camp-ground, looking for an empty site. As her guidebook had warned, even on a weekday the park was full to capacity—she of course hadn't made a reservation because she hadn't planned to camp here. Now she could only hope that today's rain, coupled with the gathering clouds, would scare some people away.

She had no luck on her first scouting trip, but did find an unoccupied picnic bench under a covered shelter, and shrugged her pack off with something that might have been joy if she hadn't been so profoundly exhausted. Before doing anything, she lay down across the bench and closed her eyes, too tired to even get out of her wet clothes. After half an hour or so, she sat up and opened her pack, pulling out her first-aid kit to douse her legs with disinfectant. The scrapes didn't look as bad as they felt—apart from the first cut, everything else could be categorized as a light scrape. She only used one Band-Aid.

The sun had dipped low enough that the northern New England air felt chilly, and McKenna shivered, leaving her pack on the picnic table while she traipsed across the parking lot into the public restroom and changed into dry clothes. Her pack contained two hundred dollars in cash, her iPhone, and the thousand dollars' worth of camping equipment she'd spent years saving up to buy. But she just couldn't contemplate lug-ging the whole thing into the bathroom with her. And as hard as the day on the trail had been, she wasn't yet uncivilized enough to strip down in the middle of a campground full of people.

Thankfully, when she got back, her pack still sat there, undisturbed. Outside the shelter, rain began to fall again. McKenna unpacked everything, spreading it out on the table. She would need all the food she'd brought to get through the 100 Mile Wilderness, the first section of the southbound AT. She removed a T-shirt and piled it with the one she'd worn today, plus two pairs of shorts and both sweatshirts. The cute skort she couldn't bear to part with; she decided she'd wear it tomorrow. She put on her fleece jacket, a little heavy for the evening, but she found comfort in the fact that she still had something warm. She had spent a decent amount of money on two pairs of long Gramicci pants—now she took one pair and placed it in the discard pile, along with two of the seven books. She kept *Walden*, and her songbird guide, and a novel she hadn't yet started, plus the little journal to record her trip.

When she repacked what she planned to keep, she hoisted her pack back on. It was still heavy, but the items she'd discarded made a difference.

A car rattled by, heading out of the campground, a group of people fleeing the bad weather. But McKenna was too tired to go in search of their abandoned campsite. Instead, she ate an entire bag of Trader Joe's Natural Turkey Jerky, then laid her sleeping bag under the picnic table. Tomorrow she would leave her plastic bag of discarded items with a sign that said FREE TO GOOD HOME.

McKenna's whole body ached. The trail had done a great job of humiliating her, but the rain on the tin roof of the shelter sounded pretty, and at least she was dry. She'd known going into this that Maine and New Hampshire were the hardest legs of the trail, and Katahdin the toughest climb. She might have failed today, but she'd failed on the hardest route up the hardest section of the whole two thousand miles. Which meant everything from here would be easier than what she'd survived today. Tomorrow she'd head to the Chimney Pond Trail, which her guidebook promised was the easiest route.

From now on, she'd be smart enough to respect the trail.

6

Sam Tilghman stood on the front lawn of his brother's house in Farmington, Maine. At least he thought it was his brother's house. He dug into the pocket of his jeans and checked the piece of paper against the crooked metal numbers nailed into the porch railing. He'd jotted it down from the computer at the public library, along with the phone number, though he hadn't called ahead. For one thing, when was the last time you saw a pay phone anywhere? For another, calling after two years seemed worse, more awkward, than just showing up. This way if Mike didn't want to see him, he'd have to tell him to his face.

It was kind of a nice house, which surprised Sam, and for some reason made him feel sad. He didn't know why. Maybe he was just tired. Not just tired from yesterday, tired from the last three months, since he'd left his father's house and started walking. Funny, his brother probably thought he'd moved as far away as possible from Seedling, West Virginia. But it turned out it was in walking distance, as long as you stuck to the Appalachian Trail and had a fair amount of time to kill. Nothing keeps you walking like demons at your heels.

There were no cars in the driveway, and no movement that Sam could see inside the house, apart from curtains fluttering upstairs through an open window. Something told Sam that if he climbed the porch steps and turned the knob, the front door would open. Sam could pour himself a glass of water from the tap (talk about luxury) and help himself to some leftovers. When Mike got home, Sam would be snoozing on the couch, or maybe watching TV. Wasn't that the kind of thing family was allowed to do? Walk right in and make yourself at home?

Sam took a couple steps back, surveying the place, trying to imagine his brother there. A trike sat overturned at the bottom of the porch stairs, and he could see a plastic playhouse in the backyard, dirty as hell but still managing to look cheerful. Sam didn't even know Mike had gotten married, let alone had kids. How did you end up with kids old enough to ride tricycles in two years? They must be the wife's—or girlfriend's—kids. What would Sam say to her if she came home first? For all Sam knew, Mike hadn't even told her he had a brother.

Sam walked around to the back of the house and shrugged off his pack. It felt good to get the weight off his shoulders, even though by now he was used to it. Someone had planted a garden, with rows of fat heads of lettuce nestled beside rising stalks of corn. There was a back deck, too, with a table that had an umbrella, and a tabby cat enjoying the shade. He and Mike had a cat once, when they were kids, until their father kicked it so hard that it ran away and never came back. Some version of that happened to all their pets. But you could tell this cat had never been kicked. It watched Sam with passive disinterest, totally unafraid.

Beyond the messy tumble of the yard and garden lay a low thicket of vegetation with a worn path inviting Sam to investigate. West Virginia this time of year would be hot, heavy, muggy. "Like living inside someone's mouth," Mike used to say. But here in Maine, headed toward late afternoon, the air was livable, a cool breeze ambling by every few minutes.

Sam grabbed an ear of corn off a stalk and walked onto the path, where it was even cooler in the shade of pine, oak, and maple. He peeled the husk back and bit into the sour/sweet kernels still a couple weeks away from being ripe. In a few minutes he could hear the burbling of a stream. Funny, the relief he'd felt at how civilized his brother's house looked; now he felt a different kind of relief, the familiarity of a dirt path, barely two feet wide, brush and woods on each side, slivers of light reaching through the increasingly taller trees. Sam had been on the trail for so long, it was like all those years growing up in a house, in the regular world, had never even happened. The woods felt more normal than his house ever had. Maybe even more safe, not that safe was exactly what Sam was after.

When he reached the stream, he saw it was bigger than he had expected, wide and fast. He took off his shirt and knelt down, splashing water on his face and under his arms, and wetting his hair. Not much of an improvement, but a little. Hopefully Mike would let him inside for a shower and a hot meal. Maybe they'd even have a washer and dryer so he could wash his clothes. Mike had taken off when he was eighteen and Sam fifteen, and Sam had already been bigger, taller. But he'd lost a good bit of weight on the trail, so maybe he could fit into Mike's clothes now.

As he pulled his grimy T-shirt over his head, he noticed a green wine bottle stuck in a tangle of moss by the shore. He fished it out of the brush, pulled out the cork, and found a note inside. It started:

> *To the Finder of this Note: Greetings. You are part of an experiment in flood dynamics, and also the poetry of streams.*

The note said that the bottle had been tossed in the stream in Avon, Maine. It asked whoever found it to mail back the answers to a bunch of questions, like where and when he'd found the bottle, in what circumstances, along with his name, address, and any other information he felt like giving.

For some reason, this made Sam happy. It seemed like a good sign. Avon was only about twenty miles north of where he was, but the note said to respond even if the bottle was found just a hundred yards downstream. It was a good mission, a friendly reentry into civilization. Maybe one of Mike's kids could help him. Didn't little kids like this kind of thing? If Sam proved himself to be a good uncle, Mike and his wife/girlfriend might invite him to stay for a while. He could get his head together, get a job, make a little money. Maybe he'd even sign up for one of those GED courses.

He tucked the note into his back pocket and carried the bottle to the house, where he could toss it into Mike's recycling bin. Then he sat on the front stoop to wait for someone to come home. It was time to focus on the future instead of the past.

Sam's past had ended one morning in March, just two months before he was supposed to finish high school.

First there was a searing and shocking pain, along with a sizzle. Sam's dad had a longtime habit of using him as an ashtray when he'd had too much to drink, but his doing it while Sam slept—when his dad couldn't even pretend to have been provoked—made something snap inside Sam. He stood up and slammed his father against the wall.

His father stared at him, his eyes glassy. Sam's rage overwhelmed him, along with a sudden new sense of his own strength. He pulled his dad up and slammed him against the wall again. Rotten whiskey and bad breath wafted across his chin. How had Sam missed it? At some point, he'd gotten taller than his dad. In his grip, the man felt small and soft. Whereas Sam felt clearheaded. He felt strong.

I could kill you, Sam thought. I could kill you right now with my bare hands and no one would blame me.

Even though Sam hadn't said the words out loud, he could

tell his dad heard them and knew they were true. No one would blame Sam, he wouldn't even blame himself, thinking of all the years his dad had beaten up on him and Mike. Their mother. Still, he let go, and his dad stumbled out of his grip, lurching forward with a rancid burp and making his way out of the room. Sam heard a soft *thud*, probably his dad landing face-first on the couch.

He couldn't remember making up his mind. Sam grabbed his old frame pack from the back of his closet, along with a couple water bottles and his sleeping bag—a good one that his grandmother bought for him the year before she died—and Mike's old green canvas tent. On his way out the door, he stopped to look at his dad, passed out on the couch.

"I'm not leaving because I don't want to kill you," Sam told him. "I'm leaving because I don't want to be a killer."

Nothing, just a muffled snore. Good riddance, Sam thought. He walked out the front door and kept walking all night long until he hit the Appalachian Trail. Then he kept on walking north.

By the time someone came home, Sam had settled into a rocking chair on the front porch. A woman driving a ratty station wagon pulled into the driveway. Sam could see two bright redheads in the backseat. The look of the mom when she got out of the car surprised him. She was very thin with no makeup, hair pulled back in a braid. Pretty, but she looked tired. She looked very much like an adult, which wasn't how Sam thought of Mike. The last time he saw him, he hadn't been much older than Sam was now.

The woman said something to the kids before trudging toward the house. For a second Sam thought maybe she knew who he was. Maybe his dad had woken up that morning in March, full of regret, and had become frantic when he found Sam gone. Maybe he'd done something a regular parent would do, like get on the phone and call everyone Sam might have reached out to. Sam had only shown his face in the small towns along the trail. For all he knew, his picture could be all over Facebook and Twitter. He might even be on one of those billboards. He was still seventeen, technically a missing child.

"Hi," the woman said tentatively, stopping at the foot of her own porch as if she needed his permission to come any closer.

"Hi," Sam said, afraid again that he'd got the wrong address. "I'm Sam. Mike's brother."

She hesitated a minute, like she was trying to work out in her head if she'd ever heard of him before. "Oh," she finally said. "Oh right. Sam. Hey. I'm Marianne."

"Hey," Sam said, and he stood up. She walked up onto the porch and held out her hand. He could tell that she'd thought about hugging him, but decided not to, and he couldn't blame her. The hand bath in her little stream was the closest he'd come to laundry or showering in over a week.

He shook her hand, then waited for her to say something like, *Thank God you're okay*, or, *Everyone's been so worried about you!*

But she only said, "Well, this is a surprise."

Sam usually felt pretty comfortable around women. They tended to like him right away. But instead of giving her a slow smile, or trying to charm her, he found himself blurting out, "So did Dad call? Have you guys been looking for me?"

She looked confused. Then she shrugged, her face rearranging itself into a kindness that Sam liked. She was smart. In one second, she understood that Sam wanted to know if anyone had been worried.

"No," Marianne said. "No, he didn't. But I'm very glad to see you, just the same."

The two redheaded kids weren't Mike's, and neither was the house. Marianne used to live here with her ex-husband. She didn't go into a lot of detail about what had happened to him, but was otherwise friendly and chatty. She gave Sam some clean sweats and a T-shirt of Mike's, and showed him the bathroom and the washing machine.

Marianne had refused his offer to help with dinner, so Sam sat at the kitchen table with the older girl, Susannah, filling out the questions from the bottle. Marianne told Sam how she worked at a day care, so she could bring Susannah and Millie with her every day. Mike worked at the Save-A-Lot, bagging groceries.

"He'll be a cashier soon," she said.

By the time Mike got home, Sam's clothes were tumbling in the dryer. Sam could tell when he came in that Marianne had already called to give him a heads-up. He looked on edge, like his long-lost little brother wasn't the most welcome sight in the world. He also looked kind of bloated and puffy, and older than . . . how old must Mike be by now? Twenty? Twenty-one?

"Hey," Mike said. "Look what the cat dragged in."

Sam stood up to shake Mike's hand, hunching his shoulders a little so he wouldn't tower over his brother. This wasn't deferential. It was strategic. Mike could be competitive, and right now, Sam needed to make sure he didn't feel threatened. He needed him to be a big brother.

Mike clapped his hand onto Sam's shoulder, squeezing a little. "What are they putting in the water back there in Seedling?" he said. "Growth hormones?"

Marianne laughed, sliding chopped onions into a wide frying pan. They sizzled as they hit the oil, and Sam breathed in the scent. Sometimes, lately, his body forgot to be hungry. But it had been a long time since he'd smelled a home-cooked meal.

Mike grabbed two beers out of the refrigerator. "Let's go out back," he said to Sam. "You can fill me in."

At the kitchen table, Susannah lifted up the pen they'd been using, giant blue eyes imploring.

"We'll finish when I come back," Sam promised her.

Things started out okay, with Mike showing him around the yard and asking him questions about the past couple years.

"Typical," he said when Sam told him about the cigarette.

Mike pulled up his shirt to show him a couple of his own scars, and reminded him about the time Dad had broken his wrist dragging him into the kitchen to clean up after dinner. When his wrist swelled up, their dad had made a deal with both of them, saying he'd only take Mike to the emergency room if they promised to say he'd fallen on his Rollerblades.

"That guy will never change," Mike said, and then drained the last of his beer.

Mike was interested in how Sam had made his way here— "You *walked*?" he said, incredulously. Sam told him how he had partly survived on food that grew on the trail, like berries and mushrooms and assorted wildflowers. The fishing was decent and sometimes he'd stop in a town to work for a day or two—offering to mow lawns or paint fences, so he could afford supplies. There were also plenty of people on the trail who were willing to share food around the campfire.

"Girls," Mike said with a crooked smile. "I see nothing's changed in that department."

"Marianne seems cool," Sam said, redirecting the subject, and right away he saw he'd made a mistake.

The barest bit of anger passed over his brother's face, like he didn't want anyone complimenting her. "She's all right. The kids are a pain in the butt, but it's a free place to live."

Sam didn't say anything. He accepted the second beer Mike handed him even though he'd barely taken a sip from the first. He reminded himself that Mike was the only person in the world who might offer him a place to stay. He thought of the girl he'd been going out with before he left, Starla, and how he hadn't gotten in touch with her because he thought she might tell his father where he was. Turns out it didn't matter. His father hadn't been looking.

Over the past few months on the trail, Sam hadn't let himself think much about Starla or any of the other kids from his class. He hadn't pictured them graduating without him, going to work in the mines, or switching from part-time to full-time at whatever job they already had. Some of them would get married. A few of the especially smart ones, like Starla, would head to West Virginia University. Knowing Starla, she was probably already packing to leave.

Marianne poked her head out and said, "Dinner's ready, guys."

"All right," Mike said, scraping his chair noisily on the deck. "Let's see what she oversalted tonight."

Marianne was already back in the kitchen giving the girls their plates of chicken and Brussels sprouts. Sam hoped she hadn't heard Mike.

Mike grabbed another beer and started to hand one to Sam.

"No thanks," Sam said. "I'm good." Mike shrugged and gave it to Marianne instead.

"These things again?" Mike said, spearing a Brussels sprout.

Marianne slid into her chair apologetically. "Sorry," she said. "It's something green the girls will eat."

Sam quickly took a bite so he could say, "Wow, this is amazing. Thank you."

He wanted to be nice, it was true, but also the food *was* amazing. Usually he wasn't a big fan of Brussels sprouts, but these were tender and crunchy at the same time. Salty, sure, but in a good way.

Mike rolled his eyes. "Sam has a special way with the ladies," he said. It was probably supposed to be a compliment, but it didn't sound like one. Mike gave Sam's head a weird little shove. Sam could see the little girls leaning closer to each other.

"What do you think, Marianne? You think my brother's a good-looking kid?"

Marianne laughed uncomfortably and took her first bite of food. Clearly there was no right answer to that question.

Mike cocked his head and pulled on his earlobe. "Got a hearing problem?" he said. "You think my brother's handsome? Blond hunk of muscles over here?"

Sam could see it on Marianne's face, the same look their mother used to have, measuring and calculating. Strategizing the best way to calm this uncalmable person.

Then Millie piped up. "I think he looks like Prince Eric."

"Prince Eric has black hair," Susannah said.

"Except for that."

Mike stared straight ahead, probably trying to remember which movie Prince Eric was in. Sam had no idea, either.

"Thanks," Sam said, with what felt like the first real smile he'd cracked in a long time. "That's the nicest compliment I've ever had."

The girls smiled back, but Sam knew right away they'd all made a mistake. In fact they'd passed the point where they could make anything *but* mistakes. Mike stood up angrily and got another beer, reaching into the fridge with such intensity, you'd think he was grabbing a weapon.

After dinner, Mike marched out of the kitchen while Sam tried to help with the dishes.

"You know," Marianne said, "it would actually help me more if you kept them occupied." She jutted her chin toward the girls, and Sam knew what she meant: keep them out of Mike's way. He picked up Millie and brought her back to the table to sit with her sister. Then they went to work finishing the note from the bottle.

"Okay," Sam said. "We already wrote that we found it in Temple Stream. Right? That's what it's called?"

"That's what it says here," Susannah said, pointing to where Sam had written it down earlier. "I can see the *T*."

"*T*," said Sam. "Like my last name."

"But not our last name," Susannah said. "Mike's not our father."

Marianne paused for a second at the sink behind them, then turned the water higher. Sam knew it was to drown out their conversation so Mike wouldn't hear. Hopefully he'd already stumbled upstairs and passed out. The one good thing about mean drunks is eventually they pass out, and nothing can wake them. It was a familiar feeling, hanging on, tiptoeing across glass, until that breath of relief.

"I have to put my address," Sam said. "Do you think this person will write back?"

"Maybe he'll come visit," Susannah said. "Like you."

She recited their address for Sam, who filled it in. Mike appeared in the doorway, leaning against the doorjamb.

"What's that?" Mike said. "You living here now?"

Millie echoed the words in a different tone. "You're living here now?" she asked, excited. "I thought you were just visiting."

"He *is* just visiting," Mike said. He reached over and took the sheet of paper off the table, crumpled it, and tossed it in the general direction of the garbage. Millie burst out crying as it landed on the floor. It made Sam sad to see the expert way in which Susannah stood and guided her sister out of the kitchen, using the other doorway. Sam waited until he heard them reach the top of the stairs before he spoke.

"Sorry," he finally said. "It just feels so much like home, I guess I forgot myself."

"What the hell is that supposed to mean?"

"What do you think it means? Want another beer, Mike? Or would you rather I pour you a shot? You can scare little kids much faster if you go straight for the hard stuff."

Mike leaned across the table and pointed a thick finger in Sam's face. "You shut up," he said. "Just shut up."

The steady rush of water shut off. "Mike." Marianne's voice was quiet.

"YOU." The word was so loud, it made it seem like he'd been whispering. "YOU STAY OUT OF THIS."

"It's her house," Sam said, his voice very low. He was remembering the way his father had felt in his hands, all that soft flesh that would have been so easy to pound. Now for the past few months he'd been walking twenty miles a day, sometimes more. He had walked over mountains, over a thousand miles. While Mike had been bagging groceries, drinking beer, getting soft. Sam was taller, younger. It would be so easy to just stand up, take him by the collar, and give him what he deserved.

Upstairs, he was sure, the girls were cowering. Sam pictured them, tiny ears pressed against the floorboards.

"I guess it's a good thing you don't smoke," Sam said, motioning toward the row of round scars on Mike's arm. Mike looked down and swayed on his feet—he'd lost the brace of the doorjamb when he'd stepped toward Marianne.

"Forget this," Mike said, and started to retreat. Then he turned back, this time pointing at Sam. "You're gone in the morning."

"My thoughts exactly," said Sam.

Mike nodded as if he'd accomplished something, then walked out of the room.

Marianne came to the table and sat across from Sam. They both sat quietly, listening to him make his way upstairs, their breath held to see if he'd start in on the girls. But all they heard was a door close. The whole house breathed a sigh of relief. The drunk was down. At least for the night.

"Why would you let him stay here?" Sam asked. She looked so tired, but she had kind eyes. Her hair looked like it had been bright red like her daughters' once, now it was a soft chestnut. Sam wondered if she had a father like Mike. When Sam was little he used to think of his father as two people, Daytime Dad and Nighttime Dad. He tried to remember how old he'd been before he couldn't look at one without seeing the other.

"It's your house," Sam said. "Why don't you kick him out?"

"He's not always like this," Marianne said. "I think it's just bringing up a lot, seeing you again after so long, and . . ."

Sam held up his hand. He couldn't stand it, listening to her make excuses.

"Maybe," Sam said. "He may not *always* be like this. But you know at the same time. He always *will* be like this."

Marianne nodded, her eyes filling with tears. Part of Sam wanted to reach out, take her hand. Comfort her. But another part knew that even though she knew he was right, and even though there were two little girls upstairs listening, nothing Sam said or did would make any difference.

Hours later, Sam lay on the couch under the quilt Marianne had given him. It was the first soft place he'd slept in months, so you'd think he'd be dead to the world. But his eyes had been open long enough to adjust to the darkness, staring up at the ceiling. Even though he'd only had one sip of the first beer, the taste lingered at the back of his throat. It made him feel sick, like somehow he had something to do with the way Mike had acted.

Mike hadn't been as bad as their dad. But then, their dad

hadn't always been that bad, either. When Mike and Sam were little—more or less the same ages as Millie and Susannah—it had gone pretty much the same way. A steady stream of beers led to their dad getting slowly meaner; the things he said, especially to their mother, meant to provoke a reaction that he could get pissed about so he could then blame whatever he did on everybody else.

Sam knew there was a good chance Mike wouldn't even remember telling him he had to leave. If he wanted to, he could stay. Either way, his brother would wake up hating himself, full of apologies.

Sam pushed the quilt aside and got up. He would've finished doing the dishes in the sink, but he didn't want to wake anyone. Instead, he fished the crumpled paper out of the trash and smoothed it out. He hunted down a clean piece of paper and a pen, along with an envelope and a stamp, and copied everything down carefully:

Who are you? Your name and address and phone are optional. Sam Tilghman. I don't have an address or phone.

Being as precise as you can, where did you find this bottle? In Temple Stream, below my brother's girlfriend's house in Farmington, Maine, tangled in some reeds in a little curve by the shore.

On what date? Somewhere in June. I lose track these days.

In what circumstances? That is, what were you doing when you happened on the bottle? I was taking a break from leaving the world behind. That turned out to be a mistake.

Add any notes or information you'd like: Just, thanks for this. Now you've got me thinking about the poetry of streams. That's a good thing to think about. Better than anything I could've come up with.

Sam slid the letter into the envelope. Outside, first light was stirring, along with a cacophony of birds, their different songs battling. For the thousandth time he wished he could tell one birdsong from another. Weird that you could sit here in a house, in a kitchen with running water and a refrigerator full of food, and listen to the same noises you'd hear in the deepest thicket of forest, with nothing but a crappy canvas tent between you and the world.

Damn, Sam thought. Life was so much easier on the trail. On the trail, there were never the unhappy events of last night, knocking around in your head and gut.

He thought about leaving a note for Marianne and the girls, but that might piss Mike off. So he just grabbed his pack, now full of clean clothes, and headed out the door. He put the envelope into a neighbor's mailbox, pulling up the little yellow flag. When a car came rumbling up the road, Sam stuck out his thumb, but wasn't surprised when it zoomed right by. If he got a ride a little closer to the trail, great. If not, he'd just walk. He'd walk as long and as far as he needed to get back on the AT, then he'd head south, all the way to Georgia.

What he'd do when he got to Georgia he couldn't say. Maybe he'd turn around and start walking north again, spend his whole life walking up and down the East Coast, staying out of the world's way. He could grow his hair long, grow a tangled beard. He'd be like that crazy guy Walden, that vagrant the thru hikers were always on the lookout for.

Another car whooshed by and Sam just kept walking. The sunlight widened into morning. The birdsong died down.

One foot in front of the other. There were worse ways to spend your life.

7

Sixty-five miles into the 100 Mile Wilderness, Mc-Kenna stood by a logging road, seriously thinking about getting off the trail.

To say that things had gotten easier since that first day on Katahdin would be true, but also misleading. Because things had by no means gotten anywhere close to anything that could be described as *easy*.

For example, at the moment, afternoon storm clouds were gathering. She hadn't been able to text her parents as promised last night, or this morning, because she couldn't get any reception. Her legs were covered with mosquito and black-fly bites despite daily and liberal dousing of bug spray—so liberal she didn't think her little bottle would last until the 114.5-mile mark, the paved road that would take her to the town of Monson to resupply. Back at Baxter State Park, on the morning of her second (and first successful) attempt to climb Katahdin, McKenna had snapped a picture of the sign with her phone:

IT IS 100 MILES SOUTH TO THE NEAREST TOWN AT MONSON.
THERE ARE NO PLACES TO OBTAIN SUPPLIES OR HELP UNTIL
MONSON. DO NOT ATTEMPT THIS SECTION UNLESS YOU HAVE
A MINIMUM OF 10 DAYS SUPPLIES AND ARE FULLY EQUIPPED.
THIS IS THE LONGEST WILDERNESS SECTION OF THE ENTIRE
AT AND ITS DIFFICULTY SHOULD NOT BE UNDERESTIMATED.

GOOD HIKING!
ATC

Strictly speaking, it was true that Monson was her best bet. But McKenna knew that, just over fifty miles in, some of these new, unofficial logging roads led to little towns. Her guidebook cautioned against going off the trail, though. Some of the logging roads petered out in the middle of nowhere, or worse, splintered off before ending up in the middle of nowhere, so you couldn't find your way back once you realized you'd hit a dead end.

Still, she took off her pack and dug out her phone, raincoat, and guidebook before sitting down to think. She turned on the phone, which had about half a battery bar left—she'd only been turning it on every couple days for a few minutes at a time. From the map in her guidebook it *looked* like this might be one of the roads that led to a town, but she couldn't tell for sure. There was no marker, just lovely clusters of Indian pipe, their white flowers bowed as if preparing for the rain.

She clicked on the compass app to see if it was any easier to use than her actual compass, which so far had only sent her into paroxysms of confusion. With the iPhone compass, all she had to do was swirl it around to calibrate. The logging road headed east, which she believed should bring her out of the mountains and trees to something resembling civilization, maybe a little town with a country store where they made sandwiches, and possibly stocked calamine lotion. Maybe there would even be pizza?

A fat raindrop landed on her phone's screen with a *splat*. McKenna held the phone to her chest protectively, wiping it off on her quick-dry T-shirt. Then she tucked it into the dry bag in her pack, put on her raincoat, covered her pack with the rain guard that was turning out to be only mildly helpful, and hoisted the weight back onto her shoulders. Tempting as the idea of a hot slice and a cold Coke might be, she couldn't risk getting lost. She had three more days' worth of supplies, which should be enough to deliver her safely to Monson. The only thing that could screw her up now would be going off the trail and into possible danger.

Eight days on the trail. Ten rainstorms—one that included actual hail. Blackfly season was supposed to be slowing down but nobody had bothered to tell them that. They particularly liked the spot right where her neck met her shoulders, and countless times a day McKenna found herself slapping one in mid painful bite.

Although it was chilly at night, the days were sweltering, and sweat already stained every piece of her clothing. Except for splashing her face and arms with water, she hadn't had a shower since the Katahdin Inn and Suites. And there was a persistent soreness in literally every part of her body, especially her shoulders, where the straps of her supposedly ergonomic pack dug in all day, every day.

Am I having fun yet? McKenna asked herself.

But her answer was always, unequivocally, *Yes. In spite of and sometimes even because of all the rustic, grueling discomfort.* She was having the time of her life.

A couple miles after "The Logging Road Not Taken," McKenna knelt at what she guessed was the east branch of Pleasant River. Back home, she'd read a blog by one regular thru hiker who said he never bothered purifying water from running streams in Maine. But a bacterial infection like giardia could destroy her whole trip, and that was another chance McKenna wasn't willing to take, no matter how pristine and cool the water might seem.

She carefully used her filter to purify a fresh supply into both water bottles. Then she spent a few minutes hunting around for a good strong walking stick. She'd hoped to find one she liked well enough to keep with her, but that hadn't happened yet—the last stick she'd been very confident with had broken mid-ford, almost sending her and her pack downstream with the current. So far, crossing rivers was the scariest part of the trip. When her stick had broken, her feet lost their grip on the rocky bottom, and something like panic had risen up in her.

Knowing that panic was a hiker's worst enemy only made her freak out more. Truthfully she wasn't exactly sure how she had righted herself and continued to the opposite bank.

Now she found another decent stick—a gnarled birch branch that was half wet. Possibly someone coming from the opposite direction had used and discarded it earlier today. She took a mental inventory of the people she'd passed who were walking northbound. She ran into at least a few people every day, and she had yet to reach an empty campsite. Everyone was friendly and openly concerned about her being alone on the trail. But at the height of summer, there were enough peo ple around that she didn't *feel* alone, not really. Even now, in the thick of wilderness with no human in sight, she felt sure that if she were in trouble and called out, people would come running from both directions.

When she leaned on the stick to test it out, it held firm, with just enough springiness that she doubted it would snap. So she traded her hiking boots for her more water-friendly Keen sandals, loosened the shoulder straps of her pack, and pulled it back on, leaving the waist belt unbuckled. Then she placed the stick into the water and started to wade across. The water rose around her to about mid-thigh, and she planted the stick firmly, remembering that she'd made it across a much faster river than this one.

One foot in front of the other, she told herself, *same as on the trail.* She just had to be a little more careful.

She was almost to the opposite bank when the rubber sole

of her left sandal lost its grip on a flat, mossy rock, pitching her forward, landing her right knee on a rock that was so sharp, McKenna wondered if it was in fact an arrowhead.

"Ow!" she said aloud, tears of pain springing to her eyes. She was close enough to shore that she could reach out her hands and grab hold of the dry ledge, pulling her legs carefully after her. Miracles do happen, because her pack had managed to stay dry—at least from stream water. The jury was still out on whether the steady, misting rain had managed to infiltrate the interior.

Safely back on shore, McKenna threw off her pack and inspected the damage. The rock had made a triangular flap of flesh on her knee, blood bubbling beneath it. She touched it gingerly and winced. If she were home, she guessed her mother would make her go for a neat round of stitches. Now she had to settle for butterfly bandages and probably a lifelong scar.

"Ow," she said again as she pulled out her first-aid kit. She swallowed a couple ibuprofen before getting to work patching up the damage. From where she sat she could see the East Branch shelter, but injury or not, she was determined to make it at least a couple more miles before stopping for the day.

Anytime anything interfered with the mileage McKenna planned to cover, she was overtaken by a surge of adrenaline, making her more determined than ever to keep going. Back in her old life, a cut like this might have taken her out of the game for a day or more. Here on the trail, there was no time to be lost over a flesh wound. As she got back to her feet, she assured herself that yes, she was still having fun, and a part of that fun was even this: getting hurt, taking care of herself, and continuing on in spite of everything.

It was nearly dark when she limped toward the Logan Brook lean-to. A troop of Boy Scouts were gathered in the shelter, watching the approaching weather. Just as McKenna dropped her pack onto the dusty floor, a shower of hail began pelting the rickety roof above them.

"Good timing," said a dad-aged man, who must have been the scoutmaster.

McKenna nodded, glad that the hail wasn't raining down directly on her head. She stood away from the group—as much as she could in the small shelter, anyway—and stared forlornly out at the weather. There were several tent sites, but there was no way to put up her tent as long as it was hailing like this. Her clothing was soaked, but she didn't know how she was supposed to change in front of ten fourteen-year-old boys and one grown man.

"You leave someone behind in that?" the scoutmaster asked her.

By now McKenna was used to this question. In one form or another, she'd had this conversation every day for over a week. "No," she said. "It's just me."

"Hiking all on your own?"

"Yup."

This answer was usually followed by more questions, like

if her parents knew, or if she needed help. How far was she going? Was she sure she could make it all that way? McKenna had always looked a little young for her age, a fact that had never bothered her as much as it did on the trail, running into concerned adults—men, mostly—who immediately labeled her as a damsel in distress.

"I'm Dan," said the scoutmaster. He rattled off the kids' names, which McKenna would never remember in a million years.

She waved. "McKenna," she said.

"That's a nasty cut."

She looked down at her knee. Blood was trickling through the gauze square she'd taped over the butterfly bandages. The injury ached with a sharp, pulsing rhythm. Since she couldn't change out of her wet clothes, she decided to re-dress the wound. Hopefully now that she'd stopped walking the new bandage would hold long enough for it to scab up a little.

"I fell crossing the river," she said.

"Long way to walk with a cut knee," Dan said.

McKenna wished his voice would sound a little less sympathetic. This distress was minor. She had it all under control.

"I'm okay," she said, and smiled at him, not wanting to be rude, but also not inviting him to be her stand-in dad for the evening. She had left her own dad home for a reason.

She scanned the room for a bunk that didn't already have a sleeping bag on it, and seeing none, dragged her pack to a bench and sat down sideways, with both legs in front of her.

She tore off the gauze and raised the knee toward her, inspecting the damage. The hail continued to pelt the roof, making it feel like they were all inside some kind of child's percussion instrument. It was weirdly cozy.

"Want some help with that?" Dan called. Apparently ten kids weren't enough for him to take care of.

"No thanks," McKenna called back, pulling off the old butterfly bandages. "I'm good."

She swallowed a few more ibuprofens, slathered the cut with Neosporin, then plastered on a fresh butterfly and gauze bandages. The dressing looked so perfect, so professional, she almost wanted to get out her phone and take a picture. Of course if she posted it on Facebook or Instagram, everyone would have the wrong reaction—worrying about the cut instead of admiring how well she was taking care of it.

In a few minutes the hail stopped, almost as abruptly as it had begun. McKenna gathered her things to set up her tent.

"Hey," Dan said as she stiff-leggedly exited the shelter. "Come back and have dinner with us. We're doing beef stew and corn bread."

Now, *that* was the kind of help she couldn't resent. Or refuse.

"Thanks," McKenna said. "I definitely will."

The next afternoon, her knee throbbing, McKenna decided to stop a little earlier than she'd planned, at a campsite by Chairback Pond, instead of going an extra three miles to the shelter. Thanks to the light rain—not as persistent but still making everything damp—she had the whole place to herself. As she pitched her tent, she reminded herself that it was early still, and other people might join her. But so far, the campsite stood empty. She managed to get her tent set up, change into warmer clothes, and get water. A couple hikers passed, waving to her as they continued on, probably looking forward to a dry night in the lean-to. By the time the sky had cleared and then darkened, McKenna sat cooking noodles on her little stove, and she was pretty sure: after nine days on the AT, this would be her first night completely alone.

As soon as the thought formed in her head, an owl hooted from a tree barely two yards away. McKenna shivered. It was a beautiful sound, eerie and low, and of course a reminder that she was never alone out here in the woods. Layers of forest concealed all manner of creatures: deer, moose, bears, bobcats, fisher cats. Several nights she had heard coyotes howling and yipping. Among hikers and naturalists, there was a running debate about whether mountain lions had returned to these eastern mountains. McKenna hated to admit she hoped the naysayers were right in that particular argument. Much as she loved animals, she didn't think her pepper spray would protect against a cougar.

The owl hooted again, and for a second McKenna considered gathering up her things and eating in her tent. Instead she looked up at the sky. The clouds had dispersed enough to reveal a blanket of stars sprawling overhead. The days of rain lent the forest a mulchy odor, but that was more of a bottom note. Out here, the top note, always, was pine. She breathed it in. She'd left her wool cap in her pack, which lay safe and dry in her tent. Her ears felt red with the cold. How could it be so hot during the day and so cold at night? In Maine, in the mountains, she sometimes felt like she walked through all four seasons in a single day.

She slurped down the last of her ramen, then put on her headlamp and collected her food to hang in a tree, a good several yards from her tent, the philosophy being that if a bear came looking for snacks, he'd go for the far-off supply instead of ransacking her tent. Bear attacks didn't happen often, but they did happen. As she packed up her stove, the little propane tank felt light—she'd be lucky to get one more dinner out of it before having to refill it in Monson.

In her tent, she pulled the gauze off her knee. It still hurt, but less than it had last night. The butterfly bandages were holding fast, no blood was seeping out, and the skin around it looked faintly pink, but not red. No sign of infection. She carefully stuck on a piece of fresh gauze, pulled on her fleece sweats, and crawled into her sleeping bag. She'd already filled her stuff sack with clothes, using it as a pillow. Usually at this time of night, in a campground full of people, she'd be reaching for a book, reading for a while as the camp noise died down. But tonight she was so bone tired from hiking with her hurt knee. Plus, the total lack of human sound was exotic and the slightest bit scary. More than the slightest bit, if she was honest with herself.

But never mind the fear. Never mind the pain or the exhaustion. She was proving that she could push through all of it. Tomorrow morning at first light she would pack up and walk at least ten miles, maybe more, depending on how her knee felt. By the next day, she felt sure, she would be able to take another picture—of the sign warning hikers coming from the south of the 100 Mile Wilderness. Those hikers would end their journey with the hardest stretch. McKenna had begun with it, and now it was nearly over. She had done it.

She fell asleep smiling, her headlamp still on, shining a tiny circle of light, all night long, on the side flap of her tent. Luckily she could get extra batteries in Monson.

8

A good ten days later, McKenna sat on the stoop of the general store in Andover, Maine, with Linda, an ex-Marine who'd started the trail in Georgia back in March. Linda was in her midthirties; she'd come home from Afghanistan four years ago and enrolled at the University of Texas. The hike was her graduation present to herself, and, as she told McKenna, she was pretty stoked to have only one more state to go before getting her certificate signed at Baxter State Park. McKenna was beyond thrilled to meet another woman going it alone. As Linda showed her the various stamps in her passport, McKenna admired her powerful biceps, covered with tattoos. Linda wore a bandanna over her cropped graying brown hair. McKenna wondered out loud if as many people asked Linda if she felt safe on her own.

"Probably not as many as ask you," Linda said, giving McKenna a quick once-over. "But you'd be surprised. People don't like to see a woman doing something like this alone, no matter how strong she looks. People were less antsy about my going to war than about me hiking by myself. This doesn't jibe with their vision of the world. It makes them nervous."

Linda tried to teach McKenna how to use her compass, the Cammenga that she'd spent seventy dollars on back in Connecticut, and couldn't figure out how to use to save her life, literally.

"No matter which way I hold it, it points north. And then it just kind of quivers. Two mornings I've set off in the wrong direction. It's easier to just use the one on my phone."

"Yeah, they should have different-colored blazes for southbound and northbound," Linda agreed.

Every few hundred yards, trees on the AT were marked with white paint to let hikers know they were still on the trail, the same color in both directions. It seemed like it should be the simplest thing in the world—north or south. But on misty mountain mornings after a cold and lumpy sleep in your tent, it was easy to point your bleary-eyed self in the exact wrong direction.

This morning, though, McKenna was well rested. Amazingly rested. Last night, for the first time since beginning the trail, she'd slept in a bed in her own room that she'd rented at Pine Ellis Lodging. Not only had she taken a shower, shaving off an impressive amount of growth since her stop in Monson, but she'd also done laundry, eaten pizza, and guzzled down a Coke. Back at home McKenna hardly ever drank soda, but on the trail it turned out to be the thing she fantasized about when she reached the end of her stamina, those tiny little old-fashioned glass bottles of Coke.

And the most decadent thing she'd done: her southbound guidebook included the name and phone number of a massage therapist. McKenna wondered briefly what her parents would think when they saw *that* charge on their statement. She decided they'd be happy to see signs of her doing something so civilized. Thinking of her parents made her realize they were due for a text. She dug out her phone.

"Hey," Linda objected, tapping the compass. "You're not watching."

"I think it's probably hopeless," McKenna said, quickly texting that she was alive and almost in New Hampshire.

Linda shrugged. "I didn't bring a phone," she said. "Just wanted to be totally cut off. You know?"

"Yeah," McKenna said. "I wanted that, too."

McKenna didn't add that she'd had a harder time weaning herself off her phone than she'd thought she would. Last night in her room, she'd broken down and logged on to Facebook. Though she'd resisted posting anything, she'd creeped on a couple pages. All her friends were fixated on where they'd be going to college. Brendan's page had been full of posts about Harvard. As McKenna read through them, she felt a pang of longing that was strong enough to make her go ahead and message him. The fact that he hadn't written back yet meant that she might have to check tonight, if she got reception at her campsite.

"This is a really good compass," Linda said. "We used the same kind in Afghanistan."

"Do you want it?" McKenna said it automatically, feeling so relaxed and pampered. As soon as the words were out she realized how much she wanted to do this, give Linda the compass. So far on the trail she'd been given meals and gift certificates for cafés in rest towns. A man her father's age had traded his excellent rain cover for her mediocre one (he'd been a north-bound thru hiker, almost done, happy to help her out on her long hike). This was her first chance to offer a little trail magic of her own.

"No way," Linda said. "You've got thirteen more states to go."

When she put it that way, a small bit of McKenna's well-restedness fluttered away on the morning breeze. Thirteen more states to go! That was like the whole original United States. She wondered what George Washington or Thomas Jefferson would say to a seventeen-year-old girl walking all the way from one tip of the country to the other.

"But I feel like there's a magnetic field in my body that just makes it go bonkers," she said. "I'm never going to be able to figure it out."

Linda laughed as she handed the compass back. "You keep it," she said. "Your phone could get broken or the battery could die. With the compass, it's like CPR. You think you don't know how to do it, but when you have to, you'll remember this little lesson."

McKenna had paid almost zero attention to the lesson, but she took the compass back and shoved it inside the front pocket of her pack. The shuttle that took hikers back to the trail pulled up, and Linda and McKenna climbed on board.

"You shouldn't feel bad if you don't make it all the way to Georgia," Linda said. "It's not exactly easy. I met this one northbounder at Harpers Ferry, he was feeling bad about giving up, but hell, he made it halfway. Over a thousand miles. That's more than almost anyone walks."

McKenna couldn't believe it. Even Linda—her fellow warrior woman!—was doubting her. "No way," she said. "I'm not stopping at Harpers Ferry. I'm going all the way to Georgia."

Linda nodded, but McKenna could tell she wasn't convinced. All along the way, people kept telling McKenna not to feel bad when she failed. She'd gotten a late start, they all told her, not adding what they were obviously thinking: *She's just a girl.* But McKenna wasn't worried, and she didn't doubt herself. Since that first dreadful day, she had steadily increased her mileage. The cut on her knee had healed to a scab and didn't hurt at all anymore. While her pack still felt heavy—especially today, after her resupply in Andover—she was almost through Maine. The hardest state! She had climbed Katahdin, and Avery Peak, and Old Blue Mountain. In addition to the scab on her knee, her legs were covered in scratches but also beginning to cord with new muscle. Her sleeping bag would keep her warm through below-zero temperatures, and her boots were perfectly broken in and waterproof. Even if it snowed in the fall farther south, she was ready.

Plus, she'd had a massage yesterday, and an ice-cream cone for breakfast today. For the first time since she'd hit the trail, she was only mildly sore instead of desperately achy. Give her a mountain to climb, a river to ford, freezing temperatures to sleep through. She could take it, and take it happily.

When they got out of the shuttle, McKenna hoisted her pack onto her back. She thought of Courtney, and wondered how things were going with Jay. If she were here, they'd be helping each other in and out of their packs the same way they'd always yanked each other's riding boots off after a lesson.

On the trail, Linda and McKenna wished each other luck and hugged good-bye. The full length of their friendship had spanned just over an hour, but McKenna felt wistful as they parted ways, Linda heading north to hike one state, McKenna heading south to hike *thirteen*.

The past few weeks, it had been a pretty good balance between solitude and company—few enough people that she rarely had to walk the trail with anyone else, and enough people that she could have friendly exchanges, discussions, and even shared meals and camping for the night. The times McKenna felt most lonely were usually late at night, climbing into her sleeping bag exhausted, not yet ready to fall asleep but too tired to read. She not only missed Courtney, but Brendan, Lucy, and Buddy, too, though enough campgrounds and sections of the trail had NO DOGS signs that it was just as well she hadn't brought a dog along.

Yesterday's luxury combined with a good early start culminated in McKenna's best day yet, nearly twenty miles. It was almost dark when she got to the north end of the Mahoosuc Notch. Her guidebook promised the Notch would be the "most difficult or fun mile of the AT," which seemed like something best tackled fresh, so she decided to stop and pitch her tent at the small campsite. There was already a group of people there, mostly girls, and as McKenna scouted out a place for her tent, one of them came over.

"I'm Ashley," she said. She was probably around McKenna's age, tall, and pretty. McKenna could tell right away that she was just camping for a night or two; she looked so shiny and clean. Even though McKenna had done laundry yesterday and washed her hair, she knew her clothes had the dingy, worn-every-day look that marked all thru hikers.

"Want some chili?" Ashley invited. "We made a ridiculous amount."

"Sure," McKenna said. "I'd love that, thanks." Any night she didn't have to choose between setting up her camp stove and cooking or just eating granola bars and turkey jerky was heaven.

"Come set your tent up by us," Ashley said. "Then you won't have to stumble home when the party's over."

McKenna set up her tent and put on her Keen sandals, much more comfortable than her heavy boots. Ashley told her she was there for the weekend from Concord, New Hampshire, with some girlfriends. "We're not hiking much," she said. "Just camping." They were all students at UNH but were home for the summer.

They had built a big fire, something McKenna had been forgoing. Campfires could lead to forest fires, and also created light and smoke pollution. She felt like a better environmentalist using her little cookstove. At the same time she had to admit the fire was festive. Three other girls sat around it—two brunettes and a redhead—and one guy. The redhead stood up and ladled out a bowl of chili.

"Thanks," McKenna said. The heat of the plastic bowl felt wonderful in her hands. She sat down and one of the brunettes handed her a spoon and a can of beer.

"Maddie is an amazing cook," said the brunette. McKenna thought she'd said her name was Blair, but she couldn't remember.

Judging from the way the one guy sitting at the opposite end of the log from McKenna was scarfing down his bowl, Blair spoke the truth. McKenna could tell the guy was not part of the original group; like her, his clothes looked dingy, his once-white T-shirt a worn shade of gray. His blond hair hung unwashed to his shoulders. He looked up from his chili for a second and turned his head toward McKenna. In that moment, she did something totally out of character. She drew in an audible breath, and then immediately turned red, hoping the girls—or worse, the guy—hadn't heard her.

He was completely, ridiculously gorgeous. His eyes were the

crazy pale blue of a Siberian husky's. He had an angular face and sharp cheekbones. His legs, sprawled out in front of him, were impossibly long and knotted with muscle, as were his arms. No wonder the girls had invited him to join them.

McKenna pulled her eyes away and returned to the chili, remembering that they'd invited her, too. They were just a friendly group. She took a bite of chili, which had just the right amount of spicy heat, along with a faint whiff of cinnamon. It was of the meat-and-tomato variety—no beans—just the way she liked it.

"Oh wow," McKenna said. She took a sip of the cold beer, the perfect complement. "This is amazing."

The girls laughed. The guy barely glanced at her again.

"Told you," Blair said, and Maddie smiled.

"So are you hiking a long way?" Maddie asked. The guy had just handed her his empty bowl, and she stood to refill it.

"To Georgia," McKenna said.

"Wow!" Ashley said. "All by yourself?"

McKenna was used to this conversation by now: the surprise, followed by doubt, followed by questions.

"So's Sam," Ashley told her, pointing at the guy.

The guy looked up again when he heard them talking about him. He grinned and waved his spoon. McKenna waved back, but also wondered if everyone *he* met worried about him being alone. He was probably never grilled about his plans and then reassured that it was an achievement just to make it as far as he already had.

"He's already done it once," Ashley added. She was sitting next to him, and her voice sounded oddly proud. She lifted her hand like she was going to pat his knee, then thought better of it. McKenna guessed they'd been drinking awhile before she showed up.

"Really?" McKenna said. "You've already thru hiked?"

"Yeah, I finished a few weeks ago," Sam said, and took another bite of chili. McKenna couldn't blame the girls for fawning over him. His voice went perfectly with his looks— deep, with a hoarse edge to it, just enough Southern accent to make it musical.

"A few weeks ago?"

"Yep. Walked all the way to Maine. Then turned around. Started walking back."

"Like Forrest Gump when he got to California," said Blair. Her tone indicated she was not as impressed by Sam's charm. Maybe, like McKenna, she was suspicious of particularly gorgeous guys.

"Or Walden," Ashley added.

They laughed. It wasn't the first time someone had mentioned a man named Walden. By now, McKenna knew that everyone had a different story about him, but generally it was said that some tragedy had befallen him and now he just walked up and down the trail, with no pack, living off whatever grew in season and sleeping under the sky. Some people swore he was a ghost. He had a quaker parrot that traveled with him, sometimes on his shoulder, sometimes flying beside him. Often, in the trail ledgers, people would write down when they *thought* they'd seen him. But one seasoned thru hiker told McKenna that when you did run into Walden, there'd be no question in your mind. You'd know the very first instant: it was him.

"Walden doesn't really exist," Blair said. "He's just a campfire story."

Sam put down the bowl of chili, walked over to the girls' cooler, and pulled out a soda. He's certainly made himself right at home, McKenna thought. She also noted he was the only one not drinking.

Ashley leaned toward Sam as he sat back down. "Have *you* seen Walden?" she asked him.

"Yeah, I have," Sam said. "I saw him twice. Once in the Smoky Mountains—that's the most haunted stretch of the trail—then in town near the Delaware Water Gap. He was eating pizza at Doughboy's, that crazy bird sitting on his head, squawking and spreading his wings when anyone came near."

McKenna didn't know much about Walden, but thanks to her dad's friend and her future employer Al Hill, she had heard about the quaker parrots. Years ago, a shipment bound for a pet store had escaped in northern New Jersey. Now these tropical birds populated the Palisades, filling the trees in towns around the Hudson. Walden's parrot was supposed to be one of these, about the size of a parakeet. She guessed it could spread its wings, though it wouldn't be particularly threatening, and they probably peeped more than squawked. But she didn't say anything.

By now it was dark. McKenna was only halfway through her first beer, but the group was becoming noticeably rowdier, the girls squealing as Sam told them that Walden's daughter had been murdered at the age of twelve at a summer camp in the Smoky Mountains.

"She had long sandy-brown hair," Sam told them. "Giant blue eyes. Freckles across her nose. In fact . . ." He stood up, facing the row of girls sitting on the log. McKenna coughed a little as campfire smoke wafted in her direction.

"She looked just like you," he said, tipping his soda can at McKenna. "A little younger, obviously."

"Obviously," McKenna said. She blushed again, from his attention, and hoped it wasn't visible in the firelight.

"So," Sam said. Now that he was standing in front of them, it felt more like he was performing. "Walden's daughter was killed. Not just killed but eviscerated. They found her one morning, by the flagpole, carved open. There was a manhunt, but no killer was ever found. Some people think it was a crazed black bear that dragged her from her cabin. But Walden doesn't buy that story."

"Did he tell you this personally?" Blair asked, sarcastic.

"Let's just say I got the information close to the source. *Very close.*"

Sam's voice was low and convincing, but it had a twinkle in it, too. It almost made McKenna want to laugh, or worse, giggle.

"Anyway," he said. "Ever since that day, Walden left the

world behind. He took to the trail, overcome with grief, and never went home again. He just walks up and down, south to north, north to south, never worrying about the weather, never carrying anywhere near enough to sustain him or keep him dry. It's hard to know how he even stays alive. But you know what keeps him going?"

"The search for the killer?" Maddie asked.

"No. What keeps him going is killing."

"He's a vigilante?"

"You'd think so," Sam said. "But the kind of grief we're talking about doesn't know logic. He wants others to feel what he feels. So while he's walking up and down the trail, he keeps an eye out. He thinks he's going to find her—his daughter, that cute blue-eyed girl. And every once in a while, along comes someone who looks just like her, all by herself, and for a second Walden's crazy heart will jump with joy, until he realizes it's not her, and then *bam*!"

Sam jumped in McKenna's direction so suddenly she started backward, almost falling off the log. The other girls laughed.

"They always find her the same way," Sam said. "Eviscerated. Guts spilling out for everyone to see. That is, if the bobcats and bears don't find her first."

McKenna laughed with everyone else. She noticed that when Sam took his place next to Ashley, she slipped her arm through his, reclaiming him. It didn't exactly make sense for Ashley to feel possessive, or for McKenna to feel flattered that Sam had chosen her to be Walden's murder victim. Maybe she should have been spooked, but she couldn't help feeling like this was Sam's weird way of flirting with her.

As if to prove her suspicion, Sam's eyes stayed on her, despite Ashley being right next to him.

Thanks but no thanks, McKenna thought. This guy is obviously trouble. Part of her wanted to inform him she'd never been scared by ghost stories. But she didn't want to egg him on.

"That chili was so great, thank you," she said to Maddie. "I really appreciate it, but I've had a long day, so I think . . ."

"Good night!" Ashley said a little too enthusiastically.

McKenna headed to her tent. The party sounds from around the campfire were increasing; part of her wished she'd pitched her tent farther away, and part of her felt glad that their proximity meant she'd feel safe from ax murderers (Walden notwithstanding) and bears (she didn't even bother hanging her food bag, knowing no bear would come close to the noise and flickering fire). She dug out her phone and climbed into her sleeping bag, hoping to find a message from Brendan. It was a bad precedent, she knew. For one thing, if she got into the habit of messaging him, her battery might run out and then she wouldn't have her phone in an emergency. But in a weird way Sam's attention had made her feel even more homesick for her boyfriend, a knee-jerk reaction to having someone flirt with her, even someone as charming as this gorgeous stranger. She couldn't flirt back. She was taken.

But she soon wished that she'd left her phone in her pack

or that she hadn't been able to get reception or—best wish by
far—that she'd never met Brendan at all. His message read:

> McKenna, hey! I was happy to see your message. Really
> glad you're safe and that everything's going so well out
> there. My head is mostly wrapped up in heading to college.
> E-mailing with my suitemates and all that.
>
> I'm glad you decided to break your rule and write
> because I've been needing to talk to you but wanting to be
> respectful. I've been thinking about how college is this big
> new chapter, and with you on this trip, I thought maybe it
> seemed like a good time to take a break? Because we're
> already kind of going our separate ways, right? Please
> don't think by "break" I mean "break up" because I don't.
> I can't wait to see you at Christmas. I just mean that . . .

McKenna stopped reading. She didn't want to read any
more, at least not now. Of course Brendan would never put it
this way, but his meaning was clear: *I just mean that I want to
hook up with other girls at college.* And why wouldn't he? Their
last night together wasn't exactly memorable, and then she'd
told him he was only allowed to talk to her once a month.
It seemed like the stupidest thing in the world that it hadn't
occurred to her that he would want to break up with her after
that.

McKenna turned off her phone and tossed it toward her
feet. The group by the fire sounded so cheerful: Sam's low,

gruff voice, followed by eruptions of laughter. She almost felt like going back out there, guzzling some beer and giving Ashley a little competition.

Tears gathered in her throat as she thought of Brendan about to head off to Harvard. Maybe he already had a girl in mind. Maybe he'd already hooked up with another girl. The tears made their way to her eyes and she pressed her forearm against them.

Even on that terrible first day, failing on Katahdin, McKenna had not cried. She would *not* cry now, not over a boy, even if he had been her first real boyfriend.

Finally, she gave in to the tears. But just a little bit, just this one night. In the morning she'd get her things together and start walking. Brendan had been her boyfriend for three months. She had more time than that left on the trail. Starting first thing tomorrow morning, she would walk that boy—and any sadness over him—right out of her system.

When McKenna crawled out of her tent before first light, what she had taken to calling the birds' time, when their musical racket escorted in the dawn, she was surprised to see Sam asleep by the fire, alone. She'd fully assumed he'd be in Ashley's tent with her.

Last night she'd thought he was several years older than her, maybe in his early twenties. But asleep, even with that fair stubble across his jaw, he looked younger. Closer to her age. She remembered Brendan's message with an ache that she tried to tamp down. *Walk off the pain,* her track coach used to say when she twisted her ankle or pulled a muscle. Today's injury was more full-bodied, a bruise that spread from her toes to her head. She needed to walk off the pain.

Quietly as she could, she pulled her gear out of her tent and started breaking it down. Sam was appealing in an obvious way. But McKenna did not want company on this walk. Being pointed in the same direction from here, no doubt they would run into each other more than once over the next couple months, but today she wanted to give herself a head start.

"That's a lot of stuff," said a gruff drawl.

McKenna looked up and there he stood, looking down at her. He ran a hand through his too-long hair, smoothing it into place, the only beauty routine necessary. McKenna suddenly became acutely aware of her unbrushed teeth and the millions of hairs that must be unraveling from her braid.

"Mackenzie?" Sam said. "That's what you said your name is, right?"

"McKenna."

"Right. McKenna." He knelt down, surveying her things alongside her. McKenna gathered up her phone and shoved it into her dry bag along with the food. She'd planned to eat something before she left, but now that he was up she decided it was better to hit the trail as soon as possible.

Over the past few weeks, McKenna had devised a very specific system for how she packed, placing everything in the exact order she'd need it, which meant her tent and sleeping bag went in first. This process required the rest of her things to be spread out and surveyed, something that helped her get her head together for the day and focus on what was ahead. More nights than not this summer, she had camped at sites with other people, but Sam was the first to join her in this morning ritual. Feeling self-conscious, she started shoving things into her pack more hurriedly.

"You like Johnny Cash?" he asked, holding up her pink T-shirt.

McKenna snatched it away and stuffed it in her pack. "No. I just like the T-shirt."

"Wow," he said, holding up her little canister of pepper spray and the whistle. "You're prepared for everything."

She grabbed them out of his hand and tossed them in with her clothes (she was too embarrassed to clip them onto their usual spot, in easy reach on the outside of her pack).

"Yeah, well," McKenna said. "I need those in case I run into Walden, so I can put up a fight before he eviscerates me."

"Won't do you much good tucked away in there," Sam said.

As he examined each item, McKenna swept it away, the usual order of her bag giving way to lopsided bulges. Luckily she had packed the tampons before he showed up! As she grabbed her Swiss Army Knife, she decided to saw off the rope bracelet that Brendan had given her. Sam watched her for a second, then went back to examining her gear.

"You have a lot of books," he observed. "Unnecessary weight."

"I need to have something to read," she said "Plus the

guidebook seems pretty practical." She didn't feel like explaining *Walden*, or her journal.

"You should at least burn them once you're done," Sam said. "That way you don't have to haul them all the way to Georgia."

McKenna stopped sawing for a moment and stared at him. His face didn't look jeery or challenging. There hadn't been a lot of religion in her childhood, but McKenna thought a lightning bolt might strike her dead if she so much as considered burning books.

"I leave them in free boxes when I finish," she said, finally pulling the bracelet off and tossing it into her garbage pile. "And then I take a new one, or buy a new one if there isn't anything good." At outposts all along the trail, there were boxes of items hikers had shed, free for the taking.

Sam leafed through her songbird book. It had been a birthday gift from Lucy last summer—a thick paperback with buttons beside each bird that played their song. Sam pressed the button next to the goldfinch.

"Hey!" he said. "I recognize this one. I never put it together with the bird, though. Every time I see one I think someone's pet canary has escaped."

"They're goldfinches," McKenna said.

"So I read," Sam said, holding up the book. "Can you tell what it is before you see it, if you hear its song?"

She nodded. "I've had the book for a while."

"Very cool," Sam said. "There's this one bird that's been driving me insane. Long note. Then a few short notes. It was pretty at first, but I've heard it so much in every state I've walked through. If something drives you that crazy you should at least know what it is."

"Sounds like an eastern towhee."

She took the book back from him and leafed through, then pressed the button. At the recorded sound, a real eastern towhee answered from a nearby tree. They laughed.

"That's it," he said.

"You can borrow the book, if you want."

"Seriously?"

"Sure. You can just give it to me when we run into each other again. If it won't make your pack too heavy."

Sam hesitated, then smiled. "Sure," he said. "Thanks. I walked all the way up here from West Virginia listening to the birds, wondering what they were called."

"I thought you said you walked from Georgia."

She expected him to look embarrassed at being caught in a lie, but he didn't. Instead, he looked amused.

"Yeah, well, I only started wondering about the birds in West Virginia."

McKenna swept the last of her things into her pack.

"You sure you don't want to stick around?" Sam said. "I bet they have a good breakfast planned. And the Notch isn't easy."

"No," McKenna said. "I want to walk a good way today."

"Want help with that?" he asked, pointing to her bag.

"No thanks. I got it." She heaved her massive pack onto her back, trying not to hope he'd be impressed.

"Bye," he said, his gaze focused intently on her.

"Bye," she said.

She had only walked a few steps when he called out to her. "Hey, Mackenzie."

Something like laughter gathered in her chest and she recognized it as happiness—at being teased, flirted with, by such a handsome guy. She seriously needed to get going.

"What?" she said, trying her best to sound annoyed.

"You don't have to worry about me cramping your style on the trail. I'll pass you in an hour or so, and you'll have the whole place to yourself."

Her happiness disappeared. She wasn't angry at Sam in particular. More at the fact that every person she ran into, male or female, couldn't wait to doubt her—to doubt her ability to hike the whole trail, to walk fast, to know what she needed along the way.

Who cares, McKenna thought. Let them doubt her. She would show them.

She didn't bother saying good-bye or even waving. She just turned, adjusted her straps, and headed toward Mahoosuc Notch.

9

Just as Sam expected, the college girls got up and made an excellent breakfast, complete with fresh eggs fried in butter, and coffee.

"You girls trying the Notch today?" Sam asked.

"Are you kidding?" Ashley handed him her half-finished plate of eggs. Sam had already wolfed his down—who knew when he'd stumble on this kind of feast again? "I tried it once two years ago and nearly broke my ankle. Why don't you hang with us today, do a mellow hike, and spend another night?"

Her voice had that lilt girls got when they were trying to sound casual, but not quite pulling it off. Last night Sam had made out with Ashley a little after the others finally stumbled to their tents. By then he'd realized that Ashley was several steps beyond buzzed, and he was feeling very conscious of the other people around. So he'd cut things short, telling her he didn't want to take advantage, in a way that would let him off the hook but still earn enough points to be fed in the morning.

"Thanks," Sam said. "It's tempting, for sure, but I got to get south."

"Right," said the tall girl. Sam thought her name started with a *B*. He could tell she didn't like him very much. "Better hurry south."

Sam sipped coffee out of a tin mug, returning her challenging gaze. What was she accusing him of, exactly? Being a player? He'd been invited last night, and he hadn't played—not much, anyway. He wondered if she thought he wanted to chase after McKenna, and then, since she basically had no reason to think that, wondered if he *did* want to chase after McKenna. Of the group of last night's girls, she was the one he'd spoken to least and yet she was the only one besides Ashley whose name he was sure of.

She had been so damned cute this morning, with her bed head and lopsided pack. He wondered how she'd do climbing through the deep pit of rocks that formed the Notch.

"Here," B said, thrusting her half-finished plate at Sam. "You might as well finish mine, too."

"Thanks," he said.

"Oh, look," Ashley said. "That girl. Her tent's already gone. Did she take off?"

"I guess so," Sam said.

"She was nice," said B.

"She was," another one of them agreed. "But I don't think she's going to make it to Georgia."

When Sam hiked the AT in the opposite direction, he'd crossed Mahoosuc Notch on a rainy day with no idea of what lay ahead of him. He'd had nothing to eat but wild mushrooms and raw scallion grass for three days. The Notch was a mile-long gap in the mountain range, crammed with giant boulders that you had to crawl over, and between, and sometimes under. It had by far been the longest mile of his northbound walk. At least today it wasn't raining, he had two full meals in his stomach, and while he wasn't looking forward to the deep, rock-filled ditches—many of which he'd had to climb on his hands and knees—at least they wouldn't take him by surprise. The sun shone incredibly hot today, though. That was the trade-off he'd made for eating breakfast and starting late. The last blackfly of the season buzzed around his head and he knew better than to expend energy trying to wave it away. Instead, he gritted his teeth and started walking.

Sam's pack was ancient—green canvas like Mike's crummy tent, with an exterior frame. It pretty much only had room for his sleeping bag and tent, a change of clothes, and the big wool sweater he'd found in a free box outside Harpers Ferry, plus a plastic garbage bag in case of rain, a few bandannas, and a toothbrush and toothpaste. Despite traveling light, it was still hard to balance as he made his way between and around the boulders, his breath heavy in his own ears.

He thought of McKenna, how tiny she'd looked marching

off with that huge red pack stuffed to the gills. How much did that thing weigh? It had amused him, seeing all the stuff she had laid out, the expression on her face as she packed—like she had to check all the boxes on her checklist. Like all that stuff could help her overcome whatever challenges lay ahead. Of course Sam knew better.

He struggled over an especially huge boulder. Reaching for a handhold, he slipped backward, his ankle scraping mercilessly against the rock and landing him back in the deep ditch. Damn. He knew he should have put on socks, but both pairs he had were so skanky and stiff. The sneakers he'd been wearing when he left his dad's house had taken a good beating by now, too. Next time he got to town he'd have to find some duct tape.

He stopped and inspected the wound, took a minute to dig out a bandanna and mop up the blood, then tied it tightly around his ankle. He could swear he'd cut himself in exactly the same place, on exactly this rock, on his way to Maine. If he was calculating correctly, that meant he was almost through the Notch.

From somewhere in the distance—a tree above the boulders—he heard a high note that had been sounding all through Maine. Thanks to McKenna he finally knew what it was. Since he was stopped anyway, he pulled out the book she'd given him, leafing through it, pressing buttons. He'd never seen a book like this before. It was sweet of McKenna to lend it to him. He couldn't help wondering how she'd done through this part of the trail, if he'd come close to catching up with her. If he was having a hard time, he could only imagine how she was faring with that gigantic pack.

Earlier in the day, McKenna's pack had made it hard to get through the Notch, for sure, but she'd started in the cool of the morning, the heat not beginning in earnest until she was almost done. The rocks were even more impressive, and harder to traverse, than the pictures she'd seen had led her to believe. She had to balance carefully, making use of handholds and then taking off her pack and lowering it to the ground. At one point, she threw her pack over two rocks and instead of climbing over, tried to slide between them. Halfway through she realized it was a bad idea. She may have lost a little weight in the past few weeks, but she wasn't so narrow that she couldn't get stuck. For a moment she thought she *was* stuck, and the adrenaline that idea inspired allowed her to kick backward, out of the wedge. Then she climbed over, pressing down so hard on the rock that she scraped the inside of her palm.

Slowly, carefully, McKenna made it through the Notch. It was by far the longest mile of her trek so far, if you didn't count that wasted first day. When she got to the other end she shrugged off her pack. Every inch of her high-tech T-shirt, which was supposed to wick away sweat, was completely drenched.

She dug into her pack for the dry bag containing her phone and food. She'd eaten two bowls of that awesome chili, but that had been fourteen hours ago by now. She'd burned so many calories on that arduous climb, her stomach was beyond growling—it felt raked with emptiness, ready to start cramping in complaint. But the phone beckoned McKenna even more than a snack. She told herself she was just checking the time, but she couldn't help also seeing the notifications of messages, texts, and e-mail. She stuffed it back down to the bottom of her pack. Wednesday and Friday, she told herself. She would text her mom and that was it. No more phone. She wished she'd thought to trade her smartphone for Lucy's plain old flip phone, then at least she wouldn't be tempted by the Internet.

From behind her, back in the Notch, McKenna heard the *teacher-teacher-teacher* of an ovenbird. And then, after a minute, she heard a cardinal's song, followed by a goldfinch, followed by a red-winged blackbird. She quickly realized it was Sam, playing with the book she'd given him.

McKenna paused. Part of her wanted to wait for him. She hadn't gotten close to sweating out all her breakup blues, and she felt lonely.

A larger part instantly rebelled against this idea. She unwrapped a granola bar, then shoved everything back into her pack and heaved it onto her still-not-dry back. She continued down the trail as fast as she could.

Because she knew the Notch would be difficult and exhausting, McKenna had only planned to go about five miles today, before camping at Full Goose Shelter. Instead she just stopped there to fill up her water bottles in the stream, not bothering with the filter, just plopping in iodine tablets. She might not make it to the Carlo Col Shelter, another six miles away, before dusk, but she could put on her headlamp, and as long as there was space in the shelter she could sleep on one of the platforms and not worry about setting up her tent. She tamped down any doubts and kept walking. For one thing, she wanted to put distance between her and Sam. For another, if she stopped to camp now, she knew she'd be in danger of breaking down and calling Brendan.

One foot in front of the other. One hour after another.

The straps of her pack dug into her shoulders, and sweat dripped off her forehead into her eyes. By the time the heat subsided—McKenna knew it had to be close to evening, but her phone had been shoved to the bottom of her pack, so she didn't know the exact time—she'd managed to finish both gritty-tasting bottles of water. She wasn't sure how much more she had to go till she reached Carlo Col, but she could hear water running, a good-sized stream, just off the trail. She decided for the first time to venture off—it was just a hundred yards or so from the sound of it, so she wasn't breaking a rule, not really. She promised herself she would only walk a straight line and would turn around if it took more than a couple of minutes.

That initial step off the trail felt terrifying, and then exhilarating. McKenna laughed at herself. Within twenty steps downhill, she had found it, probably the same creek that ran behind the Full Goose Shelter. She knelt down to fill the first water bottle and when she raised her eyes she saw a black bear kneeling on the other side of the creek in almost the exact same squat as her. McKenna thought she heard the bear inhale abruptly, as if she'd startled it.

Everything inside her froze. And then total, abject terror.

A bear. Three times the size of the biggest human she'd ever seen. Huge and furry and inscrutable, staring right at her.

Very slowly, McKenna unbent her knees and rose to standing. *Make yourself look tall*, she had read, *if you come into contact with a bear.*

Apparently the bear had received the same advice because he stood up, too, and did a much more convincing job. He was so huge and wide, she couldn't think of anything to compare him to. Hundreds of pounds of pure muscle and fur. The only instruments of defense she had, her pepper spray and whistle, were tucked into the bottom of her pack, impossible to reach. Not that she could imagine either tool being helpful at this moment.

McKenna turned and fled back up the embankment, scrambling as fast as she could, the sound of her grasping hands and feet drowning out any sense of whether the bear had decided to follow. The sight of the trail behind the trees was comforting, a destination, but at the same time McKenna knew it didn't mark any real kind of refuge—if the bear wanted to maul her, he could do it just as easily on the trail.

Just as that visual bloomed in her mind, McKenna lost her

footing. The trail quickly receded in front of her as she tumbled down, her legs scraping through rocks and brambles, sliding and rolling until her feet landed back in the stream, and her pack landed with a disheartening *crunch* beside her.

Panting heavily, she sprang to her feet. But the space across the creek was empty; the bear had disappeared much more silently and gracefully than she ever could. Her heart still pounding eight thousand miles a minute, McKenna retrieved the water bottle she'd dropped and filled it again. She plopped in iodine tablets and headed back up to the trail, noting with despair that she had rolled through a thicket of poison ivy.

She righted her pack on her shoulders and thought about jogging, which seemed fairly impossible given the uphill incline, the weight of her bag, and the exhaustion already setting in as the adrenaline subsided. The bear must have retreated, she would've been able to hear it if it were following her. So she didn't run, but just walked more briskly than usual. Her body smarted from the fall and she fretted over the rash that might spring up in a couple days. Poison ivy was not something she wanted to deal with out here.

As these complaints continued to form in her head, McKenna commanded herself to put things in perspective. The alternative, after all, was being mauled by an enormous bear. *I'm alive,* she reminded herself.

Which was more than she could say for her phone.

She didn't inspect it until she'd reached Carlo Col, miraculously finding the shelter empty. She shrugged off her pack, dousing herself with anti–poison ivy wipes first thing. Then she cooked red beans and rice on her stove. The campsite had a bear box, and she carefully packed her food into it before heading back to the shelter. Only then did she face the damage, emptying everything from her pack and spreading the contents over two platforms. The very last thing she pulled out was her phone. So much for the supposedly foolproof case. The phone was smashed, mangled, and completely dead.

Her whole body ached. The skin on her face tingled with antiseptic and too much sun. She spread her sleeping bag on one of the empty platforms and crawled into it without even filling her stuff bag with clothes to make a pillow. If she hadn't broken down and checked her phone in the first place, she wouldn't have stoked the temptation that drove her to push it to the bottom of the bag and it might still be intact. Now it was gone. She was really on her own.

She tried to keep her mind firmly on the hike, and not let it veer off to other worries. Tomorrow she'd have less than a mile to go to reach the Success Trail to the west, and then she would cross her first state line, into New Hampshire. Had it only been this morning that she had woken up at the campground with the UNH girls and Sam? It seemed miles and days away. What McKenna thought about just before she fell asleep was the fact that she'd been face-to-face with a bear, deep in the woods. Looked into its eyes and breathed in. If she could do that, she could do anything. A smile played on her lips, staying with her until she fell asleep.

. . .

What McKenna didn't know: Sam had been right behind her for most of the day, stopping when he got too close, and letting her stay just ahead of him. It was one thing to get invited by a group of girls, another to shadow a girl on her own. They barely knew each other, and though she'd acted cool about the Walden story, he realized now that it might have scared her. He didn't want to scare her even more by seeming like he was following her. He noted that she hadn't signed the trail register—a move he approved of.

Sam had heard the whole bear episode loud and clear, though he didn't know it was a bear that spooked her. He just heard McKenna scrambling desperately up the embankment, then heard her tumble down, followed by her calmer walk uphill.

Sam hung back, waiting to make sure she returned to the trail. He kept her huge red pack in his sights—like a flare signal—watching it bop through the trees. McKenna's gait was slower, a little uneven when she got back on the trail, but nothing to indicate any serious injury. From where he stood, he could hear a stream gurgling below. He walked down to the stream and sunk his drop line baited with a little piece of bacon he'd saved from breakfast. In half an hour he had a nice stack, three little brook trout. He strung them together and tied them to the outside of his pack.

Sam was pretty sure there was a shelter up ahead; since it was getting close to dark and McKenna had just had that spill, he guessed she'd stop and camp there. It would be the perfect place for him to camp, too, and maybe she'd want to share his fish. But what if there wasn't anyone else there? Wouldn't it be kind of weird and awkward?

They were two people, walking two thousand miles in the same direction. Bound to run into each other again. But for tonight, Sam figured he'd let her have the place to herself. He would rather lay his sleeping bag down at the first outcropping of rocks and build a fire to roast his trout. The heat of the day had started to burn off, a good breeze coming up as he gained elevation. It was one of those nights when it was especially good to be outside. To be alone on the trail.

10

It was a good thing McKenna smashed her phone just *after* a text had been sent to her parents. Over the next few days she worked hard to cover the miles to the next public phone at the summit of Mount Washington, the second highest peak on the entire Appalachian Trail, and not exactly an easy stretch to hustle through. It seemed to McKenna the blazes on this section were fewer and farther apart. Luckily the good weather and the weekend brought a lot of fellow hikers and campers to the trail. She made a point of checking in with everyone she passed, making sure she was headed in the right direction. When she finally reached the Summit House, she was exhausted and covered in sweat. The ground under her feet—above the tree line—was rocky. It was weird to see a parking lot, complete with cars that had made the trip up the serpentine road, but she walked past them, dumping her pack on the ground and looking out at the Presidential Range, green this time of year, and towering in endless, looming rows. How funny to face this wild expanse in one direction, and then turn around and head to a snack bar, where she bought herself

French fries, asking for her change in quarters. Then she used the pay phone to call Courtney.

Of course Courtney didn't answer the unfamiliar number, which was just as well, since McKenna had only enough change for a minute or so. The pay phone's number was printed on the front, so McKenna recited it in her voice mail and told Courtney to call back right away. "It's an emergency," McKenna said.

Two minutes ticked by. McKenna waited, munching on French fries, closing her eyes with each amazingly salty bite. When the phone finally rang, it was so loud that she jumped.

"Courtney?"

"McKenna! Where are you?"

It was so odd hearing her best friend's voice after so long. Even though she'd been hiking for weeks, McKenna had barely put a dent in her total trail mileage. The New England stretch, with all the mountains, was the most slow-going of the AT and so much time had passed that already the most normal things in her life had become completely exotic.

"I'm at the summit of Mount Washington."

"Wow. How is it going?"

"It's great."

"Really?"

"Yeah," McKenna said, working to sound insistent rather than annoyed. If Courtney hadn't sounded so dubious, she might have filled her in on the impossible first day, and the way she woke up every morning so stiff she wasn't sure she'd be able to walk at all, let alone carry a huge pack. The way hiking up a mountain left your muscles so sore that it was actually more painful to walk down (which she had to look forward to the next day). Strangest of all, she didn't feel like telling Courtney that Brendan had broken up with her. She wondered if she already knew.

"Listen," McKenna said instead, getting down to business. "My phone broke."

On the other end, Courtney gave a little gasp, as if McKenna had told her a lung had collapsed. McKenna forged through the horror, telling Courtney she needed her to text her parents in the morning, and to explain that McKenna's phone had died and that from now on Courtney would be sending the check-in texts.

"Every Wednesday and Friday before dark," McKenna said.

"But won't you get a new one?"

"Courtney. I'm in the middle of nowhere," McKenna said, even though this had been her original plan: to get off the trail at the first town that seemed big enough to have a Verizon store. She was pretty sure the phone was insured. But seriously, what had her phone done for her so far? It wasn't like dialing 911 was going to help her on the trail, she had only fiddled with the compass, and she hadn't checked the GPS once. Truthfully it was so hard to battle the temptation to check messages or go online, and when she had, she'd received the one piece of news that managed to distract and deflate her. Without her phone, she was a girl who was climbing mountains and facing down black bears. With her phone, she was a girl whose boyfriend was breaking up with her. And after all: like the rest of the world, she was going to spend the rest of her life on the grid. The broken phone was a gift and she planned to accept it.

"What do I say when I text them?" Courtney asked.

"Well, tell them my phone broke. Then after that first text, just say that we're safe, everything's fine, and tell them where we are. You'll have to fake that part. Do you still have a guidebook?"

"I can look online." They had both joined the AT website back in January. "The interactive map's pretty good."

Inwardly, McKenna laughed, knowing now that no interactive map could prepare you. "Thanks," she told Courtney. "How's everything going there?"

Courtney burst into a happy ramble, mostly about Jay and the series of graduation parties their friends were having. The ramble was suspiciously empty of Brendan, so McKenna figured she must know. Maybe he was with a new girl. She willed herself not to ask, just stood with the old-fashioned phone pressed to her ear, listening to news from a million miles away. How weird that every step she took brought her closer to her hometown when it felt like she was walking farther and farther away, to a place deeper inside herself.

The next day, hiking up Mount Franklin, McKenna heard the persistent trill of a towhee. In fact it was a little too persistent. And a little too perfect, sounding exactly the same every time, with no variation. She hadn't seen Sam since the morning she'd given him the book, and would've guessed he was miles ahead of her by now.

Sweat dripped off her forehead. This morning it had been freezing, and she still wore her fleece jacket, long-sleeved T-shirt, and Gramicci pants. She stopped to take off her jacket and quickly traded the long-sleeved T-shirt for a short-sleeved one. Then she yelled down the trail.

"That's a towhee! Give me a harder one!"

A short pause. She imagined Sam leafing through the book, looking for a bird he didn't recognize. And then the pause got longer, so McKenna thought maybe she was going crazy and it really *was* just a very vocal and precise bird, following her. But then came the distinctive, slightly alarming cough of a barred owl, not something you'd hear on a mountain in the middle of the day.

"Barred owl!" she yelled back, but just as the second word was out of her mouth, he came around the curve in the trail.

"Barred owl," she said again, more quietly, and they both laughed.

"Here," Sam said, handing her the book. "Quiz me. I've been studying."

McKenna took the book. "Hello to you, too," she said.

"Seriously," he said, still not bothering with a greeting. "Pick one. Anywhere in the book."

She flipped through and pressed the button next to the cardinal.

"No, no," he said. "I could've got that one before I even had the book. Choose a hard one."

McKenna flipped through with her eyes closed, then felt for the nearest button. The thin, whistly notes of what she thought was a prairie warbler sang out.

"Cedar waxwing," Sam said. She opened her eyes. He was right.

"You've gotten good," she said, handing back the book.

"You don't want it?"

"No, you're having fun with it." She could tell he was glad she didn't want it back.

They walked a little ways together.

"You know," Sam said, "I was worried that I scared you. With that story about Walden."

"What am I, eight years old?" McKenna said. "Scared by a ghost story? No way."

They came to a section of the trail that was too narrow for them to walk side by side, so Sam went a few paces ahead. McKenna could see him shrug under the weight of his pack. "Some people get scared," he said.

"Not me," she told him. "That's my claim to fame in my family. I'm unscareable. Always have been. Even when I was little."

He stopped and looked back at her with a wolfish but very appealing grin. "Yeah?" he said. "I guess I'll have to think of some more stories for you."

"You can't scare me, I promise."

His smile widened, then he turned and continued walking.

They went on in silence for a while, until McKenna got hungry. The sun was high, moving into afternoon.

"Want lunch?" she asked. "I've got some jerky and Power-Bars."

"No, I'm good," Sam said. "I want to make it to the shelter early. My tent's not the most waterproof, and it looks like rain."

"Okay," she said. "See you."

"Yeah. See you around, Mackenzie."

She could tell from his grin he knew perfectly well that wasn't her name. Still, she said, "McKenna."

"Right. See you around."

She sat down on a flat rock, watching him go, wondering how he'd managed to make it so far with a "not-the-most-waterproof" tent. Then she remembered that some people, thru hikers even, didn't bring tents at all, only stopped in shelters.

He must know what he's doing, she thought, almost as if to comfort herself. And then wondered why she'd think to worry about him in the first place.

Without her phone to tell her the time, and with the elimination of required check-ins with her parents, McKenna quickly began to lose track of the days. She stopped thinking of the days in terms of numbers and more by chunks of daylight and temperature. Hiking through the White Mountains was like it had been in Maine, hiking through the seasons, the climate varying wildly at different times of day and different altitudes. Mornings, she would wake up freezing, her breath visible, only to be pouring sweat by lunchtime. She could tell the approximate day by the level of traffic on the trail—something she guessed would become more dramatic as summer drew to a close, perhaps tapering off altogether as she moved south with the birds and the warm weather. Every once in a while she would hear a particularly loud and perfect birdsong, and would call out the name of the bird. But so far, Sam hadn't answered.

She wasn't exactly sure how much time passed between chatting about birds with Sam on the trail and crossing the border from New Hampshire into Vermont. She felt positively giddy as she did so; she had read in one book that New Hampshire and Maine constituted only 20 percent of the mileage on the AT but 80 percent of the work. Not that she thought the coming months would be easy—it would get colder and lonelier as the summer crowds dispersed, with fewer invitations like the one she'd received last night from a family with young kids to share hot dogs at the Happy Hill Shelter.

Approaching the Joe Ranger Road, McKenna saw a group of guys in a parked pickup truck. She noted the orange caps and camouflage, though it wasn't hunting season, and felt an involuntary nervous flutter in her gut.

She nodded at the men as she passed, taking mental note of her whistle and pepper spray hanging within easy reach on her pack. For all everyone had worried about her, she had not yet felt remotely threatened by any of the men she'd encountered on the trail. They'd all been concerned dads, or friendly buddies like the guys who'd spiked her and Brendan's sodas, or Sam. One benefit of being a girl on her own: nobody was afraid of her. Everybody was instantly friendly, willing to share food and offer help, even when she didn't need it.

But something about these guys, maybe just the fact that they were sitting in a truck observing her, made her uneasy. She didn't realize how uneasy until she'd crossed the road, back to what she considered the safety of the trail. As always, she ignored the trail ledger, walking right by it.

"Hey," a voice called to her a few minutes later.

McKenna turned back to see the three guys walking toward her. Two of them had dark hair and were short and stocky. The bald one was tall and lean. She guessed they were all in their early thirties.

"Hi," she said.

What she really wanted to do was ignore them and keep walking. But of course that would feel so rude, it would almost be like baiting them. Which was exactly what they were relying on. It always bugged McKenna, how intrusive people counted on her good manners to get her talking to them.

"You forgot to sign the trail book," the tall one said. He pointed backward at the ledger, like he was helping her out.

"Oh. Well, I'm not going far. Just a day hike."

"That's a big pack for a day hike," he said.

Apparently he was the only one who talked, which made the other two, staring at her unblinkingly, seem more ominous, like pit bulls flanking their owner. McKenna regretted the obvious lie and concentrated on not blushing. And for the first time, she also regretted not having Norton with her. These guys would probably have left her alone if she had that big snarly dog.

"Well," McKenna said. "I'll see you guys. I'm headed that way."

"Wait," the tall one said, jogging after her, and McKenna reluctantly stopped again, turning toward him, aiming for the right level of non-antagonizing irritation. "You look like you been walking a long way. Want to come on into town with us? Have some dinner? Hang out?"

When McKenna had been face-to-face with the bear across the creek, it had set off an instant panic. What she experienced facing these three guys—asking her on a date!—was something slower, more primal. She was angry that they were bugging her. She was apprehensive about their intentions. But she was also determined to do whatever she needed, strategically, to get away. It was a good thing, she thought, that their truck was down the trail, too far away for them to easily drag her into it. One of the dark-haired guys looked uneasy, like he wasn't fully committed to whatever the other two had planned. Maybe if she was firm in her dismissal, they would leave her alone.

"Thanks," McKenna said. "But I'm really just going for a walk."

"Yeah? Where you from?"

"Montpelier," McKenna said. "You guys have a good day, okay?"

"Won't be much good without you in it," he said, and took one step closer to McKenna, reaching out like he was about to grab her arm.

"Hey!" said a gruff voice, emerging behind the three men. "There you are. How'd you get so far ahead of me?"

Sam. She'd figured he'd be miles ahead by now. But he emerged from the paved road, with long strides and a straight back. She noted he was taller than the bald guy, and much broader. Sam walked right past them and put his arm around McKenna. She tried not to be relieved. She'd been handling this herself.

"Oh," the bald guy said, taking a step back, returning McKenna's personal space now that Sam had taken it over.

"Is there a problem, guys?" Sam said. There was something very foreboding, almost threatening, in his tone.

It infuriated McKenna, how quickly the three men turned and headed back to their truck. She'd been so clear that she didn't want them to bother her, and they'd persisted. Then, with a few clipped words from a guy, they toddled off like obedient children.

She stepped away so Sam's arm slid off her. Then she headed down the trail at a fast pace.

"Hey," Sam said, trotting to keep up. "Are you okay?"

"Yeah," she said. "Why wouldn't I be?"

"Seemed like those guys were bugging you."

"No. I mean, they were. But I had it covered."

"Oh yeah?"

"Yeah." She was mad at the guys, not Sam, she reminded herself. But at the same time she was mad at guys in general. A species Sam just happened to belong to.

"Well, in that case," Sam said, "I shouldn't hold my breath for a thank-you?"

"Probably not."

McKenna kept walking, fast, uphill. Behind her, she heard Sam stop, felt his eyes on her back.

"You're welcome!" he called.

She didn't turn around, just lifted her hand and waved as she walked on.

Men. Making the whole world believe that a woman couldn't and shouldn't feel safe on her own. Even a strong, tough woman like Linda, who'd managed to survive a war. It made McKenna seriously mad. Why should she have to feel unsafe? Didn't this world belong to her as much as it belonged to any man? Yes, it did. McKenna refused to let them make her feel unsafe, either by cornering her, or by making her feel like she needed one to protect her.

Sam was a little pissed himself—at the creepy guys, but also at McKenna's lack of gratitude. He had planned to head into town when he hit the Joe Ranger Road but now decided against it. Never mind if she didn't think she needed anyone watching out for her. To tell the truth, it made him feel bad that he'd left Marianne back in Maine, alone with his brother, to say nothing of those two little girls. If he couldn't look out for them, at least he could look out for this girl. So he hung back, collecting wild blueberries along the way, staying just enough behind her that she wouldn't know he was there. Making sure she was okay. Maybe she'd really had the situation with the creeps under control. But just in case, Sam wanted to stay between her and the Joe Ranger Road. Because maybe the creeps would come back. It would make him feel better, if he could see for himself that she was safe.

11

Vermont. Massachusetts. McKenna walked through both states, still summer, still plenty of people on the trail, and at the same time—plenty of room for solitude. It amazed her, the volume of hikers, and at the same time, the expanse of the trail allowing room for everyone to feel alone in the vast woods and changing landscapes. Every once in a while she would run into Sam, and they'd chat about birds, or the weather, or the distance to the next water source. Once McKenna pumped some water for him at a suspect-looking pond, wondering how he purified water.

"Do you want a couple of these?" she asked, holding up her bottle of iodine tablets.

She saw him hesitate, not wanting to take something from her—in a way that was kind of endearing. Then he shrugged assent and let her shake some pills into his palm. She could always get more when she resupplied. And Sam? She wasn't sure what he could or couldn't do in terms of acquiring things. But she did feel certain that his hike was different from hers, not a gap year, but something less luxurious.

"Thanks, Mack," he said. Somewhere in Vermont she'd told him that it bugged her to be called Mackenzie, since it wasn't, you know, her name. So he'd switched to Mack.

One night on the other side of Mount Bushnell they camped at the same site, but it was crowded. Sam stayed in the shelter and shared dinner with a bunch of guys who seemed to be there for a bachelor party, while McKenna set up her tent and tried to sleep through the noise. They didn't do much more than wave to each other.

But that night, lying in her sleeping bag and listening to the camp sounds finally die out as the natural sounds of coyotes and crickets rose, McKenna found herself wondering if maybe he'd come by her tent to say good night. Would she invite him in if he did? She imagined being with him in the small space.

She didn't wind up seeing him until morning, though.

"See you on the trail, Mack," he'd said when she headed off at first light.

All that day McKenna had waited for him to catch up and hike with her for a while. But he never did.

Four states down. And then Connecticut. By now most of McKenna's friends would be packing for their college orientations. At Whitworth, there was an outdoor club that brought incoming freshman hiking through these very mountains. She kept a watchful eye out in case she ran into anyone she knew, but lately the large groups of summer—and even the rhythm of the week versus the weekend—had started to wane. The nights had started to get cooler, but the leaves remained green, maintaining the colors of summer. By the time the foliage began to explode, McKenna would hopefully be walking through the South, the first time in her life she would miss the dazzling fall colors of home.

As she walked through her home state, the sensory details signaled summer preparing to unfold into fall, which for her, even as a small child, had always translated into school—first her parents' school year starting, and then her own. This, along with the more consistent solitude, made her feel homesick. Heading off the trail into Lakeville to do some laundry and maybe have lunch, she considered using the pay phone to call her parents. But she steeled herself against it. So far, her lies to them had been mostly lies of omission, or else secondhand via Courtney's texts. If she called them, she'd have to pretend Courtney was with her, fill them in using *we* instead of *I*. Not only would she feel incredibly guilty, but if she slipped and they found out, they would doubtless declare her solo trek from Maine to Connecticut (nearly seven hundred miles!) an impressive feat and insist she come home.

In town, she walked into the Laundromat behind a pizza place, planning to throw in a load and then eat a slice or three before switching things to the dryer.

"Hey, Mack," came a voice behind her as she opened the glass door.

McKenna turned to see Sam sitting on a bench drinking a

bottle of water. He had a way of popping up just as loneliness began to set in.

"Hey," she said. "Doing some laundry?"

"No," he said. "Almost out of coin."

They had already established that one of the reasons Sam stayed more or less at pace with McKenna and often ended up behind her was that he would stop in towns and work for a day or two to get enough money for essentials. When he ran out of money, he'd fish and forage. It reminded McKenna of the stories her dad had told her about the Pacific Northwest Trail. She guessed, though, that Sam was not on this hand-to-mouth journey as a lark. He wouldn't be returning to the kind of life her father had.

"You can throw stuff in with mine," she told him. "I won't have anywhere close to a full load."

McKenna explained her method to him—wash one set of clothes while wearing the other, then throw in the second set after she got the clean ones out. As soon as the words were out of her mouth, though, she felt self-conscious. He had just admitted to not being able to afford even a single load, and here she had this totally wasteful strategy. But Sam didn't seem bothered, just followed her into the Laundromat and threw his clothes in after she'd made her meager little pile. She remembered her weekly loads at home—clothes brimming, a different outfit every day, sometimes more than one a day if she was going out at night. She watched her favorite Johnny Cash T-shirt, now with a permanent brown stain on the back from sweating under the weight of her pack, spinning through the cycle. At home she wouldn't have been caught dead in it.

"I was going to get a couple slices," McKenna said. "Want to split a pizza? My treat," she added quickly, so he wouldn't have to worry about not having enough money.

"Sure," Sam sad. "Thanks, sounds great."

They left the Laundromat, Sam slowing his long strides so McKenna could keep up with him. Any hang-ups or embarrassment about him not having money seemed to belong to her, not him. Sam was always so good-natured and unfrazzled. Emotions unreadable behind those pale blue eyes.

McKenna reminded herself of her mother's advice, which she had always followed. *Avoid the obvious guys.* As a college professor, her mom saw girls fawning over the gorgeous ones, while the smart and studious ones went unnoticed. But it was kind of hard to avoid this obvious guy when they were headed two thousand miles in the same direction.

At the restaurant, McKenna let Sam order the pizza. "Just no sausage or pepperoni," she said. "I don't eat pork."

"Yeah? Are you a Muslim? Or keeping kosher?"

"Neither," McKenna admitted. "Just met a pig I liked and haven't been able to eat it since." She told him about Miss Piggy Pie, the potbellied pig at her childhood day camp. It had followed the kids around like a dog, and had a particular affection for McKenna, rolling onto her back for a belly scratch whenever she saw her, and often lying across McKenna's feet as she ate her bagged lunch.

"That's cute," Sam said, closing his menu. The waitress came by, nervous and flirty. Sam acted like he didn't notice, curtly ordering a barbeque chicken pizza.

"And I'll have a Coke," McKenna added.

"Just water for me," Sam said.

When the drinks arrived McKenna unwrapped her straw. The first sip of cold sweetness after days on the trail was always the best. She closed her eyes. When she opened them, Sam's hand was wrapped around her glass.

"That looks too blissful," he said. "I'm going to need a sip."

He slid the glass across the table and closed his lips around the straw. Then he shrugged and slid it back to her. "Pretty good," he said.

"Do you want one? I can—"

"No. Thanks. I'm good with water."

The pizza arrived, steaming, and they ate in silence for a good five minutes. McKenna was now used to the rhythm of eating on the trail: famine and then feast. She would go days of eating nothing but dried noodles, dried jerky, dried fruit. And then when she got to a town she would inhale everything in sight. On the occasions when *everything in sight* included something amazing—like a steaming, fresh pizza smothered in tangy barbecue sauce and grilled chicken—it was a pleasure like she'd never known in her life.

"So," Sam said when they'd each devoured two slices. He took a bite of his third more slowly, with less desperation and intensity. "What are your plans for when you get off this trail?"

"In Georgia? Well. Home to my family, hopefully in time for Thanksgiving."

"Where's home?"

"Connecticut. Not far from here, actually." She waited for him to ask if she was going to see them while she was nearby, but he didn't. Just took another bite of pizza.

"Then I have a job for a while in upstate New York," she continued. "It's with this amazing ornithologist. I'm going to help him catalog his bird research." She waited for Sam to say something, ask her a question. When he didn't, she added, "And then around this time next year, college."

She waited for him to ask which college, but he just said, "Cool."

"What about you?"

"Don't know. Might not get off the trail."

"Like Walden?" McKenna heard her own voice teasing, flirtatious almost, reminding him of the first night they'd met.

"Yeah. But you know. Without all the murdering."

McKenna laughed, then excused herself to switch the laundry. When she got back she had a new, full glass of Coke. She slid a third slice of pizza onto her plate, even though in the brief rest from eating her stomach had begun to bloat. At home, she used to hate that glutted, overstuffed feeling, but on breaks from the trail, she had come to relish it.

"So, seriously," she said. "What are you going to do when you get off the trail?"

"So, seriously," Sam echoed. He laughed a little, then went

in for his fourth slice. "You know one thing I noticed about you? You never set a fire. We should camp together. I can give you a lesson."

McKenna's jaw tightened, partly at the thought of camping with him and partly at his condescending tone.

"I know how to start a fire," she said. "I just don't. You're really not supposed to."

He waved his hand dismissively. McKenna couldn't help noticing the broad and graceful expanse of his palm, his long tapered fingers.

"Nobody pays any attention to that," he said. "What's the point of camping out if you're not going to have a fire at least once in a while? Come on. I'll spend my last two bucks on marshmallows. We can roast them tonight."

McKenna stared at him. He had a bandanna tied around his neck. The skin on his face looked super-smooth, recently shaved, and tan from these many months outdoors. How long, she wondered, had he really been on the trail? There was something about him that made her distrustful, or at least hesitant.

At the same time, she wondered what her friends might say, watching her sit across the table from this gorgeous guy, about to turn down his invitation to an overnight marshmallow roast. If only she knew more about him. In the wilderness, it hadn't seemed to matter. But here, in a situation so normal, over pizza under restaurant lights, she felt an urgent need to know.

"Listen," she said. "I don't want to pry—"

"Then don't." His words weren't exactly harsh, but definitely abrupt. Closing the subject.

McKenna shifted on the fake leather bench. Where she came from, there were rules to follow when getting to know someone. Instead of name, rank, and serial number, it was name, where you went to high school, where you were going to college. She could accept the fact that Sam didn't seem to be heading to college. She was not a conformist or a snob. But the first two pieces of information seemed like the bare minimum, and so far Sam had only provided her with half that.

He reached across the table and slid her refilled Coke toward himself, leaned in, and took a deep drink from her battered straw. It felt weirdly personal, watching him drink from the straw she'd chewed half closed. He kept his eyes on her, then pushed the glass back across the table. Like he was trying to establish some kind of truce. So she decided to press on.

"You haven't told me where you're from," she said. "Somewhere in the South? You have a little accent."

"Oh yeah?"

"Yeah."

He didn't confirm or deny. McKenna asked, "What about your parents?"

"What about them?"

"Are they, you know, supportive? Of the hike and everything."

"Oh yeah. *Super*-supportive. They're a regular cheerleading squad. A lot like yours, probably."

She couldn't tell if he was joking or not. The usual light in his eyes seemed to be dimming. McKenna shifted on the bench, then rattled off a little monologue about how she was headed to Reed next year. "That's in Oregon," she added.

"I know where Reed is," he said.

This encouraged her. Stupidly, it turned out. "What about you?" she asked. "Are you going to college after all this?"

"Doesn't everybody?" His voice sounded flat. Maybe even sarcastic.

"No," McKenna said, trying to make peace, to show him she didn't care one way or the other. "Not everybody. Plenty of successful people—"

"And even more unsuccessful people." His voice sounded almost snarly now. She was digging a deeper hole with every word.

"Well," McKenna said, trying to keep her voice light and airy, "what's success anyway? Like Thoreau said, 'The life which men praise and regard as successful is but one kind.'"

Sam put his slice down. His eyes were narrow and challenging. Warning her to change the subject.

"Did you play football in high school?" McKenna asked, taking another sip of soda. She hoped her voice sounded normal. She wanted to give him a compliment, say something that would remove the foot she'd somehow wedged into her mouth. "You have that look, like you play football."

"Want to know what look you have?"

There was a subtle change in Sam's face. A shift in the geometry of his smile. Up until this moment McKenna had been confident that he liked her, at least as a friend. And now, suddenly, she felt like he didn't. All that food turned cold in her stomach.

"I'm sorry if I—"

"You have the look of someone who always does what she's supposed to do."

Anger bubbled up, canceling out her dismay. "If that were true," McKenna bit in sharply, "I'd be hanging posters in my dorm room right now."

"So instead of your college orientation checklist, you've got your AT hiker's checklist. Fancy frame pack, check. Below-zero sleeping bag, check. Water purifier, check. Compass that you probably don't know how to use, check."

"Check. Please," McKenna said to the waitress as she walked by.

The waitress slapped the bill down on the table, her eyes stuck on Sam. Sam didn't smile back. Despite their argument, despite their being just friends, if even that, he was still too much of a gentleman to flirt with another girl while he was eating with McKenna.

But not enough of a gentleman to let their conversation go. "You have the look," he continued, "of someone who's going to get off the trail when it gets cold. You'll get off the trail, go home, and everybody will tell you what an achievement it was to hike as far as you did. Let's say, to Virginia. Even though you didn't make it the whole way like you said you were going to."

McKenna just stared at him. What the hell had she done to deserve *that*?

His jaw was set, almost trembling, like he was the one who was pissed off. She hesitated for a second, then grabbed the bill and headed up to the cash register. She paid with her parents' debit card, adding a generous tip to the receipt, and then headed for the door without looking back.

In the Laundromat, she grabbed her clothes from the dryer and left Sam's, abandoning the idea of a second load and of restocking provisions. She had a couple days' worth of food in her dry bag. If she covered decent miles this afternoon and tomorrow, she could make another stop in Cornwall Bridge. Right now she felt unsettled and angry. She needed to walk.

She spent the rest of the day on the trail waiting for Sam to catch up with her. In the evening, she set up her tent and with every move she expected him to come ambling up, throw off his crummy frame pack, and sit down. Explain himself. Apologize. It was, McKenna realized as she hung her food bag up away from the bears, the way you'd feel after a fight with your boyfriend. Not wanting to go to sleep angry.

Still full from the big lunch, she didn't eat anything but a couple nibbles of turkey jerky that night before crawling into her sleeping bag. She turned her headlamp on, planning to start reading the novel she'd traded for one of her own in the last free box. Instead, she lay in the dark, headlamp pointing dormant at the roof of her tent.

She'd felt a kind of kinship with Sam since they first met, a guy her age, hiking in the same direction. But what did she really know about him? Not where he came from. Not how old he was, except for her guess. Maybe his name wasn't even Sam. Why was he so hostile about sharing normal information? Maybe he was running from the law. Maybe he was dangerous.

She stuffed her headlamp into the mesh pocket of her tent. Listening to the crickets outside, she had to admit she was still also listening for approaching footsteps.

She squeezed her eyes shut. No, she thought, with deep and urgent conviction. Sam wasn't dangerous. She knew that as well as she knew anything in the world. But the way she was thinking about him, the way she was feeling.

That could definitely be dangerous.

Trail rhythm. Maybe it was her unease over Sam, the rattling and increasing anger she felt as two days went by with no sign of him. But for the first time, she began to think she was achieving it. She liked the phrase. *Trail rhythm.* It fit the way she'd imagined this trip would go, how she would feel, back at the very beginning. Before Courtney had bowed out, before that hellacious climb up Katahdin, before blackflies had bitten off half her flesh. Before this long, hard, and she had to admit, sometimes lonely summer had started, McKenna had had a very clear image in her mind of the girl she'd be—the *woman* she'd be. She thought she'd take down two thousand miles without so much as a stumble. The woman McKenna had *planned* on being would not let a tough uphill stretch, or a few measly insects, or a bunch of day-hiking naysayers, not to mention a too-handsome-for-his-own-good loner, get her down. That woman would scoff and then laugh, hold her head up high, and move forward with grace and determination.

She'd have *trail rhythm*.

And funnily enough, since that fight with Sam, for the first time since Brendan gave her that dry good-bye kiss in Baxter State Park, McKenna felt like the person she'd envisioned. She took in a deep breath, full of pine and damp earth. So what if the dew that hovered in the air felt a tiny bit too cold for August? The straps of her pack weren't cutting into her shoulders. If that was partly because her supplies needed replenishing, who cared? According to her guidebook, there was a killer deli in Kent, and at the clip she was walking, she'd get there by lunchtime. Despite those slices of pizza two days ago, the waistband of her shorts felt loose. She'd order a Reuben and a bag of chips and a Coke. Maybe they'd have huge chocolate chip cookies like at Joe's Corner Store back home. She would buy one and eat the whole thing. Nothing left to share, no matter who she might run into.

The market was every bit as awesome as her guidebook had promised, its shelves stacked high with top-drawer items like rice crackers, Nutella, and organic cereal bars. There was a refrigerated section with different flavors of hummus, and McKenna grabbed the one with a pool of olive oil and slices of pickled red pepper. It would stay cool enough until dinnertime. The girl behind the deli counter looked about McKenna's age.

While she made her sandwich, McKenna loaded up on everything she wanted, consciously not looking at the prices, refusing to let herself worry about how Sam would pay for anything if he happened to come into this store.

When the girl handed over the sandwich—Russian dressing staining the butcher paper, along with the chips and the exact cellophane-wrapped cookie she'd imagined—McKenna found herself asking, as if her voice had a will of its own: "Have any other hikers stopped in today? I mean, have you seen a guy about our age, kind of tall, with longish blond hair?"

"Blue eyes?" the girl asked. "The kind that look right through you?"

McKenna's heart did an uncomfortable skitter. If Sam had been here already, that meant at some point he'd passed her. Without stopping. Maybe he'd keep on walking, or even get off the trail. Maybe she'd never see him again.

What was he doing, looking right through this girl, anyway? McKenna remembered the pointed way he'd avoided the waitress's eyes. The way he'd avoided staying in Ashley's tent. She was just about to ask what he'd bought when the sandwich girl laughed, a short and decidedly unmerry bark.

"I wish," she said, wiping off the counter with an expert swish of her white cotton dish towel.

After she ate, McKenna locked herself in the store's bathroom to do some rudimentary washing up. Once she crossed into New York she could spend a night in a hotel, take a real shower, and do more laundry. For now, she stripped down to her waist in front of the sink, soaped and rinsed her face, and stared into the mirror as she brushed her teeth. It was easy to see small changes: her face was at least two shades darker, despite the loyal application of sunscreen. Without plucking, her brows were growing in a way that made her look severe but also younger. There were streaks of blond in her hair, making it lighter than it had been since she was ten or eleven, though nowhere near as fair as that of anyone else in her family. Or Sam, she thought involuntarily.

She tried to remember the last time she'd seen herself in a full-length mirror. The real changes, McKenna knew, weren't in her face. She reached behind her back and snapped off her bra. Just to see if she could, she slithered out of her shorts without undoing the button. This was no unattended truck stop bathroom; here in Connecticut they weren't messing around with hygiene. Everything shone, smelling like lemon-scented bleach. McKenna scrambled on top of the toilet to give herself something like a full view in the small square mirror over the sink.

If she expected to see a totally different body from the one she'd shown Brendan before heading off on the trail, she felt a slight stab of disappointment. Plus, the tan was not exactly photo-shoot-ready—more like Photoshop-ready, the white outline of her shorts and T-shirt standing out against her brown arms, legs, and neck. Her stomach had a slight bulge from devouring that Reuben and the chips (the cookie, saved for later, was zipped into the front pocket of her pack), but the skin it strained against was taut. Her thighs didn't look skinny, exactly, but tighter than they'd been, and stronger. Reluctantly, McKenna thought about Brendan and that last night with him, the careful questions he'd asked before each move. *Is this okay?* Hands moving, trembling a little.

Blue eyes? The kind that look right through you?

McKenna remembered Sam's hands at the restaurant. Back on the trail, the day he'd come between her and the hunters, the insides of his palms were calloused when he put his arm around her, his fingers closing around her upper arm. She felt sure that those hands wouldn't tremble. And she also felt sure that Sam would only ask permission once.

A sharp rap on the bathroom door made her jump. "Hey," an irritated voice called. "Someone's waiting out here."

McKenna gathered up her things fast as possible. Impatient suburbanites aside, if she wanted to get to the top of Schaghticoke Mountain today and into New York tomorrow, she needed to get back on the trail as soon as possible.

The hike up Schaghticoke was steep in places, but nothing compared to Katahdin or even Bear Mountain, and now she was in much better shape. Even so, it was still way later than she'd planned when she reached the summit. It was funny to be on a trail in her home state, standing at the very top. Almost as if her whole childhood, her whole life, lay spread out at the bottom of the mountain she'd just climbed. Her parents and

Lucy had no idea that right at this moment she was about to cross over into New York. She could see the Housatonic River, where her dad had taken her fishing a thousand years ago. Lucy, she realized with a pang of sadness, had never known the dad that McKenna had—the one who loved sharing the outdoors with his daughter. She wished she'd thought to send Lucy postcards along the way and vowed to start when she got to New York. Then she thought about the trouble it might cause if the postmarks on the cards didn't match Courtney's update texts.

So instead McKenna vowed to take Lucy on a hike next summer, maybe even an extended camping trip. Lucy shouldn't miss out just because their parents had become too obsessed with their careers to take time to teach her about the outdoors.

"Pretty nice view," came a voice from behind her.

Of course she knew before whipping her head around who the voice belonged to.

Sam, finally, sneaking up as usual. How could someone so big manage to move so quietly? He had his arms crossed, and his head held high, chin jutted toward her. His shave had worn off and there was duct tape patching up his flimsy sneakers. How had he hiked so far, so long, in just those sneakers? McKenna crossed her arms, too.

"Didn't anyone ever tell you it's not polite to sneak up on people?" she said, trying to hide her relief at the sight of him.

"Who's sneaking? I've been waiting up here for over an hour. I was worried you wouldn't summit before dark."

"You don't need to worry about me. I can take care of myself just fine. See?" She opened up her arms, gestured toward the panoramic vista below. "Made it to the top. Without any help from you, or anyone."

"Just barely," Sam said. Which would have been infuriating if he hadn't been grinning that almost-perfect smile, just one tooth crooked on the bottom.

McKenna's own perfect teeth, accomplished by thousands of dollars of orthodontia, felt leaden and inferior.

She pressed her tongue against the roof of her mouth and knelt to pick up the first thing she saw, a fat hedgehog-shaped pinecone lying at her feet. How much damage could a person do with a pinecone? She whipped it directly at his head, aiming for that smirk. Sam ducked—almost, but not quite in time. The pinecone grazed his eyebrow hard enough for him to bring his hands up over his face.

"Whoa!" he said. "What the hell?"

Instantly, McKenna felt bad. Apparently she'd thrown it a bit harder than she'd meant to. She closed the distance between them in three quick strides.

"I'm sorry," she said. She tugged at his arms so she could inspect the injury. "Let me see." She wanted to assure herself only minimal damage, if any, had been done. But she also just really wanted to see Sam's face up close. She was suddenly frantic with worry that he might be mad at her.

Sam kept his hands firmly in place. "No way," he said. "You're violent."

To McKenna's relief, his voice sounded playful. This was the Sam she first met, not the hostile one from the restaurant.

"Come on. I'm sorry. I didn't mean to hurt you."

"Liar."

"I didn't mean to hurt you *badly*," she corrected. "Come on. Let me see."

Her hands were closed around his wrists now, and this time when she tugged, he let his hands fall away. There was a faint pink mark above his brow, nothing major, it would probably disappear within minutes.

"I think you'll live," she said. Her voice caught in her throat slightly. She was aware of her hands still grasping his arms, mere centimeters separating them. If she stood on her toes, she could kiss that eyebrow without moving much closer.

As if he'd read her mind, Sam said, "Are you going to kiss it and make it better?"

Abruptly, McKenna released her grip and stepped back. "No," she said.

He shrugged, that infuriating grin returning, as if he could take or leave both McKenna and her kisses. But then he said, "Hey. I'm sorry, too. I was a jerk back there. I never even thanked you for lunch, or laundry, or any of it."

"Well. You're welcome."

"I'm sorry," Sam said again.

McKenna nodded.

Sam said, "So does that mean we're okay? You and me?"

"Yeah," she said. "We're okay."

"Pretty spectacular," he said.

She let out a stream of breath and walked back to the edge of the summit to retrieve her pack. At some point during their exchange, the sun had started to drop. To McKenna it looked like it was quivering, gathering up its strength for the downward plunge, orange starting to spread out and take over the landscape. It's not just the dawn that's rosy fingered, McKenna thought, and wondered if Sam would get that reference the way Brendan or Courtney would.

Without a sound, Sam appeared beside her.

"If we stay to watch, we'll have to descend in the dark."

"We'll use your headlamp," Sam said. Then he reached for her. "And I'll hold your hand."

His fingers closed around hers, and McKenna found herself stepping closer, as if she'd never been angry at all. They watched the sun drop behind the mountain ranges and light up the sky before slowly going dark. Of course Sam was right. It was spectacular.

It was slow going down the trail in the dark. McKenna let Sam wear her headlamp and she walked behind, her hand gripped in his, close enough that her face hovered inches from his back. She could smell the sweat and wood smoke on his worn T-shirt, and see his skin through the line of tiny holes that ran just above his pack, from one shoulder to the other. When they came to a campsite, they threw down their packs and looked around. No tents set up.

"Looks like we have the place to ourselves," Sam said, casting the narrow light from the headlamp.

"It's like that more and more," McKenna said. "I didn't see a single person on the trail all day."

"Summer's ending. People are headed back to real life."

"Not me," she said.

Sam smiled, and this time it didn't look arrogant at all. "Not me," he agreed.

Now that the sun had set and they'd stopped moving, a chill settled in around them, still far enough north, and getting late enough in the season, for cool New England nights. McKenna pulled out her fleece jacket and long pants while Sam pulled on his wool sweater. The cold made her realize she hadn't seen him with any outer layers and she wondered if he had enough gear to make it through the colder months.

Without necessarily agreeing on it, not in any verbal way, they blew off setting up the tent and started looking for kindling. The spectacular sunset had given way to a spectacularly clear night sky. It would be a pain to set up tents in the dark—there was no chance of rain, and opportunities to sleep under the stars would be fewer and fewer as the nights got colder. As McKenna took the headlamp back to gather wood, leaving Sam with her flashlight, she thought she could see Orion's belt, a sure sign that summer was on its way out.

Her headlamp shone the way as she headed back toward the campsite, her arms full of twigs and sticks. As she dropped the load beside him, she saw that someone had left a little bottle of whiskey leaning against a tree, with a note tied around the neck. *Enjoy.* She picked it up and twisted the top to see if the safety seal would crackle. It did.

Sam knelt by the fire pit, already arranging a tepee of sticks over some newspaper he'd been carrying in his pack. His figure was mostly visible by starlight, but he'd balanced her flashlight on a stump and she could see him silhouetted against dim shadows. His head lowered in easy concentration, blond hair flopped forward, muscles flexed naturally. No matter what Sam did, he always looked athletic, the way a wild animal looked athletic just walking across the grass, or even resting. McKenna wondered again if he'd played any sports in high school, but of course she wasn't going to make *that* mistake again.

"Somebody left this by a tree," she said, showing him the whiskey. "Trail magic."

Sam looked up. "Hope it was sealed," he said, not sounding especially enthusiastic.

"It was."

McKenna put on her sandals, then sat down on the log next to the flashlight, while Sam lit paper. The fire crackled and flared with almost magical obedience. She floated the note from the bottle into the flames, and admired the view she had of Sam's face, lit up by the orange glow. By the time he sat next to her, she was digging through her pack for food. She brought out the hummus, its plastic tub damp with condensation, and a pack of rice crackers.

"Look at that," Sam said.

She waited for him to make a crack about her fancy food, but all he did was pick up a rice cracker and say, "Thank you," in that raspy voice.

"You're welcome," McKenna said. She'd already decided to share her cookie with him after dinner.

When they finished eating and packed the remnants of the food away, McKenna was conscious of having nothing between them on the log, not even the flimsy plastic containers of food. She thought he moved just the slightest bit away from her as he reached into his pack. Was it intentional? Did he want distance between them?

She picked up the whiskey bottle and offered it to him.

"No thanks," Sam said.

"You don't drink?"

"Not much. Surprised you do."

She shrugged and put the bottle down. "I don't much. But, you know. Here it is."

Enough strands had come loose from her braid that she could feel her hair whipping against her face. She pulled off the elastic and started undoing the braid, combing her fingers through the long strands.

Sam watched her for a moment. "You're a good girl," he said, with just a hint of sarcasm.

McKenna took the knit cap out of her pocket and pulled it over her head. What had she done wrong now? He was impossible to navigate, to figure out.

"You certainly seem to have a lot of opinions about me," she said, then reached for the bottle and took a healthy swig. It shot through her body like she'd taken a mouthful of fire. She used every last bit of will to keep from coughing and spitting it out on the ground. Sam sat watching her.

"Opinions," he said. "Yeah. I've developed a few of those about you."

He reached out, as if he were going to touch her hair, but then thought better of it. McKenna picked up a slender log and tossed it onto the fire. It flared, warming and brightening both their faces. She took another sip of whiskey, smaller and more manageable this time, but it still burned her throat.

Sam eased the bottle out of her hands and put it on the other side of him. Which was just as well, because she was feeling dangerously light-headed. Enough to say, "You know, about the other day. At the restaurant. I'm sorry, too. I shouldn't have pushed you. Even though I would like to know. About you. Whenever you're ready to tell me. I mean, we're friends, right?"

Sam became absolutely still then, his eyes on the fire. He seemed to be considering when, if ever, he'd be ready to tell her about himself, and whether or not they were friends. McKenna wished she knew exactly what he'd been through. Was there someone at home waiting for a text or a phone call? Someone to wonder if he was all right, if he was safe or hungry? Even though McKenna hadn't spoken to her parents in weeks, their concern followed her with every step, and in a strange way, embraced her throughout this adventure. She worried that Sam didn't have an equivalent to that.

Not taking his eyes off the fire, Sam said, "Yeah, Mack. We're friends. Definitely. And I shouldn't have said you wouldn't make it to Georgia. Because how the hell do I know? You just have to want it, I guess. You have to mean it when you say you're going to get there."

"Yeah?" McKenna said. To her ears, her voice sounded a little husky, too. "How am I doing, then? Would you say? So far?"

She could see it. He started to turn toward her, something about his face softening.

"Fine," he said. "You're doing just fine."

McKenna pulled her hat down almost to her eyes and put her elbows on her knees, the two of them staring at the fire together like it was a huge flat-screen TV. In the quiet, she became very conscious of him sitting there, close to her, and it seemed that the main thing they were doing—their primary activity—was not touching each other.

She turned to look at him: the sharp cheekbones, unruly hair, lips that looked a quarter inch away from a smile, even when, like now, they were set in concentration. She wanted to run a finger along one cheekbone, then turn his face toward her so his blue eyes could look right through her.

"Sam?" she said.

"Yeah?"

In the stillness that followed, the quiet in which she couldn't decide exactly what she wanted to say, Sam spoke instead.

"I missed you the past couple days," he said.

"You did?"

"Yeah. And I worried about you."

"You don't need to worry about me," she said, a little defensive. Why the hell was everyone always worrying about her?

That shrug again. He still wouldn't look at her. "Okay, I don't need to worry. Am I allowed to miss you?"

"I guess you can miss me. If you want to."

Sam smiled but he still didn't look at her. Now, McKenna thought. Now would be the time for him to kiss her. To reach over and touch her face. But he didn't. He just sat staring at the fire, thinking unreadable thoughts.

How many hours ago had she felt so mad at him? Even then, she reminded herself, the resolve to maintain that anger had been wavering. And now all she wanted was to get closer. She wished she knew how. All those mountains of books at home, all that studying, all those good grades, and she didn't know how to do the most basic thing in the world, which was make a boy kiss her.

She stood up, grabbing a stick to stoke the fire. The little structure Sam had made collapsed, sending up sparks and a stream of smoke, threatening to smother the newest log.

"Hey," Sam said. "Watch it." He moved to stand up and fix it.

"I got it," she said.

She dug a little hole in the middle with her stick, letting the fire breathe in much-needed air, and in a minute it was crackling again. McKenna turned around. There was Sam, still sitting on the log, lit by the newly strong glow. An impulse gripped her and for once she pushed all second-guessing out of her head. She unzipped her fleece jacket and tossed it on the ground behind Sam. Before he had a chance to say anything, or she had a chance to think, she did the same with her T-shirt.

She meant to do her bra, too, that's how brave she was feeling, but seeing Sam's face, she stopped short. He still didn't move. His features were set, frozen, unreadable. She stood in front of him, wearing nothing but her pants, her bra, and the wool cap. I should've taken off the cap, McKenna thought, but now she was feeling mostly embarrassed and she couldn't move another muscle. She stood waiting to see what Sam would do next.

When he still didn't speak, McKenna felt like she might die of mortification. She started to believe that a silly girl whipping off her clothes without warning was so commonplace for him that he couldn't even be bothered to react.

Except for a little vein in his neck. McKenna could see it pop in the firelight, making his whole body look tense with the effort of not reaching out for her.

It seemed like hours ticked by. McKenna felt the heat from the fire against her bare back. She resisted the urge to bring her arms up in front of her. Having made this first move, she couldn't possibly move again until Sam did. Or said something. Anything.

And then finally, he did: "What are you doing?"

This was not the response she'd hoped for. The old anger rearranged itself inside her, like the fire gathering breath, but this time it was mingled with something else. Something she'd not come close to feeling, ever.

"What does it look like I'm doing?" she said, her voice a lot more vulnerable than it had sounded in her head.

That vein popped out of his neck a tiny bit more, the strained look on his face relaxing just enough to make him look wolfish. McKenna knew somehow, instinctively, that he wouldn't be able to sit there much longer. Any minute now, he would *have* to touch her.

In one graceful motion, Sam got to his feet. He stood in front of her, not touching her yet, just standing, looking down at her face. Then he pulled her hat from her head, and dropped it to the ground. He stroked her hair with both hands, fanning it out over her shoulders. It felt natural that from there he walked his fingers down her spine. No unpracticed fumbling—her bra was unsnapped in a single easy motion, falling down over her arms. She felt his lips next to her ear.

"You want to get naked?" he asked, gruff but quiet. "Then go ahead. Get naked."

"What is this?" she said. "Truth or dare?"

"It's whatever you want it be, Mack." His lips grazing her ear this time, almost a kiss.

He didn't wait to see if she'd obey, but reached for the waistband of her Gramicci pants. Along with her quick-dry underwear, he pushed them past the stubborn rise of her hips, then let them fall to her ankles. To step out of them, she had to kick off her sandals. Now she was totally naked, not a single stitch of clothing, while Sam still had on everything, including his duct-taped sneakers. He let his fingers trace her collarbone, then a straight line down to her belly button, where he let his hands separate. He moved them to her hips, then back up, the featherlight touch getting the tiniest bit rougher.

She couldn't stand it anymore. She stepped forward, closing the space between them, and kissed him. Sam moved his hands to her back, pressing her into him, her bare chest squashed against the rough threads of his sweater.

They kissed that way for what seemed like ages, Sam's hands moving up and down her body, the fire steadily warming her back. Ecstatic ages. McKenna couldn't think about where they would go next, what they would do. Something as simple as fishing out their sleeping bags could break the spell she'd managed to conjure out of the thin, wintering night air.

Finally, Sam broke away. He stepped back over the log and then lay down on the ground. She could see dry leaves immediately attaching to his hair. His arms came up the barest bit, beckoning her. She knew he didn't want to interfere with the moment any more than she did. McKenna arranged herself on top of him—jeans and wool the only things separating them. She felt his hands placing her where he wanted, and felt her own body shudder.

It frightened her, this lack of control. She didn't dare think about what she'd do next, to make this continue. Or worse, make it stop.

Sam seemed to be losing control, too. He kissed her more and more deeply, pulled her closer when she didn't think closer was possible. Just as she'd imagined, his hands went wherever they wanted to go, not stopping, not checking in. The permission he needed was in every response McKenna made, her quickening breath, the movement of her body. Even a moan. She was pretty sure she'd never *moaned* in her life. But now, this new world, the very air around her, an owl hooting from a tree, no doors protecting them from intruders, just the faith that they were the only human souls for miles. Sam's lips and the edges of his teeth pressed against McKenna's neck.

"Sam," she said, a strangled note, the first word in what felt like hours. "I think I might die from this. I feel like I'm going to die."

Brendan would have taken this as a cue to stop. Sam clearly took it as a compliment. He put his hands squarely on her shoulders, and pushed her back a little. With one hand, he brushed hair away from her face, cupped her cheek.

"You're beautiful, Mack," he said. "Do you know that? Really beautiful."

And then he reached for his jeans.

Bam. Spell broken. Because once his jeans came off, they were talking about some major life decisions. It had taken her three months to get there with Brendan. And this was the first time she and Sam had even kissed. McKenna closed her hand around his wrist.

"Wait," she said. "I'm sorry. I mean—"

Sam stopped cold. Damn. She always had to ruin everything. All the excitement, all the magic, drained away. She'd disappointed him. Worse, she'd probably turned him back into his jeering self. McKenna braced herself, waiting for him to say something about how he knew she wouldn't have the guts to finish what she'd started.

But he didn't. Instead, he reached behind her, finding her jacket in an instant, and pulled it around her. Then he kissed her. A different kind of kiss, lips just barely open, but still deep and full of feeling.

"Of course. Whatever you say, Mack," he whispered. He kissed her forehead. "Whatever you want."

Wordlessly they both stood, arranging themselves. McKenna pulled her clothes back on, including her hat, and Sam batted the leaves out of his hair. They got their sleeping bags and spread them out by the fire, zipping themselves into separate cocoons and then wriggling next to each other. McKenna rested her head on Sam's chest, and he pulled his arm out of the sleeping bag to wrap it around her. The fire rose, danced a little, and McKenna breathed in the scents of the outside world that felt more and more each day like home.

She could hear Sam's heart beating and then slowing under her ear. She'd never slept like this with anyone. In the morning, she'd finally know what it felt like to wake up in someone else's arms.

Or so she thought. McKenna's sleep was very deep, dreamless; so much so that she missed the moment when Sam slipped away. When she woke to a sun that was too high in the sky, the fire was out. Sam's things were gone, and so was he, not the barest trace left behind except the one thing she'd given him, the songbird book, lying damp and deserted beside the remnants of last night's campfire.

"Sam?" she called, scrambling out of her sleeping bag. "Sam?" she called again, though she knew he had gone. He had left her. It was obvious.

She kicked the ground where his sleeping bag had been. Incredible. All that had happened last night, and she had woken up alone. He hadn't even said good-bye. With fast and furious movements, she collected her things. Sam must have packed up the garbage, the containers for the food and the whiskey bottle were gone. How considerate, she thought, giving the spot where he'd slept one last kick.

With all her gear packed up, McKenna surveyed the campsite, trying to think where she'd gone wrong. But that led to the need to blink against tears. The sun had risen. She felt dazed, blindsided, heartbroken. But what could she do but set off down the trail? No matter what she felt, she had to do what she did every day: walk.

Her face, though, must have betrayed more than she realized. When she passed a group of day hikers—a mom and her teen-aged daughters—the mom stopped and put her hand on Mc-Kenna's elbow. "You okay, honey?" she asked.

"Yes," McKenna said, more defensive than she meant to be. "I'm fine."

"Sorry," the mom said, her voice still kind. "You just looked . . . well, you looked upset. You aren't lost, are you?"

"No," McKenna said, her voice very definite. "I'm not lost."

"Well, okay, then. Enjoy the day. Sure is a hot one."

"Sure is," McKenna agreed, wiping sweat off her brow with her forearm. She'd forgotten to keep her bandanna where she could reach it.

"Hey," McKenna said, calling after them. The three women stopped, looking back at her. McKenna could tell by the mom's face that she expected McKenna to admit she was in some kind of trouble.

"What's the date?" McKenna asked. "I've been out here for a while and I tend to lose track."

"It's Sunday, August 22," the mom said.

McKenna nodded. To say she'd lost track of time was a bit of an understatement. She had turned eighteen four days ago, without even realizing it.

12

Sam didn't know what the hell his problem was. He'd woken up predawn, the birds going crazy, McKenna's head resting on his chest, his arms wrapped around her.

"Mack," he'd whispered, his voice hoarse with emotion, then he'd kissed her hair. She smelled like campfire smoke and the outdoors. She felt completely relaxed, her shoulder blades sharp under his hands. She needed a shower. He never wanted to let her go.

And then a kind of coldness gripped him. He couldn't explain it. Three faces popped into his head: Starla, the last girl he'd slept with, his girlfriend before he took off. He didn't wonder how she was doing now. Obviously she'd be fine, going to college like she'd always planned. They wouldn't be together now, anyway, even if he was home. The next face was his mother's, made miserable by years with his father, followed by Mike's girlfriend's, Marianne, the way she'd looked so tired at the kitchen table, and so trapped. He hated thinking about Mike and Marianne and the two girls. It was Marianne's house. Kicking Mike out seemed like the obvious thing to do. A little surge of rage welled up in Sam that she hadn't done it—that she might never do it. It almost made him madder at her than at Mike.

He moved out from under McKenna carefully, laying her gently back on the hard ground. She barely stirred, her eyes still closed. It hadn't occurred to Sam before she'd stopped him last night that it might be her first time. Now, watching her sleep, it seemed obvious. She looked like a little kid, totally innocent, with nice parents somewhere, in a nice house, worrying about her.

Sam had meant to find something in McKenna's food bag for breakfast, get out her cookstove, set things up for them, brew a pot of coffee. He pulled the bag down. She was probably the only person he'd met on the trail who actually did this, hung her food in trees because of the bears. Which seemed silly to Sam given that bears tended to be pretty good at climbing.

He rooted through the bag for coffee. She was so much like a kid that she didn't even have coffee. Starla drank coffee; she smoked, too. Sam remembered the silty taste of ash on her lips. She used to run her fingers along his scars from the cigarette burns. They didn't shock her. She was a smart girl but she had her own set of problems; her dad was a meth addict who'd left when she was fourteen. She was gone now, he reminded himself, away at school. The thing was, a father like Sam's—a history like Sam's, scars and all—was pretty much in line with what Starla would expect out of life.

Over by the fire pit, this other girl's breathing sounded soft and trusting and very innocent. That's all she was, right? Another girl. Plenty of them before her. Plenty more after. He thought of her last night, slugging back the whiskey. Taking off her clothes. She didn't understand that wanting him was the surest way to wreck everything she had going for her.

Sam closed McKenna's dry bag and put the food back where she'd left it. Instead of making breakfast, he gathered his things and jammed them into his pack. He picked up the bottle of whiskey and hurled it into the woods. That's the kind of guy he was, a hillbilly from Seedling, West Virginia, and this was how he rolled. He took out the bird book and left it by McKenna's pack. She'd never given it to him, just loaned it. Now he wasn't sure if he'd see her again, so it wasn't fair to hang on to it.

It was the hottest day in a long time.

Sam had already gone through half his water by noon. Truthfully it felt good, the punishment of that heat, combined with his pace, faster than usual. It reminded him of football practice when Coach Monahan had pushed them further than they thought they could go.

It must have been a Saturday. Plenty of people on the trail, sauntering along in the most leisurely manner possible. A group of college girls were setting up a picnic in one of the campgrounds. They had a pink-and-white-checkered tablecloth and a basket like the one the Wicked Witch carried Toto off in. All Sam had to do was sit at the next bench, take a sip of water, smile at the one setting out the food. And then he had a paper plate piled with fried chicken and potato salad, a plastic cup of freshly brewed iced tea. He never could get used to the way they drank iced tea up north, sour and sugarless. But the caffeine would help give him the energy he needed to cover the miles.

"Hey," said the girl who'd given him the food. She had dark hair and a friendly, hopeful smile. "You camping here tonight?"

"Nah," Sam said. He scraped up the last bit of potato salad from the paper plate. "Thanks so much for the food. I have to get going. Lots of miles to cover today."

"How far are you going?" she asked as he headed back toward the trail, not quite deterred, not ready to give up on the chance of conversation with him.

"Thanks again," Sam called back over his shoulder, with one last wave.

How far are you going? The sun beat down through the trees. Over the next couple weeks, a maddening swirl of color would rise and then fade, falling to the ground, and his footsteps would crunch over them. Today, those leaves were still green, only the tips hinting toward orange and yellow. Pretty, but more than that they served a purpose. Their cover saved him from getting sunburnt, or worse, sun poisoning.

How far are you going? Sam put one foot in front of the other. His legs were a lot longer than McKenna's. His pack was a lot lighter. He was used to enduring pain. In no time at all, she would be miles behind him. Maybe he'd walk right off the trail and find a job in one of these little towns. Something you didn't need a high school diploma for, like clerking at a convenience store or working construction, or maybe he'd be a janitor.

The second he'd seen those girls setting out their picnic he knew they would give him food. When he saw McKenna the first time, back in Maine, she should have looked like an opportunity, planning to go all the way to Georgia, all that shiny equipment. He should have realized she'd be good for plenty of meals, plenty of warm nights. But he hadn't thought that, not once, not really. He couldn't say why. And maybe now he'd broken her heart.

But he wouldn't think about that. Anyway, it could be good for her. It might make her realize she wasn't cut out for this kind of thing, this long walk, this life with a guy like him. It'd been dark last night, so she couldn't see his scars. Maybe now she'd already gotten off the trail, walked into a town, called her mom and dad to come get her.

How far are you going? As far as possible and not far at all. He was going all the way to Georgia, and then he would turn around and start walking back again. Spend his whole life on this trail, uphill and down, seasons changing, girls coming and going. Where else did he have to go?

The sun beat down. Sam's breathing was hard and labored. By the time the air got cooler late in the day, he felt lightheaded. He wasn't anywhere near a campground, but hell, he wasn't hung up on rules, he wasn't McKenna. There was a little clearing over there just right for setting up his tent. He'd had a big lunch, he didn't need dinner.

It wasn't dark yet when Sam fell asleep staring up at the branch shadows crisscrossing his green canvas roof.

That night Sam dreamed that McKenna was in danger. He couldn't put a name or reason to the danger, he could only hear her screaming and calling out his name. He tried to call back, but his voice was strangled in his throat, the barest squeak. He couldn't reach her, he couldn't even call out to her, all he could do was listen to her voice. She sounded so scared. He had never heard her sound scared. Not even when those guys were harassing her. It must be something serious. He tried to lift up his arms, to claw his way toward her, but he couldn't move.

In the pitch-dark, his eyes flew open. He was drenched in even more sweat than when he was walking uphill in the pounding heat. Every inch of his skin tingled, that confusing moment between a nightmare and the realization that you're safe. But was McKenna safe? Sam shook his head, reminding himself that premonitions aren't real. At the same time, that uncomfortable tingle wouldn't leave his skin. He couldn't shake it.

Why had he just taken off and deserted her like that? What kind of jerk was he?

He pulled down his tent and packed everything up in the dark, wishing for one of those headlamps like McKenna had. By the time he pulled on his pack, his eyes had adjusted to the dark enough that he could find the trail, and he headed north. There was no way she'd made it farther than he had yesterday.

Any minute he'd come upon a nice legal campground and see her tent. Maybe he'd wake her up. Maybe he'd just unzip the flap quietly, peer in, and make sure she was okay. It was pretty much the only way he'd ever sleep again.

McKenna was actually south of where Sam had camped. Just a couple miles; she'd wanted to go farther but knew that would mean walking in the dark before reaching her next campground. Unlike Sam, she wasn't willing to erode the trail by pitching her tent anywhere she felt like. She had hiked all day yesterday at a ferocious pace, planning to overtake him without a word. Which of course she had done, but in a way that wasn't nearly as satisfying as she had planned—she had spent the day visualizing how she'd stride past him silently. Or maybe that would be too obvious, make it seem like she cared too much. Maybe instead she'd nonchalantly say, *Hey*, before sidestepping around him and leaving him in the dust.

Of course he didn't see her when she actually did pass him, walking by his sad little tent, which would offer zero protection if it rained. She wondered if he'd eaten anything today.

She wondered the same thing the next morning as she made instant oatmeal on her cookstove. Stirring the pot longer than necessary, she refused to think that two guys had essentially managed to break up with her while she hadn't even been in civilization. It took more effort than she would have liked, keeping both faces—Brendan's and Sam's—out of her mind. The first name hurt her ego. The second, well. This ache she felt at the pit of her stomach would go away eventually. It didn't mean anything. She barely knew him.

She just had to keep walking.

There had been a few other people camped at the site, a middle-aged couple thru hiking to Maine who were gone before McKenna had emerged from her tent. The others were a father and ten-year-old son, heading back to the real world in time to get to work and school. They said good-bye to McKenna as she started to drag her sleeping bag and other gear out of her tent to pack. She wanted to hit the trail before Sam showed up. Ideally, she would have set out at the same time as the northbound thru hikers, but she had been exhausted from hiking so hard yesterday. As she knelt to gather her things, her muscles pinged and complained, straining against themselves. It had been a long time since that massage in Andover.

"McKenna," came a familiar voice, but in an unfamiliar tone. He'd called her what he never had, not once since she'd first set eyes on him.

She stood up, her deflated tent at her feet. Sam walked toward her as if he hadn't abandoned her of his own volition, but had been kidnapped by a band of pirates and spent the past twenty-four hours sword fighting his way back to her. He threw off his pack and hugged her so hard that her back cracked. He said something, muffled, into her shoulder.

"What?" McKenna said.

"Nothing. I'm just happy to see you. I've been looking for

you all night. At first I went north because I thought you'd be behind me. But then I figured it out and turned around."

"Are you crazy?"

"No. I mean, I had a dream that you were hurt."

"You had a *dream*?"

"Yeah. You were calling out to me, and you were in trouble, but I couldn't see you, and when I tried to call back my voice wouldn't work. Do you ever have dreams like that?"

McKenna stared at him, fighting the urge to place her hands on her hips, which she knew would make her look like a scolding schoolteacher.

"Yeah," she said, struggling to keep her voice even. She didn't want to sound angry—or worse, elated and relieved that he'd come back. "I've had dreams kind of like that, where I try to speak, or scream, but can't. But you know what I've never done?"

Sam looked at her. His face was pale. There were brambles in his hair, the idiot had gone off trail again, his legs and arms were covered in scrapes and marks that would blossom into bruises before the day was through. He may have been shaking the tiniest bit. But McKenna pressed on.

"I've never hooked up with someone—someone who thought we were *friends*—and then disappeared without a word or a trace or *anything*."

He looked at her, straight on, eyes astonishingly blue in the flat morning light. Somewhere not too far away, thunder rumbled. He shifted on his leg. McKenna's eyes flitted down and she saw that his knee was bruised and a little swollen. She couldn't help it. She knelt in front of him and examined the injury. Probably he'd slipped in those crazy sneakers.

"I have an ice pack," she said. "It might help."

"Thanks."

She dug into her first-aid kit for one of her instant ice packs, and cracked it. Sam sat on the ground. When the cold spread over the plastic, she pressed it to his knee.

"I'm sorry," he said, as if there'd been no break in their conversation. "I don't know why I left."

"You don't know why."

"I woke up and you were still sleeping. I could smell your hair. My first thought was that I never wanted to let you go. And then my second thought was, I had to get out of there."

She stared at him, still squatting where she'd knelt to press the ice pack to his knee. In her whole life, nobody had ever said anything so romantic, or so confusing, to her.

"Hold this," she said. "Don't let go. Otherwise you'll just waste it."

As long as she had her first-aid kid right there, she might as well take care of his legs. She cleaned the scrapes with antiseptic pads, then put Neosporin on them, pasting Band-Aids on the two widest cuts. Sam just sat there through her ministrations. She could feel him looking at her. Another clap of thunder sounded, this one more distinct.

"Are you hungry?" McKenna asked, not looking at him.

"What I really am," Sam said, his voice hoarse, "is tired. Extremely tired."

She stood and headed over to her tent, setting it back up, this time adding the rain guard, too. Sam stumbled into the tent's opening. McKenna picked up his pack and put it in behind him. As he lay down on her sleeping bag, she laid his out right next to him. It was a nice bag, a Kelty, that would work until freezing or maybe even below. Sam sat up a little and pulled off his T-shirt, then lay back down. Thunder clapped again, closer now, and with it came a burst of rain, pelting against the top of the tent. It created moving shadows inside the small space that quickly filled with their combined breath. Sam didn't look at McKenna but at the rain, and it took her a couple seconds to realize that his taking off his shirt was a kind of confession, too.

The other night had been dark, and it had been McKenna who'd taken off her clothes—the whole thing had started with her nakedness, not his—so she hadn't seen them, the scars below his collarbone, and on his chest and upper arms. Small and round and deep.

She reached out and ran her finger from one to the other, until she rested it on his collarbone, the one scar that would be visible if he were wearing a shirt.

"I should have noticed this," she said, her voice barely audible above the pattering of the rain.

He kept his eyes focused on the ceiling of the tent as he closed his hand around hers and brought it to his lips. Then he lowered it onto his chest, gripping gently.

"That was the last one," he said. "My dad. Cigarettes. You know?"

A chill went through her, so distinct that she wanted to reach for her pack and pull on her fleece jacket. All the petty complaints about her own parents—like her dad not having time to hike with her anymore—evaporated into the dense air.

"You were right," Sam said. "I didn't get on the trail in Georgia. I hiked from West Virginia. One day, I just had enough with my dad. It was the last straw, and I had to leave. I hit the trail and started walking north, to my brother's house in Maine. But when I got there . . . I couldn't stay. The scene there . . . it was so much like at home . . ."

"You don't have to tell me," McKenna said.

Sam nodded. He looked like he appreciated it, this break in the narrative. But then he said, "Do you know what I want to tell you?"

She shook her head. Sam still wasn't looking at her. But he stroked the back of her hand with his thumb to let her know he'd detected the motion through her shadow, rain running in rivulets behind it.

"I want to tell you that I was gone for months. I walked out of my dad's house with no phone, and I never sent a postcard. Never sent any kind of word at all. I never showed up at school again. I had a girlfriend, her name's Starla. And I was on the football team, Mack, you were right about that. I had, I mean I thought I had, a life. You know?"

Again, she nodded.

"But when I got to my brother's house, he didn't even know I was lost. He hadn't heard a word about it. Nobody was looking for me."

Outside, a gust of wind joined in the tumult. The walls of the tent rippled. McKenna leaned forward and kissed Sam's forehead.

"I would look for you," she said.

He closed his eyes. McKenna touched his face, then lay down beside him, resting her head on his chest, forgetting her vow never to camp twice at the same site, forgetting the miles she needed to cover, forgetting everything in the world except these few cubic feet swarming with shadows, and the sound of the rain, and Sam's arms around her.

I never wanted to let you go.

Inside her chest, something blossomed. The way some moments stay with you forever: McKenna knew that for the rest of her life, rain on a tent flap would be the sound of falling in love. The new breadth of feeling rose like adrenaline. The person she became inside that shadow-filled tent was somebody that nobody else on earth—nobody but Sam—had ever seen.

13

They stayed like that for most of the day, hunkered in out of the rain. At one point, McKenna opened her pack and they ate what dry food she had left—PowerBars and dried apricots. They didn't kiss, they barely even talked, just clung to each other and listened to the rain.

The next morning when McKenna woke up alone, her heart seized up.

"Morning, Mack," Sam said when she crawled out of the tent.

The rain had cleared but the world around them dripped with leftover rainwater and dew. The air felt sodden when she breathed it in, and everything smelled rife with mulch. Sam had built a fire; it crackled cozily against the autumnal chill that had snuck into the air. A skillet was balanced in the flames, and Sam moved something in it around with a stick.

"What's that?" McKenna asked.

"Breakfast."

He pulled the pan out of the fire. It was filled with mushrooms and brook trout fried in the fat of the fish skin. McKenna sat down next to him and he leaned over and kissed her.

Then they ate the mushrooms and fish with their fingers. For a second McKenna thought about asking him where he learned to identify mushrooms, if he was sure they were safe. But she decided to just trust him.

They sat close enough that their elbows bumped every time they moved. There was a particular feeling she had in Sam's presence, something she couldn't exactly name. It was part happiness, part excitement—as if despite the dampness hanging over the day, everything was clearer, sharper. She felt alive, so much so that no toadstool on earth could kill her.

It was the best meal she'd eaten since she started hiking; it may have been the best meal she'd eaten in her life.

"Want to see how the other half lives out here?" Sam asked her.

On the way off the trail and down the road, McKenna smiled as she walked. She had been so curious about how Sam had managed to survive, it was exciting to finally be getting the inside scoop.

Along the trail, McKenna was constantly amazed by the way you could be in total wilderness one moment, nothing but dirt and trees, and then suddenly there would be a tunnel under a busy road, and you'd find yourself on a farm that seemed like it came from a different country or century—old stone walls, and cattle grazing.

Sam led McKenna across a field of sheep and down a country side road until they came to an orchard. There was a little shop out front that sold cheddar cheese and slices of fresh-baked apple pie that smelled amazing, but Sam told her she wasn't allowed to buy anything.

The woman at the desk remembered Sam right away. "Sure," she said, handing them each a deep bucket. "The ladders are out there. You remember the drill."

They left their packs at the back of the store and spent the day picking, climbing up into the trees and filling bucket after bucket, which they emptied into a large container.

"You okay over there?" Sam kept yelling when McKenna was hidden in the leaves.

"I'm fine," she'd yell back every time. "I'm good."

At the end of the day, the woman paid them each twenty bucks, plus a bucket of apples, a hunk of cheddar cheese, and a steaming slice of pie.

"How are we going to carry these apples on the trail?" McKenna asked as they pulled their packs back on.

Sam handed her a few. "Pack these," he said, zipping some into his own pack. They carried the bucket back to the trail and hiked a short way to a shelter where hikers were settling down for the night, making dinner, setting up tents. They sold the apples for fifty cents each.

"Now we've got enough money for food, showers, and laundry," Sam said when they'd set up her tent. The campsite was too crowded to consider a fire; they cooked instant noodles on McKenna's stove and ate them at a picnic table. She was bone tired, a different kind of tired from walking.

"I would never have thought to do that," she said. "It's impressive, the way you manage out here."

"You're impressive, too," Sam told her.

McKenna stared at him, the light around them beginning to fade. "It's easy to be impressive when you've got people to catch you if something goes wrong. You know?"

He cocked his head. "Well, I guess it's easy to be impressive when you've got no choice. And nothing to lose."

She nodded as if she agreed, but said, "I don't know if *easy* is the word I'd use."

"Have you ever worked before?" Sam asked.

"Ahem. I've worked my whole life. Well, the past few years anyway. I wait tables. That's how I paid for all my gear."

"Yeah?"

"Yeah. Don't look so surprised. Have you ever waited tables?"

"Nope."

"You should think about it. It's a great way to make money. Especially for you."

"Why especially for me?"

He looked annoyed and McKenna braced herself as his walls came up. She hesitated, trying to anticipate what he thought she meant, which was only that he was so gorgeous. He would kill in tips. But she felt so vulnerable saying anything like that to him.

"It's just, it seems like . . . women. They like you? And you know. Tips."

The wall came down. Sam laughed. "Come here," he said.

Unlike last night when they had a campground to themselves, this place bustled. In the gathering darkness conversations rumbled, laughter from one site, a mother scolding her children from another. McKenna moved closer to him on the bench, and he put his arms around her, kissing her for the first time since that morning. She could taste the cinnamon on his lips, smell the campfire on his sweater. It was a thick fisherman's sweater, oily with lanolin.

"Is this the warmest thing you have?" she asked, touching his collar.

"Don't worry about it," he told her. "I've got you to keep me warm now. Right?"

She kissed him, putting her arms around his waist, not caring that any of their fellow campers could see them. After a few minutes, darkness settled in, providing cover, and she nestled in closer, closer, closer. Until Sam put his hands on her shoulders and firmly moved her away. She hadn't realized she'd been gasping until she breathed in a lungful of cold air.

"Ready to call it a night?" he said.

She went into the tent first while he gathered up their gear. In the distance, coyotes yipped and howled. When Sam crawled in she was lying on top of her sleeping bag, still wearing her fleece jacket and sweatpants. For some reason she'd expected Sam to move slowly, shyly. But he didn't. He zipped the tent flap shut, then crawled directly on top of her, the weight of him pushing the air out of her. Before she could exhale, his lips were on hers.

For a fleeting moment she thought of the other girls who'd been in this position—under Sam, his lips on theirs. There was something expert about the way he held her. At the same time, McKenna felt sure that there was something else about the way he moved and the way he held her that belonged solely to her.

Outside the tent, the sounds of their fellow campers were dying down, nothing left but a few muffled conversations. Sam and McKenna kissed, fully clothed, until every last noise died. There weren't even any crickets left.

And then the clothes started coming off. There was no discussion. It seemed to her that ever since he'd reappeared yesterday morning, time had done a strange sort of rearranging, making itself impossible to measure. So she couldn't say how much had passed before both their T-shirts and her bra had come off. Sam pressed his bare chest against hers, both of them aware of not making too much noise, catching each other's breath as they kissed and kissed.

It was McKenna who finally pulled her sweats off, then reached for the waistband of Sam's jeans. He sat up on one elbow and grabbed her hand, slowing her down.

"Hey," he said. It was dark in the tent but McKenna felt like her naked body glowed, too visible, and she fought back a flutter of panic. Sam ran one finger from her shoulder down to her belly button and said, "Have you done this before?"

"Is it that obvious?"

"Not obvious. Sweet. It's sweet." He kissed her forehead.

"Listen. You don't have to. Anything more than this. This is fine. This is good."

"What if I want to?"

He was quiet for a second, then moved his hand along the same course it had just taken, back up toward her shoulder, this time stopping for a moment at her breasts.

"Then we will," he said. "If you want to."

She lay quiet for a moment as he stopped and moved away from her, unzipping his pack and digging inside. She heard the crinkly sound of a wrapper and then ripping. Amazing, McKenna thought, protection hadn't even occurred to her.

"Hey," she said. She put a hand on each side of Sam's face. "I think this is the first time you're more prepared than I am."

He smiled. McKenna drew in her breath and closed her eyes. Everyone had told her this moment would be painful. But it wasn't painful, not at all. It was a gathering of all her senses, the effort to stay quiet as Sam's breath filled her ears. The flat scent settling in around them, the building emotion and sensation of the way they moved, together. Of all the things she might've imagined she'd feel, nothing could have prepared her for this kind of happiness.

The following days brought a stretch of perfect weather, the kind there can only be in the fall. Even though they were walking south, away from the cool weather, the days were dry and lovely. McKenna was aware that they never discussed how far they would walk together, or what they would do afterward.

During the day, they had trail rhythm, hitting their stride together, splitting their resources—sometimes resupplying with McKenna's credit card, sometimes foraging or working for a day. Once, at an unexpectedly slammed restaurant, they jumped in to wait tables in exchange for tips and a shift meal.

"See?" McKenna said, counting out their tips afterward. A lunch crowd, mostly women, had made Sam almost twice as much as McKenna, even though he'd flubbed nearly every order.

At night, they huddled in the closeness of her tent. Thinking about that proximity would fuel McKenna's footsteps during the day. The two of them covered fifteen and then twenty miles a day. In just over three weeks they took down four states, New York, New Jersey, Pennsylvania, Maryland. They competed over who could identify birdsongs faster (at first McKenna won every time, but by the time they hit Maryland Sam was getting good enough to win more regularly). At night, they'd curl up in each other's arms. Sam would tell ghost stories, or McKenna would read aloud, her headlamp beaming onto the page of an old book or a new one.

In a free box in Pennsylvania, she'd traded one of her novels for a collection of short stories called *The Ice at the Bottom of the World*. They were strange, language-driven stories, but after they'd finished the book she knew she'd carry it the whole rest of the trip. There was one called "Her Favorite Story" about a man who canoed his dying lover out of the wilderness, trying to get to a doctor, all the while telling her her favorite story about Captain John Smith, who'd had a grave dug for him when he was stung by a stingray, "but never the man let them fill it." John Smith surprised everyone by surviving. But the woman in the story died. The first time McKenna read it, her voice shook with tears as she reached the end.

"That's what I would do," Sam said, his arms tightening around her. "I would paddle you to safety. Carry you across the river. But I wouldn't let you die."

McKenna put the book down and kissed him, her headlamp making him squint. He pulled it off and kissed her again.

She had never felt so cut off from the world, her real world. The only time she ever regretted smashing her phone was when she wanted to take a picture. As they crossed the footbridge over the Potomac into West Virginia—coming up on the half-way point of her journey—another couple about their age was walking in the opposite direction.

"Will you take our picture?" the girl asked, holding her phone out to McKenna, the river wide and beautiful behind them. The girl's face was glossy with love and McKenna felt an instant kinship with her.

"Do you think you could take a picture of us and e-mail it?" McKenna asked, handing the phone back. "I don't have my phone with me."

Sam put his arm around her. A breeze came by at the right moment, ruffling McKenna's hair, which she happened to be wearing down for almost the first time on the trail. The other night they'd camped at Greenbrier State Park and showered, then stopped in Boonsboro, where McKenna had bought new T-shirts for both of them at Turn the Page Bookstore. Possibly the corniest thing she'd ever done: hers was pink, Sam's was blue, and on the back they said, A HOUSE WITHOUT BOOKS IS LIKE A ROOM WITHOUT WINDOWS. She'd left behind her old Johnny Cash T-shirt, its color faded beyond recognition, permanent sweat stains covering the back. She hadn't even bothered putting it in the free box, just shoved it into the garbage outside the bookstore. The Patagonia skort was hanging in admirably, though, and she felt pretty—though she knew Sam would be the star of the photograph, blue eyes vivid against his tan skin, hair streaked to a gold that rivaled the leaves quaking in the trees behind them.

Who knew when McKenna would be in a place where she'd be able to check e-mail? But when she did, it would be there, this photograph of her and Sam, strong and golden, proving that this stretch of time—this idyll—had been more than just a dream.

For Sam, the four miles after that photo on the bridge were the longest miles of his life. West Virginia. Last time, going north, the reverse had been true—he'd hiked them in such fevered determination to get the hell out, and who cared where he ended up? McKenna wanted to stop in Harpers Ferry but Sam's reply was a curt "Let's wait till Virginia."

It wasn't that he worried about running into his dad, who didn't exactly spend his weekends hiking. He really couldn't put his finger on the problem. This stretch of time with Mc-Kenna, the two of them together, had felt kind of like a destination. Maybe crossing into West Virginia reminded him that after two thousand miles of walking, he'd ended up exactly where he'd begun.

"Look," McKenna said. She reached out and touched his elbow. Sam followed her point reluctantly. They only had a mile to go before they reached the state line. The last thing he wanted to do was stop.

"What?" he asked after staring into the bramble without seeing anything remarkable.

"Don't you see it? I think it's a dog." She shrugged off her pack and Sam rolled his eyes.

"Come on, Mack," he said. "We've got one more mile in West Virginia, let's get through it."

"We've got a lot more miles than that," she countered, talking about their plans for the day. Sam hadn't said anything to her about his antsiness. It was amazing she didn't realize. He forgot, sometimes—the thing people always told him—he could be hard to read.

"Hey there," McKenna said, kneeling and holding out her hand. "Come here."

It crashed out onto the trail, a scrawny, rangy hound. Sam guessed it was a Treeing Walker Coonhound. Plenty of strays like that around here, failed hunting dogs. People picked them up for a season and then purposefully lost them on the last day of shooting. This one kept his belly low to the ground as he approached McKenna, who turned carefully toward her pack. At the sound of the zipper, the dog started and backed away. McKenna rooted around, opening up her dry bag.

"You're not going to *feed* it," Sam said.

"Why not?" She held out a piece of jerky. The dog lunged forward, grabbed it out of her hand, and ran back into the woods.

"Because now it's going to follow you all the way to Georgia," Sam said.

McKenna shrugged and pulled her pack back on. She'd gotten so good at it by this point, hoisting it like the weight was nothing, a little shuffle sideways, and then righting herself like the huge, hulking thing was a part of her. She smiled at him, freckled nose crinkling, big blue eyes bright. Sam thought she looked like a photograph that might come with a frame. She looked like a girl was supposed to look, sweet and wholesome. She should have a yellow Lab or a golden retriever, not some mangy stray that nobody wanted.

"Don't say I didn't warn you when he gives you fleas."

"Deal," McKenna said, and they started walking. The path was just wide enough for them to walk side by side, holding hands.

It took Sam longer than he thought to shake the ghosts of his home state. Now that school had officially begun again, they had the trail to themselves during the week and often even on weekends. More than ever, time ran into itself, became impossible to measure, even though McKenna broke down and bought a watch in Bearwallow Gap, just for when they needed to use the iodine tablets and had to measure thirty minutes.

They got to the Sarver Hollow Shelter in Virginia a good three hundred miles after they first saw the dog. It was nearly dusk, a misty night. Sam told McKenna how he'd camped here as a kid with his Boy Scout troop.

"You were a Boy Scout?" she said.

"Sure. You don't think I developed all these mad camping skills on my own, do you? Come on, I'll show you the graveyard."

They walked down a steep incline to where Sam remembered the chimney to the old Sarver place still stood.

"My Scout leader told us the story," Sam told her. "This guy Henry built a cabin here, lived off the land for seventy years or so, all the way from the Civil War through the Depression, and then one day just took off, for reasons nobody knows."

Sam steered McKenna through the woods to the wrecked little cemetery. Most of the stones had been scratched and worn by time, but McKenna knelt in front of Mary Sarver's stone, still legible.

"Look, 1900 to 1909," McKenna said. "Sad. I wish I could do one of those gravestone rubbings. My friend Courtney and I used to do them in the old Revolutionary War graveyard in Norwich."

"There's a ghost that haunts this place," Sam told her. "You can hear footsteps in the night, and sometimes he shows up in pictures."

"I wish I had my camera," McKenna said for what seemed like the thousandth time.

"When we camped here, the ghost shook one of the kids awake in the middle of the night. He woke up screaming."

"Shut up," McKenna said, laughing. She got to her feet and brushed off her shorts.

"I'm serious," Sam said. "It was the ghost. George."

"I thought you said the guy's name was Henry."

"That's the homesteader. The ghost is George."

"Hm. Maybe that's why Henry left. George scared him off."

It was dark by the time they got back to the shelter. They didn't bother cooking, but ate the last of the latest dry food supply—there was a place in Sinking Creek where they could stock up again tomorrow. At some point in the night, wrapped in each other's arms on the platform in a dead, muscle-tired sleep, they both sat up at the same time. Outside, they heard the most piercing, mournful moan. The noise was so loud it filled the shelter. It went straight through Sam's bones, rattling.

"I don't believe it," McKenna said. "It's George."

"I'll go check," Sam said.

"And leave me here alone? Are you insane?"

"If you recall," Sam said, "that was your original plan. To be alone."

"Yeah, well, in that case I probably wouldn't have camped in a haunted cemetery."

She put on her headlamp and they got up, peering into the night. The moon was so full it made a joke out of the thin cylinder of light from the lamp. In front of the shelter, under that wide moon, sat the hound they'd met back in West Virginia. It must have been shadowing them these past three hundred miles.

"Dang it," Sam said. "See? I told you."

McKenna burst out laughing. She knelt down, patting her knees. "Come here."

The dog stopped howling and shied away. Then he stood, stock-still except for a little tail wag, staring at McKenna. As if Sam didn't exist.

"That dog's never going to let you pet it," Sam said.

"Want to bet?"

"No. Not really."

He put his arm around her and together they headed back to the shelter. Against Sam's protests, McKenna left a pile of jerky outside for the dog. Then they did their best to sleep through what was left of the night. They had a long way to go in the morning.

14

A thousand miles north, in Abelard, Connecticut, McKenna's mom, Quinn Burney, ripped open a credit card statement. Usually she just tossed them, unopened, into the antique box for her bills. But since McKenna had started hiking the Appalachian Trail, this was the most definite way to track her progress. The texts she got from Courtney were terse and vague. They didn't sound like McKenna, and she often had to fight the urge to call and hear her voice. It was important to respect her wishes, give her space. So when these statements arrived—a little map of where McKenna had bought things, how much she'd spent—it read like a narrative of what her daughter was doing.

The latest charges were in Tennessee. Tennessee! In her life as a parent, there were moments when her children sometimes did things so different, felt things so different from herself, that all she could think was, *Where did you come from?*

It was impressive. McKenna had gone so much farther than Jerry had predicted. So much farther than Jerry himself had gone on his famous summer hike. Even if she stopped now, if she didn't make it the whole way, it would be more impressive, physically and mentally, than anything Quinn had ever done herself, possibly including childbirth.

She passed the little wall hook where Buddy's leash still hung and felt a pang of sorrow. She was almost glad she couldn't tell McKenna that he'd died. Lucy's grief—and Jerry's, and her own—was enough to deal with for now.

A bit later, driving toward the university, she slowed to a stop by the Whitworth shopping center, the new gourmet sandwich shop catching her eye. It would make her late to office hours, but this early in the semester, students rarely came by anyway.

The glass door opened with a jingle. She was the only customer except for two teenagers by the window, holding hands. The boy had shaggy dark hair that curled over the back of his collar. She did a double take. The girl looked an awful lot like Courtney. She slowed, reaching into her purse for her glasses.

Until this moment, she was fairly certain McKenna had never lied to her. McKenna was a straight-A student. There had been no visits to the principal, her room had always been clean—there had been no reason to doubt her for a single minute.

But it *was* Courtney, sitting here, in Abelard. She didn't even have a tan. All these months she'd been picturing the girls side by side, identical charges on Courtney's parents' credit card statements. Why the hell had she never thought to call them?

"Courtney?" she said tentatively as she reached the table.

Courtney looked up, her big brown eyes questioning, and then fearful, as she registered who was standing in front of her.

"Oh," Courtney said. She extracted her hands from the boy's. "Hi, Mrs. Burney."

"You can imagine my surprise, seeing you here," she said, letting her voice shake for maximum effect.

"Yeah," Courtney said. "I know."

She could see the girl racking her brain, trying to come up with a story. She leaned onto the table, between the teenagers. "Courtney," she said, in the voice she used with students who had one last chance to pass her class. "You need to tell me *everything*. Right now."

Courtney let out a breath that had the barest tinge of a whimper. And then she told her everything.

Because it was the only thing she could think to do, McKenna's mom drove straight to the police station. She called Jerry on the way.

"What do you mean she's alone?" he said.

"I mean she's hiking *alone*. By herself. She lied to us. I just ran into Courtney at the deli."

"I'll meet you at the station," he said.

She waited outside for him and they walked in together. The officer they spoke to was young, barely older than McKenna. As he listened, sympathetic but clearly also a little amused, she wished they'd asked to speak with an older officer, someone with children—preferably someone with a daughter.

"How old is McKenna?" he asked, pen hovering over a white pad on which he'd so far written only: *Tennessee* and *Appalachian Trail*.

Jerry answered quickly. "Seventeen."

But Quinn had noted the date with a pang a few weeks ago and said, "No. She's eighteen. She turned eighteen August 18."

Their fight was over before it had begun. The officer shrugged and apologized. He ripped off the top sheet, crumpled it up, threw it in the trash can. He understood they were upset, but McKenna wasn't a missing person. They knew what she was doing and, more or less, where she was. And she was eighteen, legally an adult. If she wanted to walk to Georgia alone—hell, if she wanted to walk to the moon alone—there was nothing they could do to stop her.

"We could cut off her credit card," Jerry said as they stood outside the police station. "That would force her home."

She could tell, from the hard line of his jaw and how the color had drained from his face, he was furious. By now her fury had faded, and what she mostly felt was worried. A young girl, all alone in the wilderness. Who knew what could happen?

"No," she said. "I don't want to do that."

"It would at least force her to call," Jerry said. "The first time it got turned down she'd have to find a phone."

She imagined the look on McKenna's face. To have come that far all on her own and then be forced home? She couldn't do that to her. Besides, the McKenna who'd lied to them, who'd worked out this giant ruse with Courtney, that was a McKenna they didn't know. She couldn't be sure *that* McKenna would come home willingly. And then what?

"At least if she has the credit card, we can know where she is. We know she'll have resources."

Jerry pulled out his phone, furiously typing in a text.

"What are you doing?" Quinn asked.

"I'm texting her, telling her we know. In case the broken phone is a lie, too."

It felt like that part had to be true—otherwise why risk the fake texts from Courtney? But she didn't say anything, just let Jerry get his aggression out in the long and pointed text. Watching him, his blue eyes so much like his daughter's, she had to admit that in addition to her worry she felt admiration. At eighteen, she would never have been brave enough to walk two thousand miles with a friend, let alone by herself. She wouldn't be brave enough to do it now, or ever.

They had managed to raise a truly exceptional person, she thought with a mixed sense of fear and pride. Now all she could do was hope that the very thing that made McKenna exceptional would be the same thing that kept her safe.

15

Sam watched McKenna feed a granola bar to the rangy hound dog. It wouldn't go away. The last thing Sam wanted was a companion from West Virginia. Not that the dog would let Sam touch him; that was a privilege reserved for McKenna, who'd already won their bet. Sam liked to stand back and watch the ritual she went through, scrunching down and coaxing the dog toward her. He would slither over on his belly, grab the food, and gulp it down. Then he'd lower his head, cowering, as if he thought this might be the time McKenna would haul off and beat him with a nearby stick.

The dog disappeared on a regular basis, and whenever he did, Sam hoped they'd seen the last of him. McKenna was always as happy to see him come back as Sam was to see him go. Today, Sam stayed put, letting the sad little lovefest take place. No doubt the dog had a good reason to distrust humans, probably he *had* been beaten with a stick and worse. And whoever had abused him in the past, you could bet it hadn't been a woman.

The dog lay down on the ground and showed his belly so

McKenna could scratch it. God knows what kind of fleas and ticks the animal had, but she went ahead, rubbing its stomach like someone had just given him to her for Christmas. She'd named him Hank after Henry David Thoreau, who until recently Sam only knew about from half listening in eleventh-grade English. By now McKenna'd made him read *Walden*, and while it wasn't the fastest-paced book in the world, Sam liked it, especially all the bits about not conforming to society.

McKenna walked to her pack and pulled out one of the cans of premium dog food she'd started buying and lugging around for when Hank showed up. Sam tried not to let her see it, how he wanted to shake his head. The way a rich girl wastes money, not to mention energy!

After she got her things together, they headed up the trail, the dog following at a barely detectable distance. McKenna was so set on covering miles, making good time. It was already October. They had less than four hundred miles to go the southern terminus in Georgia, and McKenna wanted to get through to Blood Mountain before it snowed. Whereas Sam: he was in no rush. What was he going to do once they got to the end of the AT?

After half a mile or so, Hank disappeared into the woods. These were the moments Sam liked best, just him and McKenna hiking together, no need for conversation. It was companionable, and so comfortable, like they'd spent their whole lives together and talking was unnecessary. The trail was too narrow at this point to walk side by side, so McKenna took the lead. Sam watched her brown ponytail and her fancy pack, her good hiking boots. She sure didn't look like a girl who'd collect West Virginia strays like Sam and Hank.

That night in the Smoky Mountains, Sam helped McKenna set up the tent. For a while now they had been the only ones on the trail, during the week at least, nobody else camping, nothing but empty shelters. Even so, they usually would set up McKenna's tent, not wanting to risk a late arrival intruding on their privacy.

"Hey," McKenna said, pouring dried beans and rice into her pot and adding filtered water. It was still light, but they had climbed up to a high enough elevation that the temperature was starting to drop. She'd pulled her wool cap over her unwashed hair and wore her fleece jacket. Sam had scored a black-and-red-checked wool coat from the free box in Shady Valley, but he still could've used a hat. McKenna kept offering to buy him one, along with boots and gloves. Every time they stopped, Sam made sure he got to the free box first so he could collect whatever dried food had been left there. Hikers were always getting rid of the food they'd grown sick of, and now that McKenna was too anxious to stop—they needed to make up time!—and fishing and foraging were dropping off with the temperatures, Sam had to scramble for ways to contribute. The thing was, it was different traveling on the trail with McKenna. No girls inviting him to meals. He'd never minded mooching in the past, but these days it felt wrong, not in tune with how he felt about this relationship, the way he wanted it to be.

"Hey," McKenna said again.

"Yeah?" Sam said.

"The weather's so good. Let's have a long day tomorrow. Maybe if we start early we can have our first twenty-five-mile day."

"Not possible," Sam said. "We'll be gaining elevation."

McKenna frowned into the steam, stirring what didn't need to be stirred. He wondered if he could talk her into a fire tonight. Instead of asking, he stood up, started collecting wood.

"We had a fire last night," she said.

Sam wondered if she would have ever made a fire if she hadn't run into him. "Look," he said, pointing to the fire pit, someone else's scarred logs still in their tepee shape. "You don't have to be as careful this time of year. Fewer people come through."

McKenna sat for a minute with a look on her face that Sam loved, like there were two different people having a conversation in her head, a very smart angel and a very smart devil. In this case the devil won. Lately, it usually did. By the time they were blowing on their first spoonfuls of crunchily undercooked rice and beans, the sky was dark and a fire licked up toward the gathering stars.

"You know," Sam said, "we're making pretty good time. We don't always have to follow the trail."

"What else is there to follow?"

"Our hearts?"

She laughed. "But seriously."

"There are lots of cool detours that aren't in your guidebook. Especially in the Smokies. Cool graveyards. This is the most haunted stretch of the AT, but you have to be brave enough to venture out a little."

McKenna was looking at the fire. He saw the devil and angel again, but only in profile. He put his arm around her.

"Have you heard the legend of Spearfinger?" he asked.

"I have a feeling I'm about to," she said.

"Spearfinger is a witch who roams the trails through the Smokies. She looks like the most harmless little old lady you ever saw. She used to wear a kerchief and carry a picnic basket. These days she probably has a day pack and an outback hat."

"Mm. So what does this elderly hiker do?"

"Well, she keeps a lookout for lost hikers. Especially lost children."

"Sounds like a good reason not to go off the trail."

"Well, what she does is, she finds the lost hiker, and she's got her picnic basket . . ."

"Or day pack."

". . . or day pack full of food. So of course one thing a lost hiker's going to be is hungry . . ."

"Any hiker is going to be hungry."

McKenna had scraped her bowl clean of rice and beans. Sam knew that, like him, she was pretty sick of this reconstituted food. In the next couple days, they'd have to stop in a town and replenish, maybe find some new brand or flavor, and have a real meal at a restaurant. They'd already made an agreement not to talk about the food they wanted when they were on the trail, it was too much like torture. Once they were headed toward a town—that's when the food fantasies could start. Usually McKenna talked about ice-cold Coke and salad. *Salad!*

"Yeah," he said. "Every hiker's hungry, so it makes her job pretty easy. What she does is, she feeds them so much amazing food that they get very tired, and then she takes them in her arms and sings to them . . ."

"She takes them in her *arms*?"

"Well, yeah, that's why it works better if they're little kids. Once they fall asleep, she turns into what she really is. A witch with a sharp stone finger. That she uses to cut out their liver. Which she eats."

"Sam. That's such a cute story!"

"I thought you'd like it."

"If she's got so much food in her picnic basket, why does she have to eat hikers' livers?"

Sam shrugged. "I guess that's her favorite."

McKenna stood, gathering up their bowls. She was always busy, rinsing out her pot, hanging the food. Sam happened to know that even rangers didn't hang their food. McKenna pumped every drop of water, she packed out every crumb of garbage, and she never set a toe on a path that wasn't approved by her guidebook. There was nobody he'd ever met who kept so much to the letter of every trail rule.

"Sometimes I think you tell me these stories so I'll be scared to hike alone."

Sam came up behind her to help hang the food a little higher. She leaned back into him, the wool of her cap tickling his chin. He tied the food and let go, wrapping his arms around her.

"You don't need to be scared to hike alone," Sam said. "For one thing, you don't have to hike alone."

"You're forgetting," McKenna said. "I don't get scared."

"Everybody gets scared sometimes, Mack."

"Not me."

Sam started to nod, but then let his head tilt from side to side in only partial agreement. He tried to picture her family telling stories about unscareable McKenna. They'd be passing platters of mashed potatoes and green beans, laughing like people out of a TV insurance commercial right before disaster strikes.

What was the story about Sam in his family? Probably Mike hadn't even picked up the phone to tell their dad he'd been there. It would never occur to his brother that his dad might be worried any more than it would have occurred to his dad to give a hoot.

"How do you know all these ghost stories, anyway?" McKenna asked.

"My mom used to tell us them when she took us camping."

"Your mom took you camping?"

"Yeah."

He didn't say that it was usually an excuse to get away from their dad when he was on a rampage, and that they never had money for a hotel. You'd think when they were on the run from their drunk dad their mom would have told soothing stories, comforting ones. But she knew somehow that he and Mike would want to hear the brutal ones, that it was better to hear there might be scarier monsters out there in the world than the one they lived with.

He couldn't see McKenna's face, but could sense in her pause that she was about to ask about his mom. Before she had a chance, he said, "There was this other story she used to tell. About a settler whose daughter got lost, and he got killed looking for her."

"Oh great."

"This one's nice. Because now he turns himself into a light, a little light that leads lost hikers to safety. We're also coming into the land of the Nunnehi. Do you know about the Nunnehi?"

"Not yet."

"Very famous in Appalachia. Friendly spirit people, they were a huge help to the Cherokee. And they protected a North Carolina town during the Civil War."

"Isn't that the wrong side?"

"Sure, but that's not the point. The point is they're helpful. If you get lost, the Nunnehi take you to these houses they've got built in the rocks. They nurse you back to health and then guide you home. But don't eat any of their food if you want to go home. It'll make you immortal—but only if you stay with them. You'll never be able to eat human food again, so you'll starve to death once they send you home."

"Tough trade-off."

"So, see? It's perfectly safe to go off the trail!"

"Unless you happen to run into Spearfinger. Or in my case, Walden. Or unless you're hungry when the Nunnehi show up."

"Well," Sam said, "we're at an advantage because we know about them."

McKenna wriggled her shoulders a little, like his arms were a straitjacket around her. But she didn't get out of his grasp, just turned so the front of her body pressed against his. Sam amended his thought from earlier in the day about the best part of their days being walking together quietly. The best part came at night, when it was just the two of them together like this.

"There's this waterfall," Sam said. "In the woods around here, the Waterfall of the Immortals. It grants eternal youth and beauty. Let's go look for it."

"You don't believe in that, a fountain of youth."

"No. But I think a waterfall would be cool. And it would be fun to look for."

"It's safer to stay on the trail," McKenna said. "There's too much that could go wrong."

"'Do not go where the path may lead,'" Sam said, making his voice as somber and resonant as possible, "'go instead where there is no path and leave a trail.'"

McKenna snapped her face up toward his. "That's Emerson," she said, sounding surprised enough that if he wanted to, he could be insulted.

"No kidding?" He smiled.

"I just didn't expect you to be quoting Emerson."

"Only people headed to college get to do that?"

Sam was joking, but McKenna sputtered just the same. He loosened his grip and put a finger against her lips. Even in the dim light, he could see the dirt caked under his fingernails. They were due for a stop, big-time.

"You wrote it in the margin of *Walden*," he said.

McKenna smiled and he kissed her. She started to pull away, like she wanted to say something, but he held her tighter, kissed her more. If she said anything, *he* might say something that he couldn't take back. It had been on the edge of his brain these past few days. These past few weeks. But the words always got stuck somewhere between his head and his mouth. He pulled off her hat, kissing her neck while he untangled her braid. She shivered a little.

A great horned owl hooted, startlingly close by, followed by a flap of wings.

Sam unzipped McKenna's jacket and she pulled it off. The ground was hard, with roots traveling just under the surface in bumpy clusters, but what did they care?

"Sam," McKenna said, her body shuddering. She could be so tough and then transform, not into something weak, or even fragile, but just something so light—a butterfly, a gust of air.

How could she be so convincing in terms of her fearlessness, and then be so light and *still* so convincing? The combination impressed him, and more than that it caused a rush of emotion. His mouth was right at her ear, it would be so easy to say it, to whisper or scream it. Would she believe him, if he said it now, in a moment like this?

He pulled back, placing a hand on either side of her face. He could see it, the expression, proof that maybe she wasn't so unscareable after all. On the verge, this brave girl. And he didn't want her to say it first. He had a responsibility to protect her, to be as brave as or braver than her.

"Don't," he said when he saw she was about to say something. "I love you. I love you, Mack."

"I love you, too, Sam."

Above, another strong flutter of wings, the owl swooping down, fearless and right at home through invisible tunnels of air.

Next morning McKenna's lashes stuck together slightly, the light already apparent through the canvas of the tent. She could see her breath in the early-morning air, condensation gathering on the red ceiling. The scent of pine and juniper when she breathed in. Fall came a little later here in the South, and the changing of the leaves wasn't raging and rampant as in her hometown. But still there was color, and a mulchy smell. Sam's arm lay heavy across her rib cage. She barely had to turn her head to kiss him, his sleep almost too deep for his breath, or her kiss, to register.

Everything had changed last night. They were on new footing. These past weeks, she had done very little thinking—about the past or the future. Now, in this stillness before Sam woke, she wondered what would have happened if Courtney hadn't gotten back together with Jay. They still may have met Sam. Probably they would have become friends with him, bumping into him once in a while, and ultimately passing him since Sam would have had to stop more without McKenna, and he would have *wanted* to stop more often. She and Courtney would have talked about how hot he was, no doubt, which for Courtney would have been a reason to have a crush on him, and for McKenna would have been a reason to avoid him. But that would have been the extent of it.

Brendan probably still would have broken up with her, there was no reason for that to change. But what if he hadn't? Would she have pulled off her clothes that night by the campfire? Would she have let things progress, or stayed faithful? The thought of staying faithful to Brendan now seemed ridiculous.

She put her arms around Sam a little tighter, thinking of how he'd grown up with such a cruel father and a mother he wouldn't talk about, except to repeat her stories. She shook him awake.

"What?" he said, starting. His sleep had been so deep, she wasn't sure he knew where he was.

"I love you," she said right away, not wanting to risk his forgetting.

He didn't say anything, just took a deep waking breath, closing his eyes, then opening them again when he exhaled. Stretching a little. They were both always creaky in the morning, all those miles walked and then sleeping on the ground.

"Sam," she said. Her voice sounded more worried than she would have liked. "I don't want you to forget. I love you."

He laughed a little and looked up at her. Grabbed the hair at the back of her neck. It was still loose, still tangled, from last night.

"I remember," he said, and pulled her down toward him, kissing her before she could say anything else.

Hours later, at midday, they stood in front of an AT shelter that had a plaque with information about the Nunnehi. McKenna was surprised. Part of her had assumed Sam was making these stories up. But there it was, etched in metal, a description of the friendly spirit people: THE PEOPLE WHO LIVE ANYWHERE.

"Like me," Sam said. His voice was completely cheerful, but for some reason McKenna felt a little pang of wistfulness, thinking of Sam like that: *a person who lived anywhere.* Like at any minute he might go *poof* into the air, off to a new location.

"Come on," Sam said. "Let's go look for that waterfall."

McKenna pointed to the plaque. "It doesn't say anything about a waterfall."

"Of course not. It's not for tourists. It's for natives. Like us."

"But you know spirit people aren't real, Sam. So the waterfall's probably not real."

She threw off her pack and sat on top of it. She was hungry and tired. Her shoulders hurt. She liked the idea of being a native—in the past few months, the AT had come to feel like home as much as her own bedroom back in Abelard. But she didn't feel nearly native enough to leave the safety of the trail, the cut path tended by all those devoted volunteers, the careful blazes appearing so regularly and comfortingly on the trees.

Sam handed her a bagful of pecans he'd collected. But the idea of smashing the shells to pick out the tiny flakes of nut exhausted her. She'd rather just eat one of her stale PowerBars. She wished he didn't feel like he had to prove himself, providing for her.

"Thanks," she said.

"So what do you think? We could use a little adventure."

McKenna moved her leg aside and unzipped the front pocket of her pack, pulling out the PowerBar. She ripped it apart and offered half to Sam. He shook his head. She bit into the stale chocolate, wondering how they could have felt so close last night and this morning. Now, suddenly, they were of two completely separate minds. She'd already told him she didn't want to go off the trail.

"Honestly," McKenna said, "I feel like this is adventure enough."

"What? Me and you?"

"No. What do you mean by that?"

"You know," Sam said. "Boy from the wrong side of the tracks."

"Are you crazy?"

"Am I?"

A towhee—the bird that drove him nuts—let go with its monotonous two-note cry. McKenna, still warm in her chest from last night, felt like maybe *she* was going crazy.

Where the hell was this coming from? Why was he being so antsy and weird?

She put aside the PowerBar and picked up a rock, banged it on top of the bag of pecans. Maybe if she ate his offering, he'd stop freaking out, go back to being himself, or better yet, his new self—the one who'd appeared last night. The one who not only loved her but said so.

She opened the bag and dug her fingernails into the wreckage, pulling out pieces of broken pecans. Sam was looking at the plaque again. She tried to think about his possible reasons for wanting to go off the trail. Like the fact that he didn't have a place to go once they got to Georgia, whereas she had a family and a job she couldn't wait to get to, and then college. Maybe for Sam, saying *I love you* felt dangerous. Whereas McKenna had said *I love you* a billion times in her life. She said it on a daily basis. Not just to Brendan—which, in retrospect, she might not have meant—but to her parents, to Lucy, to her friends, to Buddy.

"Hey," she said. "I wonder where Hank went. We haven't seen him since—"

"Do you really care where that mangy hound is? Or are you just trying to change the subject?"

206

The thing was, he didn't sound angry. He didn't look upset. He looked cocky and calm and without a care in the world. His voice was lighthearted, like her not wanting to go off the trail was the funniest thing he'd ever heard. In other words, he had somehow morphed back into the very first Sam she'd met, way back in New Hampshire, entertaining a gaggle of college girls with his good looks and horror stories.

McKenna was not so good at concealing her feelings. Maybe because, unlike Sam, she actually *had* feelings.

"I just wondered about Hank," she said, "because yes, I do care about him. You know? Caring?"

"I know about caring," Sam said. Again, that smile, like everything she said was completely hilarious.

"Sam," she said, hating the cracking, plaintive sound of her voice. "It's like you're not listening to me."

"I'm listening," he said. "I hear you. Loud and clear. Stay on the trail. Follow the blazes. Arrive in Georgia at sixteen hundred hours. Forward march."

"What do you know?" McKenna said, sounding fiercer than she'd meant to.

The barest flicker of surprise crossed Sam's face and then that smile was back. It had been a while since he'd shaved, blond stubble gathering thickly along his jaw and cheeks. A sexy and infuriating smile. McKenna wished she had something other than the PowerBar or pecans to throw at him. She was mad, but not mad enough to toss away food, even if it was just smashed-up nuts that she didn't want. So she took a step toward Sam and pushed him. He stumbled back a little, eyes widening but the smile not budging. Then he righted himself, using McKenna's shoulders for leverage.

"Calm down, Mack," he said, pulling her toward him and holding her face against his chest. "It's not a big deal," Sam went on. "I want to see the waterfall. You don't. So you don't have to come. You go on. I'll catch up."

She looked up at him, her chin dragging against the scratchy wool of his black-and-red coat. "What do you mean, 'catch up'? You're going without me?"

Last night he loved her, and now he was going to desert her again? He looked down at her, brushing the hair off her forehead like they weren't arguing, like none of this meant anything to him. As much as she still felt the impulse to push him away, she also wanted to cling to him, not beg exactly, just ask him to please stay with her. *Please.* For the first time ever, she sympathized with Courtney, staying behind with Jay. It seemed like the worst thing in the world, the idea of being apart from Sam, no matter how mad she felt.

They pulled apart, both reaching for their packs, and started walking. Nothing had been decided, not aloud anyway, but McKenna could tell from Sam's cocky stride that it wasn't that he didn't care if she followed him. It was that he was sure she *would* follow him. Not for a minute did Sam think she wouldn't go exactly where he went, just like every other girl he'd ever met. So far McKenna had resisted asking him about other girls. Now, walking behind him, her face scrunched into a frown as she let herself wonder: How many had there been, exactly? And what had he said to them? Had he told them *I love you*?

The frown softened. McKenna knew, the way you sometimes just did, that even if Sam had said it to someone else, he hadn't meant it, not the way he had with her. Last night, what he'd said—what he'd felt—that had been something new. Which was probably why he was acting this way.

Maybe, McKenna thought, I should just give in. Go off the trail with him. Sam had opened himself up to something new. Maybe she should, too.

They walked for a while, Sam checking the trail for breaks in the trees, like everything had already been decided. She thought about him taking off while she walked on, sticking to the trail, counting on those spirit people to bring Sam back to her. Or else going with him, counting on them to bring both of them safely back to the trail.

Had it come to this? So in love with a boy that she'd trust in ghosts to keep her safe?

Sam reached an arbitrary point where he had obviously decided he could smash off the trail and find that waterfall. He stopped and grabbed hold of McKenna's arm, pulling her toward him.

"Don't worry, Mack," he said. He kissed her. "I'll catch up to you in a few days."

She stood, incredulous, watching as he walked through a pair of loblolly pine trees, listening as his feet cracked over roots and leaves. He'd really left her. She couldn't believe it. In fact, she *didn't* believe it. This was just his way of manipulating her, of making her give in to him by going off the trail to follow him. He was banking on the knowledge that she wouldn't be able to stand hiking alone again, or the thought of him getting lost, or worst of all: the thought of never seeing him again. Well, maybe she'd call his bluff. Maybe she'd keep walking on the trail, and see how soon *he* broke down and followed *her*.

Just as she was about to desert the spot and head on her way, a rusty voice called to her from farther up the trail. "Hey. You there."

McKenna turned and gasped. There stood a man, wiry and wizened, with a wide-brimmed straw hat, a long tangle of a white beard, and an even longer tangle of white hair falling crazily over his shoulders. Dark eyes staring at her through layers of wrinkles, but with a smart glimmer.

He could have been anywhere between sixty and a thousand years old. He had a frame pack like Sam's, but instead of bulging with a tent and sleeping bag, it looked practically empty. In his left hand he gripped a gnarled but beautiful old walking stick.

Then from under his collar came a tiny, colorful parrot. A quaker parrot, staring at her quizzically. Any doubt washed away. Here he was in the flesh, Walden, the legend of the trail, frowning at her sternly. Not in a murderous way. More like a grandfatherly way. Remembering Sam's story, McKenna almost laughed out loud.

"I wouldn't head out there," Walden said. "You know how many people try and don't come back? It's a maze with no trail to speak of. Walk a hundred feet and everything will look the same. Dozens of steep drop-offs. Bear dens. Plus there's a cold snap coming."

McKenna agreed with everything he said. They could hear Sam's footsteps, the snapping twigs, as he muscled through overgrown forest not fit for traveling.

Walden spoke again. "That waterfall is a myth, you know."

McKenna tilted her head. She wanted to call out to Sam, bring him back to the trail, and show him this amazing sight: Walden and his bird.

"I heard you were a myth, too," she said.

Walden's frown held for the barest second and then his face softened. A crusty kind of bark emerged, and McKenna realized it was a laugh. An unaccustomed laugh.

"Fair enough," he said when the noise passed.

McKenna smiled and waved, the way Sam had waved at her. Then she ducked between the trees, walking briskly to catch up with him. There was no question of waiting a few days to see Sam, or even a few hours. She had to tell him, as soon as possible, that she'd spoken to Walden! He was real.

16

Sam didn't know whether to be relieved, surprised, or disappointed when he heard McKenna crashing onto the path behind him. If you could even call it a path—the overgrown spit of dirt where someone had once traveled, where maybe people had traveled recently, was nothing like the AT. The wildness of it exhilarated him, opened up possibility. He wanted McKenna with him, sure. But he also wanted her to be able to walk away. He had been such a jerk.

He wanted to know she'd walk away if she ever needed to.

"Sam!" came the voice behind him. It was purely excited, no trace of the argument they'd been having for the past few miles. "Sam, wait up."

He stopped and waited. Just behind the next stand of trees he could see an opening. There would be a view. He wasn't sure it could match the view of McKenna, blue eyes bright, coming toward him excitedly. Something more expansive than any view opened up inside him and he set his face into the easiest expression in his artillery, the nonchalant grin.

"Sam!" she said, panting and tugging at the straps of her

pack. It was a good thing she hadn't tripped in her effort to catch up, Sam thought.

"You won't believe it," she went on. He could tell she wanted to lean forward, touch her knees, and catch her breath, but the heavy pack stopped her short. "Walden," she said. "On the trail. With the beard and parrot and everything. I talked to him."

"Walden?" Sam narrowed his eyes. One thing that had never occurred to him was to question McKenna's honesty. But *Walden*? In the flesh?

"Yes," McKenna said. "He had a pack kind of like yours. And this amazing walking stick. And the parrot, he really has a little parrot. His voice is gravelly. Stern. But he didn't kill me."

Sam laughed and McKenna tried to, but the laugh caught in her still-heavy breath.

"What did he say?" Sam asked.

He took a couple steps toward her, wanting to close the gap between them. It was so weird, he knew, the way it came and went, the need to put a wall up, and then the need to tear it down. The second always felt most imperative, because that was the one he couldn't control.

"He told me not to go off the trail," McKenna said. "He told me the waterfall's a myth."

"He's supposed to be a myth, too."

"That's what I said! And you know what he did? He laughed."

Sam closed his hands around the straps of her pack, pulling her closer to him. She tripped a little, and he caught her, holding her firm and steady. Before he kissed her he said, "Hey. I'm sorry."

He was close enough that he couldn't see her face clearly, close enough that he could feel her lips start to move against his. She was going to say *I'm sorry, too,* he could tell, but she stopped herself. Good girl. She had nothing to be sorry for.

He said, "I'm glad you're here."

"Me, too," she said. He stopped the second word short by closing the fraction of an inch that separated them and kissing her.

McKenna *was* glad. She couldn't explain why, but it didn't feel like defeat, or caving in. More like she'd traded one sensation for another. As she and Sam broke through the trees up onto a ridge—the sky opening up in front of them, clear day giving way to strangely clear gloaming—the need to cover miles, to accomplish her goal, was transcended by a fantastic sense of lawlessness. It was like with Sam's help, she'd grabbed hold of something the whole world (and her own brain) had kept from her.

"Look," he said.

He stopped at the crest of the ridge and dropped his pack. An unexpected flat spot, clear of rocks, even a perfect patch of sand for their tent. Someone had camped there before, which McKenna refused to admit made her feel better. There was a little circle of rocks, scarred ground, the charred remains of a campfire.

"Maybe we should use your stove," he suggested. She could

tell from his voice that he was trying to compromise. "It's kind of dry out here, and the smoke might draw rangers."

"No way," McKenna said. "After this day, this ridge, this view . . . we need a fire. I've gotten kind of addicted to them, if you want to know."

Sam smiled. A real smile, not the distant, infuriating smile from before. Still, she didn't quite trust it, not entirely. If there was a pattern to Sam's comings and goings, she had yet to decipher it.

"Hey," he said. "Hey, Mack."

"Yeah?"

"I'm sorry."

"You already said that."

"I know. Just, even though I'm sorry, and even though I was a jerk, I'm glad we're here. You and me."

McKenna nodded. She pulled on her fleece jacket. The cool breeze of the afternoon was starting to morph into the cold breeze of evening. They'd already filled their water bottles at a creek a mile or so back. The water had looked so clear it was almost tempting not to filter it, though of course they had. Or rather, of course McKenna had.

"Me, too." She windmilled her shoulders backward, working out the kinks from that power walk to catch up with Sam. He stepped forward and put his hands on her shoulders, digging his fingers in, massaging.

"You know what would be cool? To stay here a couple days. Do some day hikes, explore a little."

"You can't think we're really going to find that waterfall," McKenna said. It annoyed her to the extent that she could be annoyed with him when he was being so sweet, his hands feeling so good. Hadn't she already caved to one huge thing, going off the trail? How long did he expect her to stay out here?

Sam shrugged. "Who knows?" he said. "I never thought we'd run into Walden. I never thought I'd meet someone like you."

All annoyance evaporated, which would have been annoying in itself. But the endorphins from the hike were fully operational. The breeze felt so good. And being with Sam felt so good. Without further conversation, they collected wood and built a small fire, eating ramen noodles and the last of the dried cranberries. When night fell in earnest, it was the best view of the stars they'd seen on the trail. Though they'd set up the tent, there was no question, tonight they'd be sleeping outside.

McKenna went through her dry bag. There wasn't a ton of food, but she had a handful of PowerBars and some jerky. Enough to last a few days, sparsely. It would make whatever they had when they got to a town that much more fulfilling.

"As soon as we get back on the trail we'll have to make a stop to resupply and do laundry," McKenna said. "But I think you're right. It would be nice to hang out a few days. Before the last stretch to Georgia."

She watched his face carefully to see if he'd react to that, the thought of the end of the trail, and what it might mean. McKenna didn't want the end of the trail to be the end of them.

But she also didn't want to be the one who came up with a plan for them to stay together.

Still. Once they'd eaten and put away their food, once they'd zipped their sleeping bags together into a wide double bed on top of the sand, they lay side by side, holding hands, staring up at the stars. McKenna couldn't help saying, "Hey, Sam. I love you. You love me, too. Remember?"

"Not something I'd ever forget, Mack."

He turned away from the view, toward her. His hand on her face should have felt calloused, but mostly it just felt strong. And something in his face, a softening, and at the same time an urgency, like he couldn't handle everything he felt. McKenna believed him absolutely, more than if he'd spoken it.

When McKenna woke the next morning, it was gorgeous and bright. They didn't bother with breakfast; neither of them felt hungry, and supplies were dwindling. If they were going to stay camped in this spot for another night or two, they'd have to ration and forage.

"I guess it's moving past the time of year when we can find food growing," McKenna said as she wrestled with getting her sleeping bag into its stuff sack. Of all the maintenance jobs on the trail, this might have been her least favorite—getting a large stretch of cloth into a smaller one required more muscle and patience than you would think.

"Just throw it in the tent," Sam said. "Or leave it there. There's not a cloud in the sky."

McKenna looked up, though of course she had already noted the clearness of the sky, the glare from the early-morning sun. If she still had her iPhone she might have checked the weather report—if she even had service out here. But without her phone, she had learned to read the weather by being outside, and also that the weather was not always easy to read. Some clear mornings gave way to afternoon showers. She picked up her half-stuffed sleeping bag and threw it into the tent, then did the same with Sam's and zipped the flap. Then she consulted the map in her guidebook. The AT was clearly marked, as were roads that crossed it. But the expanse of land surrounding it was just that—an expanse, with green-gray squiggles to indicate rocks and trees. The map wouldn't do her any good out here. She closed the book and slid it into her pack.

"Ready to do some exploring?" he asked.

Sam's pack was smaller, so they stored its meager contents in the tent, then filled it with what they'd need for a day hike—some dry food, a couple bottles of water, the water filter, the tarp. McKenna threw in a couple of light extras, too, like the bottle of iodine tablets, just in case, plus a few outer garments in case it got cold, and then she fastened the Timex she hadn't yet glanced at to the outside of Sam's pack, which felt gloriously, beautifully light as she swung it onto her back.

"Hey," Sam said. "Let me carry that."

She couldn't resist handing it over. Her pack had become like an extension of herself; now without all those extra pounds, it felt like she'd cut her weight in half. Following Sam into the woods, walking with no heavy straps digging into her shoulders or hips, was like flying. She bounced off the balls of her feet as Sam chose a narrow, dry rivulet to follow downhill.

"How do you know the way?" McKenna asked him.

"When you search for the mythical waterfall of a race of spirit people, you do it on instinct."

Obvious translation: *I have no idea where I'm going or what I'm doing.* Sam ventured away from the dry streambed which seemed like a bad idea to McKenna, but she didn't say so, still feeling giddy with this new lawlessness. Out of habit, her eyes went to the trees, looking for white blazes, and every time she realized she wouldn't see one out here, a little spike of emotion rose inside her—a combination of panic and joy. They walked in their usual companionable and comfortable silence, the busy silence of accomplishment, she always thought of it as, except now they weren't taking down miles.

For the first time in her life, she wasn't trying to accomplish anything. She was just being. Under a clear sky, surrounded by trees, accompanied by a person she'd found in the wilderness, a person she really and truly loved.

"Holy crap," Sam said.

McKenna stopped short behind him as they walked out of the tree line to the most spectacular view she'd ever seen. It hardly seemed real. The trees had opened up to a wide stretch of dust bordering a steep outcropping of rocks—a wall of sharp shale that dropped down to a gleaming lake, so clear and pure that it offered the sky right back to itself, mirror images facing each other.

"It's like a gift," McKenna breathed. "A reward for going off the trail."

Sam put his arm around her and gave her a little squeeze. "You hungry?" he asked.

"Starving."

He took off his pack, but instead of unzipping it he walked toward a stand of blooming trees with red flowers and started picking the small red berries that covered the branches.

"You're sure those are edible?"

"Positive. Ash berries. My mother used to make ash berry jam. It's a weird flavor, but I'm craving some variety, aren't you?"

While Sam collected the berries, McKenna got the tarp out of his pack and spread it on the ground, pulling out select items to go with them. She pushed aside any dubiousness about those red berries—they looked like something your mother would warn you not to eat at the park. Hadn't Sam steered them toward this amazing spot, this beautiful moment?

He joined her on the tarp, his shirt folded and filled with berries, which he spilled out in front of her to join the granola bar and purified water and salmon jerky. McKenna had bought salmon jerky for a change of pace and *hated* it—she thought it tasted like dried cat food—but they were toward the end of their provisions, so it would have to do. Sam picked up a berry and put it in her mouth. Her face immediately went into an involuntary squint; it was unbelievably tart and made her shoulders shudder. But after half the granola bar and a nibble of the fishy jerky, she found herself craving the taste. Just introducing that small bit of something new, instead of the same tastes she'd had day in and day out, made the picnic seem special. She wrapped up the rest of the bag of jerky and put it and the PowerBars away for later.

She lay back on the tarp, staring into the blue-lake sky. "I wish we could get down to that lake," she said.

"We should try."

"No." The word came out short and final. "It's too steep. We'd have to search too long for a way down, and it would take forever to climb back up."

"Could be worth it. For a swim."

McKenna closed her eyes. "This time of year, at this altitude? That water is probably forty degrees. Can't you quit while you're ahead?"

She heard a little rustling as he swept the remnants of their lunch back into his pack, and his face came to hover in the space above hers. "Yeah," he said. "I think I can."

Eyes still shut, she reached up and touched his chin, the beginning of a beard. "It's like we're the last people left on earth."

"Would you like that?" he asked.

McKenna thought in an idle way—everything felt idle at this moment, like nothing but the sun and Sam's nearness mattered anymore—that his voice sounded vulnerable.

"Yeah," she said. "Sometimes I think I would like it. And other times, the thought scares me."

Her eyes opened, taking in Sam's face blocking everything else from her vision. He was too close for her to tell if there were tears in his eyes, or if things were just blurry because he was so close.

"Well," he said, "it doesn't scare me at all."

As if to prove his point, he pulled off his clothes, and then hers, and they made love with the clear blue reflections hovering above, below, and all around.

Afterward they dozed, neither of them was sure for how long. It could have been ten minutes or two hours. McKenna was in the midst of a very peaceful dream: she and Sam, down at the lake, standing naked on the sand as the cool mountain water lapped over her toes. In the second between believing it was true and realizing it wasn't, McKenna thought she'd never wanted anything as much as she wanted a swim in that pure, cold water.

It was the crash that woke her up, a rumbling sound that took its time so that she almost thought it could be the waterfall, appearing magically, either beside the lake or right there where they lay.

A second crash made McKenna sit up, grabbing for her clothes. The sky no longer reflected the lake, it was completely dark. In her heightened dream state McKenna thought of the word *eclipse*, but it wasn't an eclipse, just a storm, swept in without warning.

"Sam," McKenna said. Unbelievably, he still slept. She stood to pull on her pants and kicked him lightly but urgently. "Wake up. It's about to—"

More magic, the sky opened before she could say the word. No preambling drizzle, just a faucet turned on full blast. They were soaked in an instant.

"Damn it," Sam said, jumping to his feet and gathering up the tarp and his pack in one motion. Fast as they could, they got their things together and then ran. McKenna let Sam choose the direction, assuming that he knew where he was going, that he'd lead them back to their tent.

"Wait," she yelled as he started to duck between the trees. A crash of light, with no time to count from the clap of thunder that preceded it; it was like they happened simultaneously. McKenna might not have been a Boy Scout, but she knew what that meant.

"We can't stand under the trees," she said. "The lightning!"

"Would you rather stay out here and be the only targets?" he yelled, then reached for her hand, pulling her along the ridge. They ran for a while, the pack slamming on Sam's back, before finally ducking into an outcropping of rocks beneath a low ledge, neither the lake nor their campsite anywhere in sight.

They huddled close together while the storm raged, holding

the tarp over them for extra protection, their breath coming fast and furiously. McKenna had to admit she hadn't really felt afraid, and didn't feel afraid now. So far it had been a day of existing inside her body, following her emotions, and living in the *now*. Kneeling with Sam, watching the storm, only heightened that sense, the two of them wet and shivering, the display of light and sound gorgeous and humbling. They were merely two creatures in the forest, waiting out Mother Nature. McKenna didn't worry about the wet clothes, all they had to do was make it back to their campground to change. The very fervor of the storm meant it would probably pass quickly.

As it began to die down, they even laughed a little.

"That was amazing," Sam said. "I've been out here . . . hell, I've lost track of how long I've been out here, and I've never seen a storm like that."

As the rain slowed, Sam held his hand out from under the tarp, catching the drops in his hand and then slurping them down. McKenna did the same.

"We should have put out a water bottle and caught some," she said. "Water that we wouldn't have to purify."

Sam rooted in his pack and pulled out his still-full water bottle—at lunch, they'd been drinking from McKenna's. "Where's mine?" she said.

"Can't find it. We must have left it when we ran."

McKenna imagined it, rolling over the edge of the ridge when they pulled up the tarp, landing beside that lake. In the dim light following the storm, it almost seemed like that lake had been a mirage, or a trick, so weird that they could run away so quickly from something so huge.

"Oh no," McKenna said. "The filter's gone, too."

She pawed through their things, hoping she was wrong. But they had few enough things that she knew she hadn't missed it. They had left the filter behind.

"Don't worry," Sam said, ducking out from under the tarp. "We have your other bottle at the tent. And we have the iodine tablets."

She stood up and shook out the tarp, then jammed it into the bungee cords Sam had strapped on his pack's exterior—no point getting the inside of his pack wet. Overhead, water still dripped from trees in loud and persistent drops, but the outpouring from the sky seemed to have ended. It was oddly quiet, the clouds still hung overhead, empty but not quite ready to float away.

Sam took a few steps, looked around. There was no discernible path, just thick trees to one side and the wall of rocks on the other. Where there should have been footprints signaling the route they'd taken, everything was mud, the rain having cleared off the top layer of silt, leaving a blank canvas.

"Maybe if we follow the rock wall, it will lead us back to the ridge with the lake view," she said. It made sense that if they got back to that ridge, all they had to do was walk along it, and eventually they'd get to the spot where they'd picnicked.

"But there's probably nothing there to mark the spot," Sam said. "I'm sure the water bottle would've rolled away, and we took up everything else. It makes more sense, I think, to go through the woods."

"Where everything looks exactly the same?"

He turned his head, blue eyes narrow and, McKenna thought, looking a little superior. Still, it made her feel better that they also looked calm and in control. He wasn't worried.

"Maybe it looks the same to you," he said, and strode off into the trees. McKenna paused for a second. The sight of his back, lovely as it was, had the potential to become a sore subject. Still: her out-of-mind calm hadn't really left her yet, so she took a deep breath and pulled his pack on. It wasn't as liberating as walking without anything, but compared to her usual load, it felt almost like nothing.

Sam kept walking, turning his head this way and that, choosing routes between the trees that seemed increasingly arbitrary. As the clouds overhead finally blew away, revealing a sky that was darkening past late afternoon, enough sun crept through so that her clothes began to dry—thank God and REI for quick-drying technology. Sam wasn't faring quite as well; his cotton clothes still looked sodden. He stopped short at the base of an ash berry tree, looking up into the leaves, trying to figure out if it was the same one they'd snacked at before.

"This is just one tree," McKenna said. "The one we found before was a whole stand. And we could see the view from there, remember?"

"I know," Sam said. "I was just wondering if we should collect some."

Truthfully, McKenna's stomach had not felt tip-top since eating those berries. Maybe they weren't poisonous as in drop-dead-the-second-you-eat-them, but she wasn't convinced they were *food* in the strictest sense, either.

"Thanks," she said. "But I'm good. Right now I just really want to find our campsite."

An image formed in her head of the place where they had left her tent and pack with almost everything she had been hauling all these months, the gear that had become like an extension of her body. Her tent, her sleeping bag, her cookstove, her billfold with just-in-case cash. She had not been this far away from her things since going out to dinner with Brendan back in Maine. As natural as the earlier part of the day had felt, as liberating as it had been to leave everything behind, now she couldn't believe she'd been talked into it. Not only was she far away from her things, she didn't know how to get back to them. The trees surrounding them, the stupid poisonous ash berry tree included, had no white blazes, nothing that would help them get back to everything they needed to survive.

"Don't panic," Sam said, though she hadn't said a word.

"Who's panicking?"

"Nobody." His voice sounded too firm, like he was issuing orders.

"Okay, then," she said. It took a lot of effort to make the words come out calmly. "If we're not panicking, what are we doing?"

"Walking. Walking and looking."

"Any particular direction?"

"This way," Sam said.

The certainty in his voice rankled McKenna because she knew it was a lie. Still, she didn't say anything, just tugged habitually on the shoulder straps and walked after him.

An hour later? Maybe more. Enough time had passed while walking with no idea where they were that the heat of panic had begun to take hold. Even so, McKenna stopped and got her fleece jacket from Sam's pack.

"Do you want your coat?" she asked him.

"No thanks." His face had taken on a gritty and lockjawed expression, like no matter what, he wouldn't admit they were lost.

"It's actually pretty dry," McKenna said, feeling the itchy wool. The clothes Sam wore still looked damp. The air around them was getting colder. He must be freezing.

"No, I'm fine. Let's keep walking. I think we're close."

Which was total bull. The woods surrounding them looked nothing like the place where they'd camped, they'd gotten so deep into the forest that there was no sign of an opening on either side. Even if they *were* close to their campsite, there was absolutely nothing to indicate it.

By now, she'd had it with Sam pretending he knew what he was doing. So she said, "Oh yeah? Why do you think that?"

Sam didn't say anything, just veered—randomly, McKenna

was sure—through some trees to the left. She remembered the view from the lake, layers and layers of peaks and forest. Now they were folded into those endless and indiscernible layers.

Finally, she couldn't help saying, "I knew it. I *knew* we shouldn't have gone off the trail."

She'd expected him to stop then, to turn, to argue. For example, he could point out that she hadn't seemed to *know* that when she'd run after him spouting off about Walden, or in her lawless euphoria the night before. She hadn't noticed it on their picnic, or in talking about making their way down to the lake, or naked and without a care underneath him and the blue sky. But he didn't, he just kept walking.

As her panic spiraled, McKenna found that she couldn't stop talking.

"It's getting dark. We're going to freeze out here. We're just going in circles. We hardly have any food left. There are no blazes. Do you know what every disaster story I read about the AT had in common? They all went off the trail."

That wasn't what she said exactly, not in that order, anyway. There were other sentences threading these thoughts together. She'd never been a nervous talker, but now that she'd started, she couldn't stop. She felt like if she let the words slow down, if she shut up (as the stiff, tense muscles on Sam's back told her he wanted her to), all those words would translate from theory into reality. She wouldn't be talking about their disaster. She'd be living it.

"It's getting dark," McKenna said again. "In a little while it *will* be dark, and we're just out here, exposed, with hardly anything to eat and just one water bottle—"

"Shut *up*," Sam finally said. He stopped short and turned. A vein in his forehead that she'd never seen stood out, blue and furious.

"No!" she shouted. "I won't shut up. I'm petrified. We could die out here, Sam!"

"Is that how fast you go from one point to the other? You're either safe and happy, or you're right on the verge of death?"

"It's like you don't get it. This is *dangerous*. This is the wilderness out here, with animals and elements and we have *nothing*, we walked away from everything that's—"

"Everything that's what? You know when I walked away from everything? Coming up on eight months ago. Coming up on my whole damn life. You're worried about being lost? You're worried about being cold? Hungry? What you'll do next? Welcome to my world, princess."

McKenna swallowed, thinking of all those months Sam had been on the trail alone with no money, none of the advantages she'd had. Not to mention all those years in the house with his wild-card, alcoholic father. She reached out, trying to soothe him, but he was too far gone. He turned, snatching his arm away from her, and kept walking.

But not for long. If their argument was too far gone, then so was the day. Not much time had passed when Sam had to admit defeat, leaning against a tree and sliding to the ground, which was still wet. McKenna took off his pack. There was enough space to lay down the tarp. She handed Sam his jacket, and pulled on her hat, grateful that she'd brought it. She wished he had one. Mad as they were at each other, they huddled together, clinging tight. It was the only chance they had of staying warm.

17

Sam couldn't sleep, and not just because it was so cold. He'd taken off his wet T-shirt and wrapped up himself and McKenna in his wool jacket. She slept on his chest, even though she'd been almost too pissed to look at him. Her forehead felt cool, but when he reached under her shirt to check, the skin on her back was warm. She was sleeping so soundly. Maybe that was what happened when you grew up in a house where you knew you were safe. You learned how to sleep. Or else maybe it was just that her conscience was clear. Unlike Sam's.

He knew this was all his fault. He had walked off the trail and dragged McKenna along with him, even though she knew better. He'd treated her like she was being a priss. He'd teased and goaded her into doing what might just lead to their death.

He had seen it in her eyes, a kind of panic, even though she didn't *really* believe they might die out here. Why should she believe in something like that, her own mortality? Not only had McKenna lived in the kind of world Sam could hardly even imagine, with safety nets made of money and love. But she'd always followed her very carefully thought-out plans. Danger was something that didn't exist for her. It was just something abstract that you had to avoid, not something that was *real*.

But the thing was: out here, this time of year, with so little food and possibly no water (unless they could find a pure source—since they no longer had the filter and only a limited number of iodine tablets), they would have to get back to the trail, or they could die—of dehydration, starvation, exposure.

They could die.

Sam almost didn't care, he definitely wouldn't care if he were alone. But he couldn't stand the thought of bringing McKenna down with him.

Very carefully, he moved his arm out from under her, and laid her onto the tarp. The first shreds of dawn reached up above the trees. He might not be going to college, but he'd had high school English, he knew about the rosy-fingered dawn, and it had never looked more like fingers to him than this morning. The knobby shafts of pink light would have been beautiful if he hadn't been so scared. Where were those lost traveler spirits when you needed them?

He looked through his pack for the fishing line and a couple scraps of jerky. If he could find a stream, maybe he could catch a few trout for breakfast. While he was at it, he'd keep his eyes out for a way back to the trail. It would be better to lose all their stuff than to wander in circles searching for it. He dug his knife out of the front of his pack. It wasn't white paint, but he could still make notches in the trees to work as blazes.

Back at their old campsite, in McKenna's giant red pack,

she had pens and the leather-bound journal that he knew she hadn't written more than a few words in. But they hadn't brought those with them yesterday. So Sam picked up a stick and wrote in the dirt to the right of McKenna's head, large letters so she'd see them as soon as she opened her eyes: WENT FISHING. WAIT HERE.

He left the pack, the food, the water. Several steps away, he made his first notch in a tree. Maybe his spirit hadn't been broken just yet, because setting off with the hopes of waking her up with a string of fresh fish made him smile. "Hey, Mack," he'd say. "I found the way back to our campsite. But first I'm going to make breakfast."

The relief he pictured on her face was more than enough to keep him going.

McKenna bolted awake an hour later. She looked straight ahead, and then around. She didn't look at the ground next to her.

"Sam?" she called.

The trees answered with stillness, no wind, no leftover raindrops, not even that damned towhee. Even the birds were smart enough to stay out of this part of the forest. She jumped to her feet, kicking the tarp sideways so that it half covered, half erased Sam's note in the dirt.

"Sam? *SAM, you idiot!*"

If a girl screams for her boyfriend in the forest and nobody hears, is he a complete jerk? Is she certifiably insane, certifiably moronic for ever having listened to a single word he said?

McKenna squatted down on the tarp and put her head in her hands. Way back in June, sitting in the Whitworth Student Union with Courtney, she'd talked herself into the idea of hiking the Appalachian Trail alone. And she *had* hiked it alone, all the way through New England. And then she'd hiked it with Sam. The two of them climbing up and down mountains together. A couple on a camping trip: much more like what people would expect than a girl walking alone. But for McKenna, the road with Sam was the road less traveled.

And look where it had led.

She took her head off her arms and shook it, hard. Panicking wouldn't help. Falling into despair wouldn't help. Her stomach was past rumbling, it just gaped with a crampy pain. At least before performing his standard disappearing act, Sam had left her with his pack and some supplies. As she rooted through, she found herself worrying about him. He hadn't taken any food or the water bottle. She wondered if his clothes from yesterday had dried.

McKenna took a deep breath and closed her eyes. Even though the last thing they'd done last night was fight, she shouldn't jump to conclusions. He'd left his things behind, hadn't he? Including the water bottle? He couldn't be so angry that he was willing to undertake a suicide mission. Maybe if she sat tight and waited, he would come walking back through those trees.

She pulled out the packet of salmon jerky and ate two pieces, though she could easily have devoured the last of it, despite the awful fishiness. She took a few careful sips of water because who knew how long it would take to find another source.

After just enough food to make her realize how completely ravenous she was, she lay back on the tarp, closed her eyes, and waited.

And waited. And waited. And waited some more.

She couldn't bear it—the way the sun was rising, and how she was unable to do the only thing that ever made her feel better: move.

Sam didn't seem to be coming back, though hours passed. Maybe he was lost. Maybe he had deserted her. Either way, she couldn't sit here for the rest of her life, or the rest of her life could be considerably shortened.

Gathering up her things, she forced herself away from fear and toward determination. *I will see my family again. I will get back to the trail and walk the rest of the way to Georgia.*

In the widest stretch of dirt leading off between the trees, the closest thing to a path, McKenna could see Sam's footprints. She set off to follow them. At some point, the footprints stopped; they didn't disappear, just tapered off, blending into a confusing assortment of other footprints. For a moment, the multiple prints comforted McKenna—this must be a part of the woods where other people had walked—but she quickly realized they probably belonged to her and Sam from yesterday. They must have been going in circles, like those kids in *The Blair Witch Project*. Courtney had made McKenna watch that movie, and McKenna had rebelled against the blatant attempts to terrify her, refusing to lose a wink of sleep remembering the over-the-top images. Now, five years after watching it, she finally felt afraid. What could be worse than walking in circles through the woods, trapped, never finding your way out? She wondered if that movie had taken place in the Smoky Mountains.

She stopped, shrugged off Sam's pack, and took a very tiny sip of water. The loss of the other water bottle and filter was brutal. Thank God she had the iodine tablets, but they would only help if she found a new source. Having only one bottle meant she would have to find a new source every thirty-four ounces. She remembered laying all her gear out on her bed back at home, surveying it with Lucy. The giant water jug she'd filled and then pronounced too heavy to carry. Of course she'd been right, there was no way she'd have made it this far with all those gallons. But just now, the tiniest bit of water wetting her dry lips, she remembered how carelessly she had glugged all that water into her bathtub, the sound it made, and the bubbles that formed under the collapsible plastic. To live in a world with a roof, always a few steps away from a faucet, seemed like a luxury only found in dreams.

"Sam!" she called at the top of her lungs. The sound bounced back to her in an almost echo, the forest especially still after such a loud noise. Nothing.

"SAM, YOU IMPULSIVE ASS! ARE YOU OUT THERE?"

More of nothing, just nothing, not even creatures rumbling behind the trees. It made her feel something too close to despair to think about her house, or her family. Or even Sam. So instead she decided to think about the stuff she *had* brought along, the stuff she'd carried all this way and left at the campsite yesterday. Her Keen sandals, her worse-for-wear-but-still-cute skort, the compass she hadn't learned how to use, the bird book, the copies of *Walden* and *The Ice at the Bottom of the World*. Her cookstove and pot, plus her gloves and her cash and the Visa whose bills went to her parents. The stuff of survival. In her mind, she apologized to every last item, swearing with grim determination that she'd get back to it.

"Compass, Keens, books," she muttered as a sort of mantra, walking furiously, the second-nature rhythm of one foot after the other. "I will get back to you."

But hours later, exhausted, the sun breaking her heart as it started its trip to the other side of the world, McKenna didn't know if she'd made any progress at all. The patterns of trees and branches, the lack of a path, the trunks of trees: it all looked the same. When she *could* see through the trees, it was only layer upon layer of lush mountains that would have been beautiful if they hadn't represented an endless expanse for her to stay lost in.

The campsite could be steps away or it could be miles. If she had that compass now, she would definitely figure out how to use it. She imagined it in the palm of her hand, the gorgeous brass weight of it, pointing her back to the trail.

She refused to think about Sam, in his duct-taped sneakers, without water. Wasn't that his own doing?

The only high point of the day came when she found a stream. In that moment she'd experienced something like joy, downing what was left in her bottle and then filling it back up. The water looked so clear and felt so cold, she was almost tempted not to waste iodine tablets. She thought that was something Sam would do, she could almost hear his voice next to her, making fun of her for thinking such precautions were worth bothering with. *You're going to die of thirst waiting for the pills to work.*

She plunked the tablets into the bottle defiantly, then rested for thirty minutes, grateful for the one bit of technology she had left: her watch. Then she drank long and deep, replenishing herself before dipping the bottle again, filling it to the brim, and adding two more tablets.

Hours later, the sun had made its final bow, and McKenna trudged on in darkness. She heard an owl in the distance, and stumbled over a tree root, landing in the dirt, catching herself with her hands and scraping her palms. Sitting up on her knees, she gave it one last try for the day.

"Sam!" she yelled. *"Sam! Are you out there?"*

The forest answered with that same infuriating stillness, the birds all gone to bed, the crickets and frogs all gone for the winter. McKenna pulled her cap down over her ears, and reached for the sweater Sam had left behind, not bothering with the tarp or food, but forcing herself to take a few swallows of water before closing her eyes. Sleep rushed in at a remarkable pace, the full force of her mental and physical exhaustion taking over.

Then, from somewhere off in the distance, a sound. Almost like a voice, like someone calling out. She sat up and listened, waiting for it to come again.

"Sam!" she called into the darkness. And then, from her diaphragm, as loud as she could: "SAM!"

Nothing. It must have been her imagination. Or the owl. She lay back down and fell into a dead sleep almost before her head hit the cold, hard ground.

Twelve hours earlier: Sam sauntered away from where McKenna lay sleeping. Every ten feet or so, he stopped to mark a tree. If felt like something McKenna would do, taking precautions. It took him longer than he thought it would to find water; by the time he reached the mountain stream, the sun was high in the sky. He peeled off his wool coat and knelt down, cupping his hands and slurping the water, then splashing it onto his face before drinking more. It tasted cold and perfect and clean. Then he baited his hook and dropped the fishing line. Much as he'd enjoyed the water's temperature, now he hoped it wasn't too cold for the fish.

As he waited for a bite, he imagined McKenna, who must be awake by now. Maybe she'd be making a fire, confident he'd be bringing back breakfast. He tried to remember if they'd brought matches with them when they left their campsite.

Finally something bit, but when he pulled it out, it was a tiny trout. If a ranger had come along, he would have written him a handful of tickets—for fishing out of season and without a license, for keeping an undersized fish. Which would have been fine with Sam because then the ranger could lead them to safety, and Sam wouldn't pay the tickets anyway.

It had to be close to noon by now, so one undersized trout would have to do. He'd already left McKenna alone too long; she'd be getting antsy and worried. Sam killed the fish with a knife through the eye. He'd always thought it was mean the way his father and brother would let the fish flop and gasp their way to death, drowning in oxygen.

The last tree he'd marked had been about ten paces back. The question was, from which direction, exactly, had he taken those paces? The trees surrounding the stream looked more alike than he wanted to admit.

Over there—that tulip tree, he was sure he'd walked right past it. He hooked the fish to his pocket and headed that way. Three or four trees down, a magnolia, he'd made one of his etches there, he was sure of it.

Time ticked by. He walked from tree to tree. Here! He was sure he'd made the mark on this oak, a piece of bark freshly shaved, revealing pale white wood underneath. But when he walked in the direction he was sure he'd come from, noting the sun's position in the sky, he realized the mark might have been natural, made by a squirrel or woodpecker. He should have thought of a more distinctive way to mark the trees, something more clearly man-made.

"McKenna?" he called, hoping he was closer than he realized. All he heard in reply was a rustle, some little rodent running away. The air was cold but Sam brushed a clammy film of sweat off his forehead. He should have taken another drink of water from that stream. Noticing a patch of edible violets, he ate a handful, then pocketed a few more handfuls to give to McKenna along with the fish. Not much of a breakfast, but still a breakfast—with protein even—to keep them going until they could find their campsite.

He wondered: How long would she wait for him? Sitting tight, being still, was not her specialty. It wouldn't take her long to decide he was lost and come looking for him.

After what seemed like a few hours, he decided to scrap the plan of finding his way back to where they'd slept. No way McKenna would still be there. By now she'd have marched off in full rescue mode. Picturing it made him smile a little. He'd do what she was doing—try to find his way back to their first campsite with the fire pit. They'd either meet up there or bump into each other on the way.

Turning around in the right direction—he was sure of it now—he set out walking, feeling bad that McKenna was stuck carrying the pack, and also wishing they hadn't lost that second water bottle.

Every once in a while he'd call out, "Mack!" but it was so

depressing not hearing any reply that before long he stopped. He found an ash berry tree and ate a few handfuls, but that, along with the flowers, only made him hungrier. If he hadn't eaten anything, his body would have clicked into that mode of no expectation, which he was pretty familiar with by now. But the thin flora opened up his stomach to the idea of food without doing much to satisfy it. He wouldn't eat the fish, though, he was saving that for McKenna, and anyway he had no way to start a fire. He went ahead and ate the berries, since he was pretty sure she didn't like them anyway. Then he continued walking. He'd find McKenna by late afternoon, and they'd eat the fish together.

Sound travels strangely through forests, with rock walls and trees of varying heights. Sam thought he heard McKenna's voice, but when he called back, he didn't get an answer. Either the wind was carrying sound in his direction but not vice versa, or he wanted to hear her voice so badly that he thought he had.

By the time the sun sank to late-afternoon level, the fish had started to stink. Sam sat down on a fallen log and pulled it off the hook to examine it. His head was dizzy with dehydration. His hunger had reached the bearable point where his body was tamping down the sensation, but he knew he was going to have a hard time continuing on without any calories. This did not make the idea of a raw trout any more appealing, but he took out his knife and cut into it, picking out flaky pieces of flesh and downing it like pills, not chewing, just trying to get the protein into his body. Directly across from where he sat there was a small ring of mushrooms growing out of the dirt, yellow mushrooms with little brown flecks. He thought they might be blushers. The caps were a little small, but maybe that was because of the altitude. Sam threw what was left of the raw, semi-rancid fish aside and plucked a couple mushrooms from the dirt. He'd only eat a couple, enough to keep him going.

About half an hour later, as he tried to figure out what he'd actually eaten, his brain wasn't making the right connections. Trees started multiplying.

"Who the hell put so many trees in this forest?" he said out loud, and then laughed. He tried to lean against one, but it turned out to be the one damned spot for miles without a tree. He stumbled, crashing sideways. When he hit the ground, he heard it, very clearly this time:

"SAM, YOU IMPULSIVE ASS!"

He knew he was out of it enough to hallucinate McKenna's voice. But he probably wouldn't hallucinate the *impulsive ass* part.

"Mack," he yelled, but the voice that came out of his dry throat was a sad little squawk. His stomach churned. Suddenly, he wasn't sure if he'd be able to get to his feet. When he opened his mouth to try again, instead of McKenna's name, out came a steady gush of vomit. He turned onto his hands and knees, retching, until his body had completely emptied. Then he crawled a few feet away and collapsed face-first into the dirt.

Time had done a funny slide. He couldn't tell how long he'd been out here. It was both good and bad that he'd puked, getting rid of the poison, but also getting rid of any nourishment, any fluids. He felt bone-dry. He was exhausted and depleted. He needed to get up.

The mushrooms may have left his body, but they hadn't quite let go of his brain. The sun widened and narrowed through the trees. He imagined it jeering at him. A big joke.

For the first time in his life, something mattered, and Sam had managed to screw it up so royally. If McKenna were here she would point out how well he'd done all those months on the trail, and now that he'd gone off it, everything was going to hell. But it wasn't McKenna, it was the sun that went ahead and scolded him.

"You thought you were invincible," the sun said. "You thought the rules didn't apply to you. You thought you were smarter than the whole damn world."

"I'm sorry," Sam whispered, and when he passed out, it felt like falling straight through the earth, letting it close on top of him, covering him up forever.

Later—he wasn't sure how much later—Sam opened his eyes to flatter light and a clearer head. He took a moment to blink up into the trees, feeling relieved that he was still alive, and then dismayed at everything he would have to do to stay that way. He was so tired.

Still, he got to his feet and did the only thing he could think of. He started walking. He thought about calling out to Mc-Kenna again, but remembering the earlier croak of his voice, he decided to preserve his energy until he knew she was close by.

Sam himself was wrecked. And yet his body moved, doing what it had been doing for so many months now, moving forward. Sam thought that if his heart stopped beating right here, his body would keep walking, one foot after the other, until his flesh decayed, peeling off his bones, his skeleton continuing its never-ending march.

Jeez, he thought. *You're turning into one of your own damn ghost stories.*

Paying attention to the darkening sky and the dropping temperature, Sam waited until the last possible moment to untie the wool jacket from his waist and button it to his chin. He wished he'd taken McKenna up on her offer to buy him a hat. Not to mention boots—the duct tape was flapping on the ground as he walked. He wished a lot of things, none of which would do him any good as the sky got dark.

"Mack!" he finally called out. The sound of her voice was the only thing that could convince him to keep moving. The sky was so damned dark, no houses, no electric lights anywhere to light it up. He started to sink to the ground again, he would just lie down for a quick nap and hopefully not freeze to death.

And then he heard it again. *"Sam! Are you out there?"*

He scrambled to his feet. Damn. McKenna needed to yell again. Didn't she know that? Once for him to hear. Then again for him to figure out the direction she was calling from.

"MACK!" he yelled. *Mack, is that you?*

No answer. He walked a few feet forward in the dark, planning on calling out again, but before he could gather his voice, he was plunging downward. So instead of saying *Mack*, he just kind of screamed, his back scraping against rocks and roots. He couldn't tell how far the drop was.

He landed with a horrible *pop*—the noise a snapping branch would make, except in this case the snapping was somewhere inside his body, in the vicinity of his ankle.

She must have heard him. *"Sam!"* This time it rang out, clear and definite.

"Mack," Sam said, the sound pitiful. Maybe he could've mustered it, if he really tried, but he didn't want to draw her toward him and bring her tumbling down the same rocky incline. Stay where you are, Mack, he thought. Don't risk your life searching for me. I'm fine right where I am.

As if he'd summoned them, a pack of coyotes picked up from somewhere in the woods, their yips rising over one another's and up toward the moon. McKenna would hear them and think she'd imagined his voice. She'd be tired, her mind playing tricks on her.

And then the pain moved from his ankle to shoot through his whole body, taking over, leaving no room for other thoughts or even worry. For the second time that long and horrible day, Sam passed out cold.

18

McKenna woke up floating above a clear, wide lake. Her first impression, when she opened her eyes, was that she was right on the verge of plunging out of the sky and into the water.

She sat up and scrambled back. In the dark of both the starless night and her own exhaustion, she'd apparently decided to sleep right on the edge of a cliff. She had put on her cap and pulled on Sam's sweater, all at the edge of a thousand-foot drop-off, jagged shale cliffs leading down to the water. Sam's pack sat at the edge, too, leaning forward a bit, like it was about to take a swan dive. It would have been a gorgeous and panoramic view to wake up to, if it hadn't come with the realization that all night long, she'd been sleeping so close to a literal edge. Maybe she'd started out a few feet away and rolled closer as she slept (she couldn't believe that even in her depleted state, she wouldn't have sensed that gaping cavern). If she hadn't woken up at just that moment, she might have taken the final roll.

What would it have felt like, waking up in midair? Falling, falling, falling, to the freezing water below.

Probably it would have felt a lot like yesterday. The knowledge, grim and terrifying, that she could very well die.

It was barely after dawn, a fine mist of dampness covering everything. Her nose and cheeks felt cold and stiff, and she could see her breath. Hugging herself in Sam's sweater, she wondered how he'd fared without it. At least he'd taken his wool coat. She imagined the tips of his ears, bright red, maybe even frostbitten.

No, that was dramatic. It was cold in the mountains, definitely, but not yet near freezing. Dire as their situation seemed, they were lucky in some respects. A few weeks later, and they might have been caught in a snowstorm instead of a downpour. There might really have been no way to survive, alone out in the elements, without even each other to cling to.

Part of surviving would be facing these, the lucky aspects, recognizing the things that would help her continue to move forward. For example: the lake! Wasn't the lake a landmark? Two days ago, she and Sam had picnicked by its edge. She might not have her compass, or know how to use it. But if McKenna was facing the lake, she was sure they had come here from the right. Unless they'd managed to walk all the way to the other side of it?

She had no way of knowing if she was sitting anywhere close to the place where they'd been. The edge of the lake could span miles. McKenna took a sip of water, deciding to save what little food she had left. Her stomach had stopped expecting food anyway, and eating something now could just make things worse. The last thing she needed was for one morsel to set off mad cravings, fantasies of cheeseburgers and pancakes, great piles of spaghetti and cold bottles of Coca-Cola.

She took off the sweater, which she'd worn over her fleece jacket, and stuffed it into the pack. The very real possibility that Sam could be dead washed over her, so shocking that she couldn't even manage to be afraid.

What should I do? she asked herself, heading in the direction they *might* have come from in the first place. Should she look for Sam? Or should she try to find her way back to the tent, and go for help? Even if she found the tent, she wasn't confident she could make her way back to the trail. And even if she did make her way back, it could be hours before she ran into anyone, or managed to find her way to the nearest outpost in her current state.

In her mind she heard it, the *crack* of her phone as she'd slid down that embankment. What an idiot she'd been not to get a new one. But then, looking around at the thick layers of trees and peaks, she realized there was a good chance she was in one of the few places left on earth where she wouldn't get reception. The real idiocy had been in coming off the trail in the first place.

McKenna walked on. This walking wasn't like on the trail, where you knew you were taking down miles, heading toward a specific destination. Another surge of fury toward Sam rose up inside her, but was immediately tamped down by the sight of something amazing, a stream. Maybe the same one she'd found yesterday. Or maybe the one she and Sam had stopped at on their way here. The uniformity of forest made it so hard to find your way. But she reminded herself of her plan, to recognize blessings when they appeared. She glugged down the rest of her water and knelt to refill the bottle, diligently plopping in two iodine tablets and tightening the lid.

"Sam," she called out, just for the hell of it, her voice barely rising. She'd called in vain so many times yesterday she didn't believe he was even out there anymore. For the first time it occurred to her: Sam might not even be lost. Maybe he'd figured out the way back to her tent and was waiting for her there. Or maybe he'd arrived at the campsite, taken what he needed, and headed back to the trail.

Even as these bitter thoughts formed, McKenna dismissed them. Sam might have his issues, sure. But she knew the person she loved wasn't a figment of her imagination. The person she'd spent the past months with would never desert her so cruelly. Because he loved her. She knew he did.

"Mack!"

She heard it. Not *maybe* heard it, like yesterday. But she *heard* it, the voice calling out.

"Sam!" she yelled. *"Sam?"*

"Mack!" came the voice again. It sounded loud and strained, a last-ditch effort, a final exertion of energy. *"Mack!"*

Any tiredness disappeared. She ran in the direction of the sound.

SAM.

MACK.

SAM.

MACK.

McKenna found herself at the edge of a sharp incline, a ten-foot wall of rock that would have been nothing for either of them in the daytime.

There at the bottom, in a pathetic heap, lay Sam.

Her mother always said that McKenna never got scared. But if she was honest with herself, way back when she sat in the Student Union with Courtney and decided to do this hike alone, she had felt scared. She'd felt scared when she knew she was falling in love with Sam. And she'd felt scared ever since they'd been lost out here, realizing that they could die if they didn't find their way back. She'd never been more scared in her life than yesterday, when she'd woken up to find Sam gone.

But none of that compared to how she felt right now, at the sight of Sam at the bottom of this drop-off. His face was white and he was shivering. His lips were colorless and cracked, with red sores starting to break through. He looked like he'd lost twenty pounds since she'd last seen him, only thirty-six hours ago. He looked like he could die right here in front of her.

He must have stumbled down it in the dark. She had to get to him. She leaned forward and slid the pack ahead of her, then crab-walked down carefully, bracing herself with her feet and the palms of her hands.

"That was impressive," Sam croaked when she reached him.

McKenna swallowed her fear—terror, really—because it wouldn't do them any good. She pulled her hat onto his head.

Then she raised her water bottle to his lips. Sam drank more deeply than she'd ever seen, glugging it down in such fierce pulls she worried he'd drain the entire thing, or that he'd drink too much and heave. Gently, she pulled it away from him. The sour scent of vomit clung to him. She put her hand against the side of his face. It felt like a sheet of ice.

"Sam," she said. "What the hell happened?"

"Wanted to get you some food. Didn't you see my note?"

"Note? How could you have left a note?"

"In the dirt. Right by your head. So you couldn't miss it."

He was shivering so hard, teeth chattering, like the warmth gathering with the morning sun couldn't reach him. McKenna pulled off her jacket. The faculty adviser from their hiking club had always told them the only way to warm up someone who had hypothermia was skin-on-skin. Her body was the warmest thing around. But she couldn't bear the thought of having to expose him before the warmth would work.

"Look," she said. "I'm going to take your clothes off."

"Do you really think this is the time?"

"Very funny." She untied his shoes, those ridiculous damn sneakers, working off the duct tape and what was left of the canvas. His bare feet were full of so many blisters on blisters, she wondered how he'd been walking. "Once we get you warmed up we can figure out a way to hike out of here. Sam. Jeez."

In her hand, his ankle, so many colors she couldn't count them, and looking three times its regular size, the ankle bone not visible.

"I think it's broken," he said, his voice small.

McKenna dug through her pack—Sam's pack, really—she wished she had one of those instant ice packs, sitting useless back in her tent. She was sure she'd thrown in some ibuprofen. Finding it, she tamped out four pills and pressed them into Sam's mouth, giving him just enough water to get them down. Again, he tried to drink hungrily, an uncontrollable glugging, like he'd die if he couldn't get as much water into his body as possible. McKenna wondered if he'd had anything to drink at all since she'd last seen him.

But questions could come later. Right now she had to warm him up. She stripped off the rest of his clothes and piled the sweater and two coats on top of him. Then she covered him with the tarp and stripped off her own clothes and climbed under everything with him, pressing her body—the exact right temperature a body should be—against his. Sam shivered against her, she could feel his teeth against her neck, chattering, his body becoming violent as his temperature rose. She wrapped her arms around him and held him as tightly as she could.

Desperate as she felt, she continued to feel thankful for small pieces of good luck. She had managed to stay warm last night, and had carried that warmth with her to Sam. After half an hour or so she could feel his body calming, warming against her own. The sky above their heads was blue and clear, no clouds, no threat of rain.

She had found Sam. He was alive, and so was she. Not only

that, but he hadn't wandered off and left her. At least not on purpose.

It was hard to say how much time passed. Enough for the sun to broaden, its rays reaching down and warming the top of her head—she pulled her cap off Sam so he could feel it, too. He lay still now, the shivering having subsided. His eyes were tightly closed but she couldn't tell if he was sleeping or reveling in the sensation of being warm again or trying to block out what must be massive pain from that mangled ankle. The tiniest bit of color had come back to his face. He still looked pale, but his skin looked fluid again, as if those sheets of ice had melted. She pressed her hand against his cheek, imagining that she could feel blood pulsing underneath her palm, moving through his veins. She kissed him and his eyelashes parted, allowing her to see that burst of color, the pale but vivid blue, brighter than the clear sky.

"Hey," she said.

"Hey." And then he kissed her back, his lips still dry but already mending. McKenna felt a surge of hope. They were so strong from these months on the trail. And they were young. Everything about them would regenerate quickly. They would bounce back. Every part of Sam would mend, just as his lips were mending. Their bodies pressed together for warmth and comfort. But also for love.

"I love you," she told him.

"I love you, too. I'm sorry. That was the most boneheaded

thing I've ever done, walking off like that. And I've done a lot of boneheaded things."

"No. It's okay. You wanted to get food. You weren't thinking straight. You meant well."

"Right, good intentions. That means we're on our way to hell, right?"

The warmth that had been gathering so consistently in her chest chilled for an instant. Then she said, "Sam. This is no time for pessimism. Pessimism could get us killed."

"I'm not being pessimistic," he said. "I'm being realistic."

"A realist is just a pessimist who thinks he's right."

"Who said that?"

"Me. Right now."

"Yeah, well." Sam winced, as if he'd moved the wrong way. McKenna had never broken a bone in her life, so she couldn't imagine how painful that ankle must feel. "That's very smart of you to say, but it doesn't mean we're not screwed."

McKenna climbed out from under the tarp and put all her clothes back on except for her jacket, which she stuffed into her pack. Sam sat up, too. He cut the right leg of his jeans with his knife, making room for the swollen ankle, and pulled them on. When they were both dressed again, McKenna put her hat back onto Sam's head.

"My dad always says the most important thing to keep warm is your head," she said.

"You know what? My dad used to say that, too."

McKenna sat next to him, offered a sip of water. This was

the closest thing to nice she'd ever heard him say about his dad.

"He wasn't always so bad," he said, as if reading her thoughts. "You know how I told you my mom took us camping? Well, way back in the early days when we were little, my dad used to take us camping, too. I mean, we'd go as a family. You know how I kept telling you all the things I learned from the Boy Scouts? Well, I was never a Boy Scout, Mack. I learned all that stuff from my dad."

His face looked different, more vulnerable. She reached out and placed a hand on his shoulder, holding him steady. "Sam," she said. "Let's save the confessions for later. Okay? Let's make them when we're in a hospital, and you're doped up on painkillers with a cast on that ankle, and we've got a roof over our heads and eighty more years ahead of us."

She stopped short of saying, *Don't act like this is your deathbed. Because I won't let it be.*

"Mack," he said. "Haven't you wanted to ask what happened to my mother?"

"I was waiting for you to tell me."

"She was cleaning this lady's house, she did that sometimes when she could get the work. And she came across a cabinet with all these pills, anxiety meds, Valium and Ativan and Xanax. She carried them down to the kitchen and poured herself a glass of water and swallowed every last pill. She threw the bottles away and rinsed out the glass—she was always considerate about little details like that. She didn't like to leave messes for other people. Then she walked out of that house, I guess so nobody would find her in time to save her. She walked into the woods and lay down under a Kentucky coffee tree. And I guess all the anxiety went away."

McKenna's hand held on to his shoulder.

"I was fourteen," Sam finished.

McKenna lay down next to him, pulling the tarp back over them. She didn't say anything—everything she could think of felt too trite, too much like something she'd heard other people say. So she just held him.

After a while she finally said, "Sam? I'm going to tell you I'm sorry about what happened to your mom when I know we're safe. But for now? No more confessions. No more energy spent on anything except getting out of here."

"There *is* no way out. Not for me. I can barely move. I definitely can't walk. And I won't drag you down with me."

"Well, then you better try harder. Because I'm not leaving without you."

"I shouldn't have called out to you," Sam said. "I was so freaking delirious. Otherwise, I wouldn't have."

"Well, I'm happy for delirium, then," McKenna said. She pushed the tarp off him. "We're both walking out of these woods."

Sam sat up. He carefully moved his legs, wincing again from the pain. McKenna gave him a couple more ibuprofen, hoping they wouldn't upset his stomach. She found some thick sticks and fashioned a makeshift splint, using liberal amounts of Sam's duct tape. They ate the last of the awful salmon jerky, had a few more sips of water, and got to their feet.

"I'll get you up this cliff first," McKenna said. "Then I'll come back for the pack."

"I hate this, Mack," he said. "I want to be the one helping you."

"So you wish my ankle were broken?"

"No," he said. "Though you have to admit, it would be easier for me to carry you than vice versa."

McKenna frowned and draped his arm around her. Sam almost laughed. "I'm not saying you're not superwoman. If you've proved anything, it's that you are. But I still don't think you can piggyback me up there."

He was right. Just testing the smallest bit of weight he'd allow her, she quickly realized she couldn't carry him at all. She might be able to support him if they were walking, but not while scaling a wall.

"Here," she said. "You do it without using that ankle. I'll be right below you, to spot you where you need it."

They made their way up slowly, McKenna just below Sam; twice he slid down and automatically used both legs to stop himself, crying out in pain. But finally they got out of the little ravine. They stood at the top of the ledge, panting, each taking a tiny sip of sustaining water. Then McKenna shimmied back down to get the pack.

"I'm just going to slow you down," he said when she returned.

"Stop it."

"I'm going to kill whatever chance you have of getting out of here. Which is the same thing as killing you."

"Shut up."

"But—"

"Shut *up*. First, *you're* always leaving. Now you want to make *me* leave."

"Mack, I—"

"No. We're in this together. Whatever happens, we stick together. I'm not leaving you ever again. Got it?"

"Got it," Sam said, but he didn't sound happy about it.

"I'm going to go look for a walking stick. If you use me on one side, and the stick on the other, maybe you can walk without putting weight on the ankle."

"Which will have us moving at the rate of an inchworm."

"It will if that's your attitude." McKenna was trying to use the stern voice her track coach used when spirits were lagging. But just as Sam's voice, trying to be wry and realistic, was tinged with something past despair, so was her own with the sound of rising panic.

And hopelessness.

Yesterday she'd had a goal: to find Sam. That first goal achieved, her goal had become getting him warm and then out of his little ditch.

The next goal seemed impossible. They hadn't been able to do anything but walk in circles when they were both well. Now Sam was badly crippled and they were both starving. Just finding water would be a challenge, let alone getting back to the trail.

And worst of all: nobody would be looking for them because nobody knew they were lost. Nobody *would* know they were lost, not for another month or more, when she didn't show up in Georgia. And even then: How would anyone know where she'd gone off the trail? Walden had seen her leave, but she was pretty sure he wouldn't wait around to see if she came back. And at this point she wasn't completely confident she hadn't hallucinated him. She'd never signed the trail registry. Even now, in this desperate moment, Courtney could be sending her parents a cheerful text, telling them everything was fine and dandy. They might still be getting those texts as her corpse rotted, as her skin and bones were bleached and battered by sun and rain, and eventually covered up by the year's first snowstorms.

And Sam? He'd been gone since last spring and no one had come searching yet.

"Hey," Sam said. He must have noticed she wasn't looking for a walking stick, just standing there, not moving.

"Yeah?"

"'I came to the woods deliberately. So when I died, I wouldn't think that I'd never lived.'"

McKenna blinked at him. That was Thoreau, Sam's own version of the first lines of *Walden*. Much as this moved her, she would not cry.

"Is that how it goes?" Sam said.

261

"Kind of."

She thought of the book, the words that had started it all, waiting for her back at their campsite. Along with "Her Favorite Story," about John Smith, who'd survived, and the man who'd failed to save his dying lover.

"Tell me how it goes," Sam said in a slow, coaxing voice. She recognized what he wanted, which was not to keep himself alive, but to make sure she lived.

"I will," she said. "When we get back to the book. I'll read it to you."

"Promise?"

"Promise."

And McKenna walked a little ways searching for a stick long enough for Sam to lean on and thick enough to bear his weight, all the while making sure she didn't go far enough to lose sight of him.

In Abelard, Connecticut, her mom had a better idea than McKenna realized of where she was. Since finding out McKenna was hiking alone, she hadn't been waiting for the credit card statements, but rather monitoring the card online every night after dinner. Charges became like smoke signals. She'd see that McKenna had spent thirty dollars at a grocery store. Forty dollars at a restaurant. Fifty dollars at someplace called Turn the Page. When Quinn saw a charge, she would Google map the town, clicking on the + sign again and again, as if she could zoom in directly to where McKenna was, see her walking along the sidewalk. In her classes, she had lectured vehemently against NSA and drone technology, but now she thought she'd gladly send an army of drones to follow McKenna, keep tabs on her, keep her safe.

She often found herself trying to analyze the charges with Jerry. "Forty dollars seems like a lot at a diner," she'd say. "Maybe she met a friend. Maybe she's not alone."

"Maybe," Jerry would say. He had become infuriatingly Zen about the whole thing, refusing to worry. Or at least refusing to admit he was worried.

But now she was more worried than ever. There hadn't been a charge in over a week, not since McKenna had taken out two hundred dollars in cash in some North Carolina town.

"Doesn't really mean anything," Jerry said when she couldn't keep quiet about it any longer. "When I was on the trail, two hundred dollars would have lasted me the whole summer."

"Yes, honey. But that was thirty years ago." If he mentioned his time on the trail one more time, she might have to kill him.

"Listen," he said. "She's a smart girl. Resourceful. And she's all grown up. We're just going to have to trust that she can take care of herself."

19

More than a thousand miles away from home, night had fallen. On a low tree branch, not two feet away from where McKenna had stopped short, eyes were reflecting what little light the stars offered. Sam stumbled against her, muttering, as if he'd already drifted to sleep on his feet. They'd managed to walk all day with Sam leaning on her, hopping forward while he braced his other side with the walking stick. Half Sam's weight plus the weight of his pack had McKenna longing for the relative ease of her giant red pack, stuffed to capacity.

The movement was so awkward, the weight so heavy on her muscles and bones. Plus she had no idea if they were making any progress or getting any closer to finding people. She knew the smartest thing to do when you're lost is sit down in one spot and wait to be found. But since nobody knew they were lost, that would just be waiting to die. As it was, by the time it got dark, McKenna felt like they were *walking* to die, continuing forward until they would both collapse in a lifeless heap.

She didn't say any of this to Sam, but she could feel his own resignation as he leaned on her. He had already given up. He was only moving forward for her. And now they were moving through the dark.

"I wish we could find the lake again," McKenna said. Then worried this sounded like an accusation, since it was his calling out that had led her away from the lake.

Sam hadn't said a word in hours, since they'd filled up the water bottle in a muddy puddle that morning, so she kept talking. They had to trust that the iodine tablets would do their work on the silt and debris, taking sips as rarely as possible. For hours, she'd been sure they were moving back in the direction of the lake, but if that were true, they would be there by now.

In the dark she wasn't sure of anything. The pair of eyes shining back at her could be an owl or a bobcat. She took a step forward and heard a low growl, polite enough to warn her.

What are you doing here? Crossing into my territory, snarled the animal. Definitely not an owl.

McKenna tightened her grip on Sam and pivoted him around, crashing through trees in the opposite direction. She knew they needed to stop soon or she'd risk breaking an ankle, too. Or worse, she thought, remembering how close she'd slept to the drop-off by the lake. But she wanted to at least find a break in the trees, an overhang or a soft spot to lay down the tarp. A barrier between him and the cold ground would protect Sam from another bout of hypothermia.

"This would be an excellent moment for one of your spirit stories," McKenna said. She didn't expect him to say anything, wasn't sure he'd ever say anything again.

But then he did speak. Or rather, he made a croaking sound as if it had been years since he last spoke instead of hours.

"Look," Sam said.

McKenna stopped. Her eyes should have been accustomed to the dark by now, but she was so exhausted. Everything was a blur of branches and shadows and leaves. If McKenna lived to get out of here, she would never buy another pine scented product in her life.

"Oh." She gasped, realizing what stood before them.

It wasn't a stand of low trees, but a house made out of logs built into a rock wall, with a patch of grass growing on its roof. For a moment McKenna felt a surge of hope that someone might be living inside, someone who could help them.

She placed her palm at the small of Sam's back to make sure he was steady, then she stepped forward to poke her head through the doorway.

"Hello?" she called, though she could see it was empty.

She leaned against the hut's wall. The wood felt so cold and hard, as if it had petrified thousands of years ago.

"The Nunnehi," Sam said, sounding clearer this time. "This must be one of their houses."

"It can't be," McKenna said. "The Nunnehi aren't real, remember?"

The structure looked perfectly real, though. McKenna dropped her pack, then went to help Sam inside. In the distance, coyotes had started their nightly bash, yipping and howling, no doubt beside some body of water McKenna and Sam hadn't managed to find. As Sam sat against a corner of the wall, McKenna spread out the tarp.

He let out a low groan, and she searched in her pack for the ibuprofen. She shook the bottle—not many pills left. Still, she gave him four, hoping it would eat into the pain enough for him to sleep. Pulling off his sneakers, she didn't try to examine his ankle. It felt taut in her hand, and bigger than it had this morning.

"It's like he sent us in this direction," McKenna said. "That bobcat."

"What bobcat?"

Sam must not have seen, and she hadn't told him. Her mind was fogging with exhaustion. For a moment she felt like this hut was just a figment of her imagination, that they were really still stumbling through the woods. Or maybe they were lying at the bottom of a ravine, unconscious. Maybe they were already dead, and this was just the last electrical activity of McKenna's brain, a final moment after her heart had already stopped.

She touched the cool wall again to reassure herself, then she pressed her hand to Sam's chest, his heart beating audibly from exertion, and maybe excitement, too, at discovering this place. It was real. They were both alive.

She took a sip of muddy water, then handed the bottle to Sam. He took a conservative sip. Maybe it was better that the water tasted so gross and muddy, it kept them from glugging it down the way they wanted to. Her eyes had adjusted enough to see Sam's lips, as cracked and dry as her own. Through the awkward hobbling and stumbling of the day, neither had peed, not once, and now that they'd stopped, McKenna still didn't need to. Dehydration was settling in, their bodies clinging to every last drop of moisture.

Sam dragged himself onto the tarp. McKenna knew she should help but she was so tired. She thought she might fall asleep right there against the cool wall. Her body ached in places she hadn't known existed; it took every ounce of strength she had not to finish the ibuprofen herself.

"Sam, you have to eat something."

She pulled out the last bit of food they had, their last PowerBar, twisting it in half, then quarters, then eighths. She put an eighth in her mouth, and held another out for Sam. He was muttering, maybe already asleep. She crawled over and pushed the food into his mouth. As he chewed, thankfully, McKenna pressed the back of her hand to his forehead. He felt warm and clammy.

She lay down next to him and rolled the leftover piece of tarp over them both. That tiny bite of food had only made her stomach come alive, gnawing with hunger, pleading for more. She sat up and took another sip of silty water, making herself stop so there would be some left in the morning. When she'd purified this water, there'd only been five iodine tablets left, but the water had been so murky, she'd had to use two of them. If she only used one from here on out, that would mean they had three bottles of water left. And that was only if they were lucky enough to find another water source.

"Whoever built this place, they wouldn't have built it far from water. Right?" she said, thinking out loud.

Sam jerked, a painful spasm. "Spirits don't need water," he croaked.

McKenna closed her eyes, willing herself not to argue with him. She imagined Sam and his brother in the woods listening to the ghost stories their mother told them, their eyes wide.

It was only fun to feel afraid when you knew you were safe.

But the Nunnehi. They restored lost travelers. *If you're going to show up,* McKenna silently told the Nunnehi, *now would be an excellent time.*

Her bones hurt. She closed her eyes and listened to the coyotes, trying to hear the music of water behind their howls. Against her eyelids the animals danced and played, as a roaring waterfall crashed around them. Of course that waterfall wasn't for humans. Only coyotes and bobcats and bears.

Shafts of light came leaking into the hut too soon, unwelcome. McKenna woke to a stab of fear at the prospect of another day, not knowing how she'd get through it. The first thing she did was reach over and touch Sam to make sure he was still breathing. She had no idea how she'd keep him going until the next nightfall.

Had it really been just four days since they'd wandered off the trail? It felt like a thousand years ago.

She sat up. Footsteps, distinct and definite. The sound of another creature approaching. Maybe it was a hiker, with an iPhone and GPS. Or maybe even a ranger? As McKenna's excitement rose, she jumped out from under the tarp and tried to peer through the slats of petrified branches. Just as fast as it had leaped, her heart sank as she heard distinctly nonhuman snuffling. Whatever was out there, it panted and huffed and snorted, using its nose as guide.

"Oh no," she whispered, and then bit her tongue. A person might not have heard her at that decibel level, but an animal might. A bear might have already smelled the chocolate peanut butter PowerBar that sat unwrapped at the other end of the hut. McKenna thought about throwing it through the doorway so it could take it and amble off.

But it was their very last morsel of food, and she wouldn't part with it so willingly to any creature other than a bear. If it was a coyote, she could possibly scare it off using Sam's walking stick. Even if it was the bobcat from last night (though if it were, it was likely rabid, as they didn't stir in the daylight), McKenna thought she would be brave enough to challenge it.

She got onto her hands and knees and crawled to the doorway. The animal was getting closer, its huffs and puffs louder. McKenna picked up Sam's stick, but didn't have a chance to decide whether to wield it like a club over her head or like a spear by her side ready to stab. Before she knew it, the animal was in the hut with them: a furry brown head, gleaming white teeth, huge brown eyes, and a goofy, doggy grin.

"Hank!" McKenna yelled, and threw her arms around the dog's neck.

Sam watched McKenna through bleary eyes. You'd think that dog had shown up from AAA, with a cell phone, a gallon of water, and a five-course meal. That stupid dog, a fat tick swollen above its eye. Not only could it *not* do anything for them, it would probably expect a can of Iams and a handful of beef jerky.

The thought of food—any food—would have been painful if Sam's ankle hadn't been throbbing so badly that the pain wasn't just in his ankle, but in his whole body.

"Hey," he said, not even recognizing his own voice. "Mack. Any more Advil?"

She moved away from the dog, but just a little, her hands still on his back like he might vanish if she let go.

"Is the pain really bad?" she asked.

"It's pretty bad," he admitted.

McKenna pulled out the ibuprofen. As the bottle shook, she looked at Sam. He didn't say anything. She had to know that he knew they were running out of everything. He wished she didn't feel like she had to protect him.

"Here," she said, pressing three pills into his hand instead of four.

The dog stood in the archway wagging his lopsided tail. His muzzle looked wet, water dripping off.

"Mack," Sam said, jutting his chin toward the dog. "Hank. Looks like he just had water."

McKenna looked at Hank. The little hut was so small, she barely had to reach out to touch his mouth.

"Hank," she commanded, like he was Lassie. "Where is the water? Hank, take me to water."

The dog just stared at her, kind of grinning, wagging his tail and waiting for her to feed him.

"The water must be close," Sam said. "If you scout around a little." He saw her hesitate, not wanting to leave him. "I'm so thirsty, Mack. And I can't drink any more of that mud. I just can't."

The look he'd come to know so well came over her face. Determination. Like she was standing on the starting line at some high school track meet. Sam wished he could close his eyes and will her back in time, a thousand eyes on her perched on the blocks, safe and sound.

"Okay," she said. "I'll look around a little. But I won't go anywhere I can't see the hut."

"Okay," Sam said. She ducked outside and he lay back, panting, wishing he'd asked for a sip of what water they had left. The only thing Sam had to be glad for was that at this point he was the only one who seemed to know they were doomed.

It didn't take long for McKenna to come back with the bottle of water, all cleaned out, the water inside clear and perfect. Sam noticed she only dropped one iodine tablet in. Of course they were running low on those, too.

"Here," she said, ripping off another tiny piece of PowerBar and handing it to him. He ate it, though at this point there didn't seem much purpose to it, either rationing such a small amount of food, or eating at all. Part of Sam wanted not to eat or drink, to just give up and be done with it. Done with walking, done with trying, done with everything. He swallowed the cardboard morsel and lay back. Out of the corner of his eye he could see McKenna checking her watch, waiting for the water. He must have drifted off, because it didn't seem like any time had passed before she was putting her hand under his neck, lifting the bottle to his lips.

Her face had become so familiar to him. More familiar even than the trail, this place he'd been living for so long, because unlike the trail, McKenna's face didn't change. It stayed the same sweet, freckled, blue-eyed face, only the expressions varying. Right now she had one that he hadn't seen before, a new kind of worry. He could read her thoughts, about how they had to get moving, they had to use the daylight.

For so long, she'd been waking up and walking. Sam knew it hadn't occurred to her yet that there wasn't a point anymore. Finally they'd come to this little place where they could lie down and rest.

Rest and wait for the end. Maybe it would be peaceful when it came.

"Sam?" McKenna said. Behind her, the dog barked. The tick was gone from above its eye. McKenna, taking care of everybody.

"Mack," he said. And he drifted away from her.

He could see light on the other side of his eyelids. Something shining in through this world of pain. A voice. It sounded familiar.

"Sam?"

He wanted to take his hand out from under the tarp, close it tight around hers, feel her bones beneath his grip. But he couldn't move. This pain in his ankle had turned into a blanket laid on top of him, compressing every organ in his body. His breath would only come out in short raspy bursts.

"Sam?"

Other words, following his name. Hopeful, urging words. She wouldn't admit what she must know: Sam was done walking.

"Mack," he managed to croak out. "If you want to walk, you're going to have to leave me."

"No way."

It was the last thing he would ever have to do, so he gathered the little strength he had left. He sat up on his elbows, looked at her, and concentrated on making his face very grave, his voice definite. He'd have to convince her, otherwise she'd just sit with him until the end of time.

"Listen," he said. "This place, this hut. Whoever built it, it's bound to be a landmark, right? The rangers will know about it. If you can get back to the trail, it's not like before. You can tell them where I am. You can send them back to get me."

She looked dubious. At the same time he saw it, the antsiness, the need to get out of there, to move.

"I can't walk," Sam said. "And you can't carry me. If you don't get help, I'm going to die here."

That was it. The magic words. She nodded. He let out a breath and lay back, feeling like he'd just run a marathon on his wrecked ankle. McKenna handed him the water and the last of the PowerBar. He took a sip but said, "No. You eat that. You'll need the energy."

Something had come over her. She ate it without protest then said, "Maybe Hank knows the way out. Maybe if I follow him."

Sam laughed. The life this girl had known, and all the endless optimism it had given her.

"Yeah," he said. "Maybe."

"You take the water," McKenna said. "I mean, drink a lot. Who knows how long it'll be, before we can come back with more."

Obediently he let her lift the water to his lips. He drank and drank. Then he lay back and listened while she gathered up the things she needed. He felt her lips on his forehead, and was glad she didn't say *I love you*. That would have sounded too much like *good-bye*.

He lay on the tarp, listening to the sound of her leaving, the sound of her low voice talking like that stupid animal might know what she was saying.

Sam's body shuddered.

It came out of him like a fountain, every drop of water he'd managed to get down. When he was done puking, he used his last bit of strength to roll over to the other side of the hut.

"Safe travels, Mack," he said.

Or maybe he just thought it. Time began drifting, floating, a kind of darkness that filtered in and out. It became very hard to know or feel anything.

20

It didn't seem possible to McKenna that they had walked this long.

Maybe it was just exhaustion and hunger—subsisting for days on what, put together, would constitute one tiny meal. But she was convinced that if someone had been watching their progression from the lake to the hut, they would have seen her and Sam walking in circles, the same paths, the same streams.

Hank seemed to know where he was going, crashing determinedly through the trees. Sometimes McKenna had to turn sideways or take off the pack altogether to follow him.

"Hank," she called, pulling on her pack after squeezing between two gnarled birch trees. She scanned the stretch of tree trunks ahead of her. No sign of him.

"Hank!"

The sound of rustling, galloping back to her. He sat in front of her, staring up and wagging his tail. McKenna knelt and patted him ferociously. He licked her face. She questioned, for the thousandth time that day, the wisdom of following a feral dog who would probably take off when he realized she didn't have any food left to offer him.

"If I could think of something else to do," she told the dog, "I would do it."

Hank nudged her pack with his nose, as if asking for food. She shook her head. "Nothing there," she told him, and petted him again, hoping affection would be enough to keep him beside her. She got up and pulled the pack on. Hank bounded off into the woods and she did her best to stay with him.

Uphill. They definitely hadn't gone down an incline this steep. At the same time, she wasn't sure of anything. Her whole life, McKenna had never been hungry. Well, that wasn't true. Once she and Courtney had done a terrible fast together, drinking nothing but a concoction of vinegar and lemon juice for days. It was miserable, but at any moment there was a refrigerator in the next room, a convenience store on the corner, a restaurant down the street. What a mockery of life that stupid fast seemed now. If she was lucky enough to get back to the world, she would never diet again.

The climb leveled off, and Hank stood waiting, as if he now knew that it frightened her to lose sight of him. "Thanks," she said. "Thanks, Hank."

When she got her breath back, she took a step, signaling that she was ready to walk again. Hank took off. What must Hank eat when she didn't feed him? Squirrels and rabbits? She wondered, if he caught one, would he bring it to her, and would she have the stomach to rip off a piece of raw meat for herself? At this point, she thought she would. As she walked, her eyes raked the ground for any sign of vegetation, anything that might pass as food. The only thing she saw was the occasional withered mushroom. Maybe at some point she would have to risk that. But she wasn't there yet.

Up above, a cloud drifted and then settled in front of the sun. The sun itself was already making its move toward the other side of the world. Another day of walking, of moving, without getting anywhere. It would be another night of hunkering down until exhaustion surpassed terror. Would she just continue this way until she died?

Back at the hut, was Sam already dead?

A sob rose in her throat. She couldn't consider that. She was so tired. And so hungry. From behind the trees ahead, Hank barked. She stumbled forward. And there it was.

Their campsite. Hank sat right beside McKenna's tent, the rain flap firmly in place. There was the fire pit with the charred remains of the fire they'd built. There was the stretch of sand where they had laid their sleeping bags, and slept so peacefully without knowing what lay ahead. It seemed like a million years ago.

"Hank!" McKenna said. "Good boy. Good boy."

Truly she had never been so thankful for anything in her entire life. Even as she looked around, she refused to let despair sink in over the fact that she had no idea which direction they'd hiked from when they'd first come to this place. She still didn't know how to get back to the AT.

But she would worry about that later. Inside that tent sat her red pack and the food they'd left behind to sustain them over the next days, plus a water bottle, full to the brim. Her fingers trembled as she fumbled with the zipper of the tent. Hank burst through the flap, straight toward the pack, wagging his tail, ready for the food she had inside it. McKenna's fingers shook again as she unzipped her pack and plunged her hand inside to pull out a plastic baggie filled with granola bars. She unwrapped one and gave it to Hank, who swallowed it in two bites. McKenna's first couple bites were equally urgent and ravenous, barely chewing, choking down the nourishment. Then she took a sip of water and lay back on the cool nylon floor. Hank sniffed at the baggie and she unwrapped another bar and fed it to him. The sleeping bags she'd thrown into the tent so carelessly, days before, might as well have been feather beds. She gazed up through that beautifully familiar ceiling, not thinking about anything, just eating, replenishing, swallowing.

Food. Calories. The abatement of hunger and more than that, the cessation of starvation. She was going to live.

She closed her eyes, the physical relief in the slight bloat of her belly was so strong she thought she really might start to cry.

From outside the tent, she could hear a noise building—far away at first, only vaguely familiar, and then more and more distinct. It took a few seconds for her mind to place it, the slow movement of rotors. McKenna sat up as the sound came closer.

A helicopter.

She scrambled outside and looked up. It wasn't close enough

to see yet, but it was coming closer, and it sounded low, maybe even low enough to see her out here in the clearing, with no trees to obscure the view.

The new infusion of calories merged with the biggest shot of adrenaline McKenna had ever felt. She jumped up, waving her arms back and forth.

"I'm here!" McKenna yelled. *"I'm here!"*

There was no indication, that anyone had heard her, and of course how could they over the noise of the rotors. The helicopter flew in the opposite direction. McKenna dove into the tent and grabbed her pack, searching frantically for matches, willing herself to calm down so she could focus on what she had to do. The stack of kindling that Sam had built still sat beside the fire pit, she arranged it into a tepee as fast as she could. And then, with nothing else that would catch as quickly, she grabbed *The Ice at the Bottom of the World.* Ripping out pages but preserving "Her Favorite Story," McKenna stuffed the papers into the tepee and lit them. She could still hear the helicopter's rotors, their noisy beat and whir. It headed back in her direction as her little fire emitted the thinnest wisp of smoke. The helicopter dipped down lower, but then headed away from her again. Was it looking for something? Was it looking for *her?* Again she jumped, waving her arms.

"I'm here!" she yelled, because she needed to say it, even though they couldn't hear her. *"I'M HERE!"*

And then she sat down. Even if the people in the helicopter did see her fire, now rising higher as she fed it more pages, why would they think she was anything other than a wayward camper, building a fire to cook dinner? Why had she never bothered to learn the simple signal (she guessed it was simple, since she didn't know what it was) for SOS? Even if they *saw* her, they might just interpret her jumping and waving as excitement over the sight of a helicopter, a silly kid.

McKenna thought all these discouraging, despondent thoughts. And then she stood up and waved and jumped and screamed till her voice couldn't scream anymore, and her throat felt as rasped and ruined as every other part of her body. By then the helicopter had flown away, with no sign that it had seen her, let alone recognized that she needed help.

McKenna collapsed on the dirt beside her fire, gasping and panting. She didn't move until after the rise and fall of her chest had finally subsided, and the sky had become dark except for the stars. She stared up at the same view she and Sam had watched together just a few nights ago, back when they were immortal. Mere hours ago, she'd been convinced that all she needed to do in this world was get back to this spot, this campsite. Reunited with her stuff, she'd remember the way back to the trail and get help to find Sam. Everything would be all right.

"Hank?" McKenna said, suddenly remembering how she'd found this longed-for spot.

Nothing.

"Hank?"

She sat up. From the moment she'd heard the helicopter's

rotors, she had forgotten about the dog. Probably all of her running around and screaming had terrified him. She walked over to the tent and looked inside, hoping to find him cowering there. It was empty. Sorrow and panic, her new familiars, seized her chest.

"Hank," she said, her voice too destroyed to call out. She had no idea how to get to the trail. She and Sam had hiked for hours to get here. And also, she felt guilty. How smart Hank had been, to lead her back to this spot. She imagined the dog, a hound after all, following her scent through the woods, and then over rain-worn miles to find her. And all McKenna had done by way of thanks was feed him a few stale granola bars and terrify him.

She remembered then the three cans of Iams she'd been carrying over Sam's protests. They had pop tops. McKenna got one out of her pack and cleared her throat.

"Hank," she said, in a sweetly high-pitched voice. "Come here, Hank!"

She unsealed the lid with as much of a *pop* as she could manage. On cue, Hank bounded out of the trees, skidding to a stop at her feet, tail wagging, all forgiven. A noise that McKenna had completely forgotten existed, a laugh, prickled out of her wrecked lungs. She knelt down and fed Hank by scooping the congealed meat out with her fingers, and letting him lick a handful at a time.

Lucy had told McKenna on numerous occasions that physical contact with animals lowers blood pressure. McKenna would have to tell her little sister, if she ever saw her again, that she was right. Gross as it may have looked, this ritual with Hank calmed her down, slowed her heart rate. When she was done, she gave the can to Hank, who flopped happily beside the remains of the fire, licking and chewing the last drops. All McKenna wanted to do was eat some more of the food she didn't have to cook—the second packet of awful salmon jerky, the granola bars and dried fruit. But she knew she had to save those things for the walking she'd have to do the next day, and maybe the next. Who knew how far she'd have to go, how long, and when she'd next be in a place where fire was possible. So McKenna forced herself to build up the fire. She cooked a pack of Alfredo noodles and ate them directly from the steaming pot, trying not to think about Sam on the floor of that hut, wishing she could share every bite. If it hadn't been for the thought of him, the freeze-dried Italian cuisine would have been the most delicious thing McKenna had ever eaten in her life.

When she was done, she cleaned up her campsite. She even hung her food, because she hadn't gone this far to get mauled in her tent by a chocolate-loving bear. She did everything the way she had when she'd been alone on the trail. Sticking to a strict ritual of *the right way* was the only thing left that made her feel safe.

She lured Hank back into the tent with another small bit of jerky, not willing to risk his being gone in the morning. She might be exhausted, her whole body beaten up from the outside in, but at least her stomach was full. Even though her heart felt too dark to admit it, the truth was McKenna still had hope.

Back at the hut, Sam's stomach was not full. He couldn't remember the last time he'd peed. He couldn't remember much of anything. There was a girl, her face would swim in front of his, but it would change into different people he'd known, sometimes men, sometimes women. He'd come to hover in a space between sleep and waking. At points he felt sure someone was holding him, a scent like lavender would surround him, and a hand pushed back his hair. His mother must have held him like this, right? That's what moms did when you were sick. Maybe it was a spirit person, nursing him back to health, and soon he'd stand up and walk out of here.

Where was *here*, anyway? Was it day or night?

He fell asleep, without dreams, and then opened his eyes to remember everything, his body so full of pain he wished it would crack open, a thousand little pieces for nobody to find.

Sleeping was best. Second best was that space in between, the different faces, the hands stroking his head.

Sam didn't have the strength to ask the question that kept running through his head, not panicked anymore, just wondering: *Is this what it feels like to die?*

McKenna woke before first light. No time to wait for the sun to come up. She unzipped her tent right away and Hank bounded out. Before packing everything up, she fed Hank, then filled Sam's bag with his few extra pieces of clothing, his tent, the bird book, his sleeping bag. She wished there were a way for her to carry his pack along with her own. Leaving it there on the ground, like a piece of his body, was almost like saying good-bye to him all over again.

From behind her, Hank stood at the edge of what almost looked like a path, wending through the trees. He wagged his tail. McKenna was sure that she and Sam hadn't come from that direction. She walked a few paces, and then walked toward where her tent had been, trying to remember if this had been it, the first vantage point. She closed her eyes, opened them again.

What she remembered about walking into this campsite was Sam's back, the straight line of his shoulders, his smile when he turned to her, the feeling of lawlessness and how it felt like being delivered from her whole life. Which didn't help her one bit now. In the future she would need to remember to take note of directions even when she was in the passenger seat. Although she felt like crying, could almost feel her tear ducts trying to operate, nothing sprang to her eyes. She reached for the water bottle and took a sip. Tired of waiting, Hank turned and crashed into the trees.

"Hank!" she called, sure that he was going the wrong way. But obedience wasn't Hank's thing. McKenna walked as fast as she could to keep up with him, immediately heading up a steep ledge that she *knew* they hadn't come down; she would have remembered. If this shale wall had been any more vertical she would have needed rock-climbing equipment to scale it.

As she climbed up over the top, sweat dripped down her face. The dog was trotting ahead so fast and so blithely, almost like he wasn't even aware she was following him. She didn't want to risk taking off her jacket and losing him. *Slow down, Hank.*

She was determined to keep him in her sights. It was only because of Hank that she'd found their original campsite. When you find something that works, McKenna told herself, you stick with it. She wiped the sweat off her face and trudged on. The dog eventually stopped to drink at a wide, deep stream, and McKenna threw off her pack and filled her water bottle. She had exactly one iodine tablet left, and she decided to save it for when she came upon more questionable water. This water ran so fast and looked so clean, she splashed a few handfuls on her face before drinking deeply, her lips on the surface of the water. Then she filled her bottle and bribed the dog to rest awhile with the last can of Iams.

The last. She'd eaten the last bag of noodles last night. She'd managed to choke down the last of the horrific salmon jerky for breakfast. Everything was coming down to the last, she was running out of time.

When Hank finished eating, he drank a little more, then walked right through the water, swimming across the middle, and scrambling back to shore. He stopped and looked back at McKenna, waiting politely for her to cross.

"Crap," she said.

She stepped cautiously into the current. Pebbles crunched under her boots; the water that had felt so bracing and refreshing hitting her face felt alarmingly cold when she was faced with the prospect of wading through it. She turned back to shore and picked up a long, thick stick, almost as long as her body. Stepping into the stream again, she plunged the stick toward the center. The water would be up to her waist.

She drew in a deep breath and stepped forward. Before she even had a chance to get her footing, the current hit her, knocking her sideways, soaking her and her pack. McKenna scrambled to right herself as the current pushed her downriver; she scraped her palm across a sharp rock trying to catch herself, only to have another rock gash through her pants. Safely on shore, Hank barked and ran after her.

As the current brought McKenna downstream, she fought down panic. If she drowned in this river nobody would know where to find Sam, or even that he was lost. The pack prevented her from rolling onto her back in the dead man's float she needed, but as she drifted past a snarl of tree roots, she managed to grab hold of them and pull herself out of the current. Back on the cold ground, she lay sideways, Hank standing over her, dripping and then spraying her with more water.

McKenna could hear Sam's voice in her head: *That's what you get for letting a dog be your Sherpa.*

"I know," McKenna said, staring up into the concerned, drooly face. "It's a stupid plan. But it's the only plan I have."

She pulled off her sopping fleece jacket and tied it to the outside of her pack, hoping it might dry in the sun. Then she followed the dog for the rest of the day, not bothering to stop when it got dark.

Dark. Again. Another day of traveling, walking, and finding nothing. For all she knew, Hank was leading her deeper and deeper into the woods. How many more nights would she have to live through before she was rescued or before she died? Nothing in the world could have vanquished what little hope she had left like the sun going down.

She had her sleeping bag, but it was soaked. She couldn't bear the thought of stopping, of digging out all the warm gear she'd rendered useless. When finally even Hank refused to go another step, collapsing in a heap on a pile of leaves, McKenna put on the fleece jacket—it had dried, thank God—and lay down next to him. For a moment she thought about climbing into the pile of leaves to try to keep warm. But then she remembered snakes. It almost would have been funny, if she hadn't been so tired.

21

Laughter. At first McKenna thought she heard it in her dream. It was that kind of sleep, her body so deeply submerged in exhaustion it was like swimming up from the bottom of a deep lake, reaching the surface. When her eyes finally fought their way open, in the second it took for her to remember where she was, she recognized the sound and knew it was real.

People. Laughing. Voices.

"Dang it. I knew I left it in here somewhere. Can you point that flashlight this way?"

Beside her, on his bed of leaves, Hank let out a low, threatening growl. McKenna wished she could shush him. At the same time, she could barely understand why she wasn't on her feet stumbling in the direction of the voices, flagging them down. *People.* Didn't this mean she was saved?

More low laughter, as one of them tripped, cursing. McKenna realized she was plastered to the ground in terror. She squinted through the dark, trying to make out the men, trying to assess them. She realized she was hoping to hear a woman's voice.

When McKenna was little and her family went to a crowded place like a carnival or a museum, her mother would bend down in front of her and say, "If you get lost, get a grown-up to help you. Go to a mom with her kids if you can find one. But if you can't find a mom, find a lady."

Last summer, when McKenna took Lucy to Six Flags, she'd said those same words. Lucy had rolled her eyes, too old to hear it.

"Hey," one of the men said now. "I think I found it."

There were two of them, she was pretty sure, both with thick Southern accents. McKenna knew she should get to her feet. *Help,* she would say. *I'm lost. My friend's hurt.*

What kind of monsters would they have to be to hurt her instead of help? They had flashlights, they must know the way back to *somewhere.* They would lead McKenna out of the woods, they would use their cell phones to call for help.

The night hung black and dark, no sign that morning was anywhere near. How long had she been asleep? By the time the sun rose, a team of rangers could be on their way to Sam, find him just in time.

I have to risk it, she thought. *I have to risk it for Sam.*

And yet her body wouldn't budge. Except maybe to flatten herself a little more, closer to the ground, so she wouldn't be visible.

"You gonna finish telling that story?"

"Already told it. Girl's a bimbo. But I'd do her again if I had the chance."

"You'd do anything that's breathing."

Laughter again. Was the tone really sinister, or did it only sound that way after what they'd just said? It probably didn't mean anything. Some men talked like that. Especially when there wasn't a woman around to hear. But McKenna's spine had turned to ice, her nervous system froze, not letting her move. In her pack beside her, buried in all the wet gear, was her canister of pepper spray and her whistle. Who would hear, if she blew that whistle? Nobody close enough to come running.

"Dang it, Curtis, can't you work that thing any faster?"

McKenna pushed up the slightest bit on her elbows, peering through the trees in front of her. She could smell cigarette smoke and she could see their heads, covered by wool caps. One of them had a rifle over his shoulder. Something else glinted just beyond them, glass and metal, and then she heard the sound of liquid glugging into glass. It must have been a still. She remembered what Brendan had said, way back in Abelard, mentioning guys who kept stills in the woods as a possible danger.

She flattened herself again. Her heart was beating so loudly she worried they would hear it. Hank snarled again, also lying low. McKenna made a firm, frantic gesture with her hand, as if that would keep him quiet.

Just because they had a still. Just because they were cursing. None of it meant they were dangerous. Probably they were just normal Southern guys, out joking around. They wouldn't hurt her. They'd want to bring her to safety. It was a chance for them to be heroes.

For the first time, McKenna let herself think: *What would have happened back at Joe Ranger Road if Sam hadn't intervened with that group of guys?* Probably nothing. They would have bothered her for a bit, harassed her, scared her, and then left her alone. It had been broad daylight. It had been nothing.

But what if it *hadn't* been nothing? Wasn't that the main reason people didn't want her—a girl—to travel alone?

"Here you go, Jimmy, get me some more of that moonshine."

Hank snarled. But he had snarled at Sam, too. The dog didn't have a particular sixth sense for character. He just didn't like men.

Back in West Virginia, Sam likely knew where to find a still. He might have come sneaking through the woods at night with a friend, stumbling and swearing.

"Curtis. Did you hear that? Sounded like a dog."

"Hope it weren't that bobcat."

"You could get its coat."

McKenna heard a *click* as he did something with his rifle. She could try to talk herself into it all she wanted, but she knew she would never stand up and ask them for help. Even if the greater chance was that they *would* help her. Even if not calling out, not going to them meant that she and Sam might never be found. She couldn't risk it.

McKenna was strong enough to climb a mountain and fail, and then climb it again the next day. She was strong enough to make her way, starving and hurt and exhausted, through as many days and nights as she needed. She was strong enough—she knew she was, even if it hadn't turned out that way—to hike the whole Appalachian Trail, all by herself.

But she could not bear the thought of standing up and facing these two strange men. She couldn't risk being left out here afterward, in pieces.

But then, she might not have a choice. Because now here they came, toward the sound of Hank, whose growls had started to escalate. McKenna tried to calculate whether it would be best to try to roll under the leaves—too noisy—or to slide backward through the next stand of trees, out of sight. Even if she managed to hide herself, her pack would be left behind, proof that she'd been there, that she was still there, somewhere.

Suddenly, Hank leaped off the leaves, crashing through the trees. Standing in front of the two men, barking, he almost looked menacing. McKenna took advantage of the sound and rolled sideways, burying herself as far under the leaves as she could. The thought of snakes didn't bother her at all now.

Please don't hurt him, she pleaded silently. *Please don't hurt him.*

The men both burst out laughing. "That coat won't get you any money," one of them said. "Git. Go on. Git!"

They sounded almost playful. She closed her eyes and pressed her face into the ground. If it were daytime, would she feel differently?

Bam. A shot rang out. McKenna froze, listening for a yelp, but instead heard the sound of Hank running.

They must have shot into the air to scare him away. Surely it would have been easy to hit him, if they'd wanted. McKenna lay stock-still.

"Curtis. You coming?"

"Hold your horses."

This was it. Her last chance. She could stand up. Walk over to them.

"You put that safety back in place now! I don't want to get shot on my way out of here."

The leaves covering her didn't make the slightest rustle. It was possible even her breathing had stopped. Curtis and Jimmy walked away, drunken feet crunching leaves and twigs. McKenna listened harder than she'd ever listened in her life, trying to determine their direction. She must be close to a road or trail for them to have come in here for a party. Then again, they may have set up the still in the most remote place possible. She thought about crawling out of the leaves and following them at a distance. But her body still wouldn't move.

She stayed there until morning, when a tentative Hank returned and snuffled at her through the pile of leaves. Only then did McKenna sit up, grabbing the dog's muzzle and kissing him between his eyes. Hank ducked away from her and backed up.

McKenna stood, brushing leaves off. Had she slept? If she

wasn't sure, then she must have. She tried to blink and found one eye swollen shut—something must have bitten her during the night. Gingerly, she pressed her fingers against her eyelid.

"Okay, Hank," she said. "We must be close. Right? Today is the day we walk out of here."

Hank wagged his tail. McKenna bent to unzip her pack, her whole body crackling and protesting. She felt like she was a hundred years old. In her food bag, nothing but four cereal bars. Screw it. She ate two and gave one to Hank. She guzzled down the last of the water.

"See that, universe?" McKenna said.

Now there couldn't be any question. Today she would make up for last night's cowardice by thumbing her nose at her situation. She would not hoard provisions like she'd be roaming these woods for days. She was going to walk out of here.

McKenna stepped through the stand of trees that had separated her from Curtis and Jimmy. The still sat there, primitive and complex at the same time. McKenna couldn't second-guess herself for not asking them for help. She would not let herself think about the state Sam must be in, the barely helpful over-the-counter painkillers gone by now, dehydration and starvation setting in. Today would be his second day with no water or food.

She examined the ground, trying to see if the men had left any footprints, but it was too dry and dusty. Over to the right. (West? East? South? North? Along with her pack she'd been reunited with the compass but it was still impossible.) It looked like some branches had been pushed aside and Hank started off in exactly that direction. After the bushwhacking of the past days, the ground beneath her feet looked almost like a path. McKenna let hope rise as, every half mile or so, she saw a discarded cigarette butt on the ground. She fought down a swell of love toward Curtis and Jimmy, even though if they showed up again, she'd probably rush back into hiding.

Her swollen eye throbbed. She may have been feeling more optimistic with her progress, but she hadn't come upon anything that resembled a water source, and it was getting into late afternoon.

Sisyphus, McKenna thought. *I have turned into Sisyphus, pushing that boulder uphill, only to have it roll back down as soon as I get to the top.* She wished she could remember the crime she'd committed to land her in this unending hell of walking and searching but never finding. Maybe, in keeping with Greek mythology, the crime was simply hubris.

Up ahead, she heard a rustling through the leaves, and battled the all-too-familiar feeling, the combination of fear and hope. As the culprit—a raccoon—ambled their way, McKenna also felt the familiar combination of relief and disappointment. If it wasn't something that would kill them, it also wasn't something that would help her get the hell out of here.

Hank backed up a few steps and growled. In return the raccoon made a noise that literally made McKenna jump, despite her exhaustion and the weight of her pack. It was a huge noise, much bigger than the one Hank had made. Almost like a roar.

If the bear McKenna had faced from across the creek had made exactly the same noise, it wouldn't have surprised her at all.

The raccoon teetered up on its hind legs and stretched out its arms, looking alarmingly human and alarmingly . . . *wrong*. Raccoons were a common nuisance at her house; they delighted in countering all her dad's efforts at securing their garbage. Apparatuses that made the garbage collectors curse and exclaim would do nothing to hold off the raccoons . . .

But raccoons were nocturnal. In this, the midafternoon, they should all be tucked away. McKenna didn't know much about raccoons behind their black masks and nimble little hands. But she did know that.

And she knew that it was not normal behavior for a raccoon to menace a dog and a human. It should be running in the opposite direction.

But he didn't run away. In fact he walked closer on those two crazy feet, waving his little hands like an angry drunk.

This raccoon had rabies.

You have got to be kidding me! McKenna wanted to scream to the skies, and would have, if she didn't think it would inflame the adorable beast, rendered deadly dangerous.

Hank flattened his ears against his head and bared his teeth. "Hank," McKenna whispered furiously. She tried to call him back to her. There was no telling where Hank had come from, or how long he'd been on his own, but she was pretty sure his vaccinations weren't up to date. McKenna wasn't exactly prepared to get rabies, either. She squelched down the momentary urge to get between the two animals.

At her feet there was a small round rock, perfect for lobbing. If the raccoon weren't sick, it would certainly scare him away. But in his present state, it might only encourage him to leap for them. Which, from the looks of it, was exactly what Hank was preparing to do—dear Hank, ready to protect her, not knowing the risk of a frothing, premature death.

McKenna took several steps back. "Hank," she whispered. "Hank, come."

Hank dragged his belly backward, along the ground, toward her. And the raccoon fell forward, onto all four paws, took a step toward them, and roared again—this time even louder than she'd expect a bear to roar. McKenna didn't wait to see if it would lunge, she just turned, banging through the trees, running.

But it was only that first surge of adrenaline that allowed her to run with the pack, maybe a yard or two, after which she had no choice but to dump it. The sound of her footsteps drowned out whatever was going on behind her, she threw the pack down not knowing if Hank and the raccoon were battling, and ran until the dog caught up with her, zigzagging in front of her and turning off in the opposite direction.

She followed him. She wouldn't allow herself to think about how far she was traveling from the life force of her pack. She just ran, following Hank until night fell again.

McKenna stumbled forward onto the ground, her eyes facing the dirt. She covered her head with her hands. "I give up," McKenna said into the ground. "I give up."

Hank snuffled back to her. He peered into her face, licked her. She refused to pick up her head. The dog barked.

She couldn't give up. She was Sam's only chance. She had to get to her feet.

Standing, she looked over her shoulder, as if she could measure the distance back to all her belongings, refusing to remember how happy she'd been to find them. And now she was facing her third night alone, this time with no jacket, no sleeping bag, no food, no water.

Hank barked again. He turned around and started trotting. There wasn't any point in stopping. If she was going to die of exposure or dehydration or starvation, she would do it on her feet. Hank bounded through the trees and McKenna walked forward into one of the strangest sensations of her life.

All these days, these past awful days, walking from one piece of forest into the next. But this time, as the dusk settled in around her, she saw stars gathering not through trees, but in a wide and insistent sky.

I've been here all along, the sky told McKenna, *and so has the world.*

Here it was, a small piece of the world. Through the dusk, with her one open eye, she could see a clearing. A little log cabin with a chimney and smoke. Sitting out front, in an Adirondack chair, was a man she'd met just once before, though she'd heard about him many times. A man with a long beard and a hat, and she knew that somewhere on his shoulder was a tiny parrot.

McKenna walked forward, waving her arms over her head, as if she needed that gesture for him to see her.

"Walden!" she called, as if she'd been looking for him this whole time.

For a moment he sat staring at her, so placidly that McKenna worried this tableau was a mirage. Maybe it was only a product of her delusional state, a hallucination, this perfect cozy cabin and a man she sort of knew, but felt absolutely certain that she could trust.

Walden stood up and walked forward and rested his hands on her shoulders. "Good God, girl. I told you not to go off the trail."

His voice was gruff, so harsh and scolding, it jolted her into reality. She was here. Walden was real. A stream of words came babbling out of her, about the past few days, but mostly about Sam.

"He's hurt, I had to leave him, I didn't want to but I had no choice, he can't walk, I left him at this place, this petrified wooden shelter with grass on the roof, he doesn't have any water, we have to go back and get him . . ."

Walden draped his arm over her shoulder and started walking toward his cabin, propelling her along with him. "Night's falling," he said, "and you're a mess. You're not going back into the woods now."

McKenna broke away from him. She looked around at the unreal surroundings. This scene that would have looked rustic to her a few months ago now looked like the most welcoming piece of civilization, bright as a shopping mall. She had to get Sam here, too.

"We have to go back," she said. As her eyes roamed the clearing she realized that Hank had bolted. "We have to get Sam."

"And we will," Walden promised. "We'll get him. I know just the place you're describing and I'm going to radio the park ranger. But right now it's dark. Even I'd get lost if I tried to go looking."

McKenna paused, part of her was desperate to run back to Sam, bring him directly here, but of course she knew she could never find her way back.

"Come on," Walden said, his voice unexpectedly gentle. "Come inside."

Is it possible to feel defeated and triumphant at the same time? No, McKenna decided. It was not. Walking with Walden into his house, her relief was tamped down by worry. Sure, she had managed to save herself. But if Sam weren't saved, too, the only result of surviving would be a life stretching out before her, eighty years or more of knowing: she had left him in the woods to die.

22

At first light, two rangers bushwhacked through the woods. There was no trail to speak of, but they both knew the area well. It wasn't the first time kids had gone searching for the waterfall, or other remnants of the Nunnehi. Usually it was kids from somewhere close enough to be called local.

"You'd think thru hikers would know better," said Claire. She had just graduated from Purdue's School of Forestry and Natural Resources last year and started working for the Park Service in August. This was her first rescue.

Pete, on the other hand, was a native North Carolinian. He'd grown up in the Smoky Mountains—didn't need a fancy degree to learn what was what in the forest. He'd long since lost count of the idiots he'd fished out of these woods.

"None of them know better because they all think they know everything," Pete said.

He'd been picking up cigarette butts with a pointed stick, putting them into the pouch he wore on his belt. One thing Pete hated more than anything in the world was smokers—the way they hurled butts onto the ground without any regard to nature. The one thing you were certain to find in the most re-mote parts of the world was cigarette butts. Pete felt sure that if he ever got around to climbing Mount Everest, he'd reach the top, take in the view, look down, and see a cigarette butt lying at his feet.

Pete checked his compass. Claire was using her GPS, con-stantly noting their coordinates. "This kid's going to be a wreck if his girlfriend's story pans out," Pete said.

"Poor thing. She was hysterical."

"Guilt will do that to you. She knows they were both damned fools."

Overhead, a helicopter swooped, also looking for Sam. There were other park rangers, all of them trained EMTs like Pete and Claire, scouring different parts of the woods. The ra-dio on Pete's belt crackled, people in various spots thinking they had seen signs that the two kids had been there.

"Plenty of signs here if one of them's a smoker," Pete grumbled.

A little farther on, they came upon a fire pit with a frame pack sitting next to it. "This must be the place where they camped," Claire said.

"She cleaned it up nice," Pete said. "Makes our job easier."

They didn't have time to stop. Pete knew it would be hours before they reached the old Cherokee hut, and there was no guarantee the kid would still be there.

"I keep hoping someone else will radio that they've found him," Claire said after they'd walked a few more hours in silence, concentrating on making good time. Pete could tell from her voice that she was scared to stumble on a corpse.

"Don't worry. Nobody ever died of a broken ankle. Hasn't been quite cold enough for someone to freeze to death. And if the girl's timeline is right, this'll be his third day without water. Dehydration shouldn't have killed him yet." He knew his voice sounded gruff, complaining, even while he was trying to be comforting.

"But all those things together . . ." Claire let her voice trail off. She turned up her radio as some rangers chattered. One of the helicopter pilots thought he'd seen something, but it turned out to be a deer.

"Too much tree cover," Pete said. "Waste of time and fuel. They'll never see anything."

Claire picked up her pace, moving past him, and Pete continued the conversation without her. "It's true a bear could get him. Even a pack of coyotes, in his weakened state. And I guess exposure can set in more easily, with everything else that's going on."

He really didn't think she'd hear him, but she stopped, her face pale.

Then Pete saw it, the hut, just where he knew it would be. Of course all those other rangers with their helicopters and GPS satellites couldn't find this place. It took someone who'd grown up in these woods. He felt sure he could have found this place blindfolded.

"Hey," Pete yelled. "Kid! You in there?"

Claire had already ducked her head inside the door. Pete was right behind her.

There was a tarp laid out on the ground, and a black-and-red wool coat. Other than that, the tiny hut was empty.

McKenna sat in Walden's rocking chair, listening obsessively to the radio. Her eyelid was still swollen, but only half-shut. She almost wished she hadn't let Walden talk her into eating the pancakes he'd made—every time a voice crackled through the static, she was sure she'd puke it all up. McKenna pushed her now-fruit-scented hair (did *Walden* really use this shampoo?) out of her face and leaned forward, pressing her ear to the speaker.

Walden, it turned out, did not actually live *on* the trail. He was not a wise old vagrant, or a grief-crazed serial killer. He told her he got a good chuckle whenever he got wind of one of those stories. It also amused him to see entries in trail registries, people gushing over catching a glimpse of him. Truth be told he was nothing but a retired English lit professor who lived in this cabin, and he'd hiked the AT in both directions more times than he could count. These days, he mostly stayed near his house. "Old bones aren't what they used to be," he told her.

The radio was silent for a second. Somehow McKenna could sense it was the kind of silence that came before news. Important news.

A voice crackled through the static. "We found the hut. Tarp's here but no kid."

She was on her feet before she even realized she'd moved. "Walden!" she yelled.

He'd already left once this morning to retrieve her pack. He'd found it so quickly, she thought he was the one—not all these rangers—who should be out there looking for Sam. But Walden seemed intent on guarding her, making sure she didn't take off back into the woods. He was outside now, doing who knows what, but she was sure he wouldn't have gone far. She didn't want to leave the radio, she had to hear what happened next; but more than that, she needed to tell Walden. So when he didn't come, she ran outside.

Her breath and words came out in short, almost indecipherable gasps. "On the radio. I heard. The hut. It's empty. They found the hut but not Sam."

Walden maintained his poker face. It occurred to McKenna that might not actually be his name, she'd just been calling him that and he hadn't corrected her.

"That's a hard thing to hear," he said. "But it's still a good sign that they found the hut. He can't have made it far. They're going to find him soon."

"I need to go out there," McKenna said. "I can call for him, maybe the dog would come back and help." Hank had not reappeared since delivering her to Walden.

"They've got dogs out there already, tracking his scent. Trained dogs. And helicopters. Rangers who know what they're doing, who can give him medical attention. You'll just be in the way."

"I can't stand doing nothing," McKenna said. "I'm going crazy."

"Better to go crazy than get lost again. You think you'll help your boyfriend if those rangers have more than one person to search for? You don't have a broken ankle, which only means you'll cover a lot more ground. Get even more lost than he ever could."

McKenna sank down to the grass at Walden's feet and covered her face with her hands. She knew he was right. But she also knew she couldn't stay here waiting for news. Her body was crawling with helplessness, and with the not knowing.

Apparently, the old man didn't appreciate her fragile state. "What you need to think about, young lady, instead of marching off into the woods again, is calling your parents."

The pancakes roiled anew in her raked, raw stomach. She couldn't even begin to think about getting in touch with them, everything she'd have to confess.

"Lucky for you," Walden said, his voice softening the tiniest bit, "I don't have a phone. So you're going to have to wait. At least a little bit. Here," he added, thrusting a water bottle under her nose. "Keep hydrating."

Sam was pretty sure this was it.

He could hardly remember when or why he'd pulled himself out of the hut. All the stories he'd been telling McKenna, almost as jokes—ways to amuse himself, to impress and entertain her—now they were flitting around in his head, moving in front of his eyes. Spirit people holding him, talking to him. One even lifted a cup of water to his lips, Sam could swear he felt the cool dampness, it was real, until he tried to drink, and only gagged on his own deathly dry throat.

Deathly. That was the word, it had hovered so close around him when he was inside those four walls. As if other people had crawled in there to die and now it was his turn. The air felt sick with it, he could smell it—his own body, churning away at his insides, getting to work consuming whatever was left of him, at this point only craving water to wash it all down, to wet the cracked rasping dryness of his lips. He couldn't feel his ankle anymore, couldn't feel his leg at all.

She would want him to stay there. That's what had kept him there. Waiting.

At some point, while waiting, you realize that it's never going to happen. Sam couldn't say when that point arrived because he'd lost all track of time. Maybe McKenna had left a couple days ago. Maybe a couple hours. Maybe weeks. Maybe he'd been here in this hut his whole life, or at least since he'd left West Virginia. When was that? A million lifetimes ago and maybe just yesterday. Maybe he'd walked right out of that mean SOB's house, and gone right to this hut.

He'd been here ever since, making all that crap up about hiking to Maine and back. About meeting a girl. About there being someone out there, someone who gave a hang, searching for him.

Sam's eyes blinked open. He hadn't known they'd been

closed. There was a little Tinkerbell kind of light, floating just outside. He couldn't stand up, but he could roll over. He could slither out on his belly, into the sun. He hadn't realized how cold it was, that he was shivering, until he slithered like a snake out of a hole into that patch of warmth.

He squinted. He saw the stick McKenna had found leaning against the hut, and he pulled himself up onto it. Staggered a few steps, then fell. Righted himself. At least he might be able to get to water. If he could drink a little water, he could last another couple days.

Tinkerbell danced and flitted. This direction and that. He wished she would stay still. He wished she would talk to him.

What would he give to hear McKenna's voice right now? He laughed at the thought, he'd give anything, but of course he had nothing left. What he wanted more than surviving himself was to know she'd found her way to someplace safe. He could stand being out here in the woods, freezing cold and dying of thirst, as long as he could imagine McKenna dry and fed and clean. That's what he would give. His life for hers.

Tree roots. Yeah, you'll find them in the woods for crippled idiots to trip over. Sam fell, no water in sight, and this time he knew he wouldn't be getting back up.

He couldn't say how much time had passed, hours or days, until another mirage: voices. Unfamiliar voices that knew his name. Sam didn't even bother yelling back. It was enough jack-assery for one day, for one lifetime, dragging himself away from the one place anyone knew to find him, to follow a bit of light that of course abandoned him. Even if he'd *wanted* to answer, there was no voice left in him, everything had dried up, every last calorie gone and used. He was done.

"Oh my gosh," the voice said, a female voice. "That's him."

"Is he breathing?" a male voice asked.

Sam tried to focus on the face hovering over him. Two fingers pressed against his throat, another hand resting on his chest. Brown eyes, brown hair. Young, frightened, hopeful. Maybe this was really happening. If he were going to hallucinate a girl, he felt positive he would hallucinate McKenna.

"Yes," the girl said. She was wearing khaki, a badge, a ranger uniform. This made him less hopeful. Much as he loved McKenna, he also might hallucinate a ranger.

Another one appeared, a guy, his frowning face blocking out the girl's. A beautiful sound, the top of a canteen being unscrewed. Cold metal against his lips and then, like life entering his body after he'd given it up completely: water.

"Take it easy," the girl said, soothing. "A little at a time. Not too fast."

Sam pulled his head away. Breathed deep. Went for the water again. Dampness washing over his dry lips and throat. The world lurched into focus. This was real. The man had put down his pack, pulling off what Sam guessed was a collapsible stretcher. The girl gave him another sip, then moved down to his feet to examine his ankle. Sam winced as the pain returned. The man threw a blanket over him.

"You're a real true-blue ass. You know that?" the man said.

"I know," Sam croaked. And then, because he'd never been so grateful in his whole life—and now his life would, in fact, continue—he said, "Thank you. I know I messed up. But thank you."

Back at Walden's, McKenna had returned to her perch beside the radio. Different voices crackled through, lamenting spots coming up empty, sometimes the sound of helicopter rotors nearly drowning out everything she heard. Until finally she thought she heard a light female voice nearly as elated as she would have felt, announcing:

"We found him! Severely dehydrated, not completely lucid. Ankle really bad. But he's alive!"

Coordinates, details coming through. McKenna pressed her hands against her cheeks, hardly daring to believe it was real. She turned her head. Walden stood there; for a moment she thought he was frowning, then she realized it was only his permanent scowl and somewhere underneath it was a movement, a smile.

McKenna stood up. "Where will they bring him out? Can we meet him there?"

"We don't want to get in their way," Walden said. "We'll head to the hospital."

He already had keys in his hands. McKenna nodded and followed him outside.

23

How strange and at the same time how normal, the buzz and glare of fluorescent lights. After all, McKenna had lived in the civilized world for nearly eighteen years before she took to the trail. Even while she was hiking, she had walked back into civilization and sat under lights like these in restaurants, walked under them when stocking up on groceries. All that time living between the layers of the Appalachian Mountains, civilization and its lights, cars, air conditioners, and machines lay, if not in easy reach, at least in mappable reach, a simple matter of consulting the guidebook and walking the prescribed number of miles.

Until she went off the trail.

She sat by Sam's bedside in the hospital, machines beeping, bustle visible through the glass door. Sam slept, wearing a plaster cast that went nearly up to his knee and a saline drip to replenish all the fluids he'd lost, plus antibiotics to combat the giardia he'd tested positive for. McKenna had tested negative for the bacteria, but because she'd also drunk unpurified water and been in such close contact with Sam, they gave her pills to take as a precaution. When she filled the prescription at the hospital pharmacy, she'd automatically made a mental note of where she would keep them in her dry bag to protect them in case of rain.

It was impossible to believe that she wouldn't be returning to the trail. This moment, here in the civilized world, felt like another rest stop. It didn't feel like the end, even though her parents were on their way, and even though Sam lay here, in the hospital bed, sleeping and drugged, with that heavy cast. Sam would not be walking anywhere, not anytime soon.

She reached over and stroked the heavy blond hair off his forehead. Sam looked pale, as if everything vital had been drained from him. McKenna traced the bones in his face with the tip of her finger. When she first saw Sam, she'd thought he was gorgeous, intimidatingly so. Now his face did not intimidate her. It only made her heart swell, a painful ache that also made her feel more herself, more human. Not because his face was beautiful, but because it belonged to him.

Sam, the person she'd come to know so well, brave and vulnerable, often wrongheaded, but so smart and resilient, so unique. So willing and able to live outside society's rules, rules that imprisoned everyone within the same damn life.

I went to the woods because I wished to live deliberately.

The truth was, McKenna felt a lot of emotions sitting there with him, listening to the hospital machines beep, and the fluorescent lights buzz. The strongest emotion, apart from love, was relief. To see Sam lying there—wounded and depleted, true, but alive, and warm and safe. It overwhelmed her. According to the doctors, his body would be replenished in just a few days. The ankle, of course, would take longer. But he would be all right, he would survive, hopefully even flourish. After everything he'd been through, not just these past few days but his whole entire life, Sam deserved to flourish.

McKenna had been so afraid, first that she would never find help, and then that the rangers would never find Sam, or that if they did, they would find him dead. Now the sight of him and the promise from the doctors that he would be all right flooded McKenna with such deep and urgent relief that if she started crying over it now, she might sit there for days, crying. Producing enough saline water that they could simply hook Sam up to her tear ducts.

I went to the woods because I wished to live deliberately, to front only the essential facts of life, and see if I could not learn what it had to teach, and not, when I came to die, discover that I had not lived.

Behind Sam's eyelids: motion, movement. The drugs and exhaustion were apparently not too heavy to combat REM sleep. McKenna watched the eyeballs roll beneath his lids, the flutter of his pale lashes. What was he dreaming about? His dad? His time on the trail? Her?

She withdrew her hand and sat back, rubbing her knees. She was still wearing the Gramicci pants that would always have round, dark stains over both knees from all those nights of kneeling in the dirt in front of the fires Sam had talked her into building.

If McKenna was honest, among the emotions she felt was anger. Anger at Sam for all the things he'd talked her into, most notably leaving the trail, walking into so much danger. Not pretend danger, but *real*. It had almost gotten them killed. But more than at Sam, she was angry at herself for not standing firm, for not listening to her own inner voice. Much as she loved him, much as—in ways—she felt grateful to him for his friendship and everything he had shown her about life, she wished she had been strong enough to listen to herself instead of him. McKenna had listened to Sam as if he had something to teach her about what was wrong with herself, what needed to be changed. When really, she didn't need to be changed, not by someone else.

I did not wish to live what was not life, living is so dear; nor did I wish to practise resignation, unless it was quite necessary.

The back of her neck itched from a cluster of bug bites— spider? mosquito?—that she hadn't even noticed until she got to the hospital and all that adrenaline subsided. By now her eyelid was almost back to normal. She scratched the bites on her neck the way her mother had taught her a million years ago: around the bites, not letting her nails break into the actual swelling.

It made her guilty to think it, but McKenna felt strong. In front of her lay Sam, broken by their experience. The rangers had found him collapsed, delirious, near death. Whereas McKenna had walked out of the woods on two feet. She had escaped whole and unhurt. The only treatment she needed was a good meal or two, lots of water, and a dose of possibly unnecessary antibiotics. Scrapes and bruises and bug bites, sure. But otherwise whole and healthy and fine.

Part of this was luck, McKenna realized. But another part. That was McKenna. Her strength and perseverance and smart, reasonable brain. She had managed to get out of the woods on her own—well, with a whole lot of help from Hank, but that in itself had been her decision, to trust that crazy hound dog. She wondered where Hank was. She hoped he was okay and wished there was a way for her to see him again, to thank him.

McKenna couldn't help but imagine it. Returning to the trail. Going back and finding Hank. Now, for real, the tears gathering in her throat started to rise. She fought them back, not wanting to wake Sam, not wanting to be crying if someone else walked in. Because the truth was, the same feeling that had overtaken her that day on Mount Katahdin was rising up inside her now. The feeling of a goal unmet. The feeling that she had decided to accomplish something, and now she would have to take a deep breath and leave it unfinished.

Hiking from Maine to North Carolina was an impressive feat. But it was not hiking the entire Appalachian Trail. Her passport lay in her pack, almost but not quite finished. She would not be a thru hiker. She would not have her certificate. Everything she'd done, everything she'd been through, and in the end she'd only failed, as surely as if she'd given up on that very first day.

McKenna leaned forward, resting her head on the tops of her

knees and covering the mosquito bites on the back of her neck with both hands. They itched terribly. Maybe the doctors—who were dying to treat her for something—would give her something to make them go away.

I wanted to live deep and suck out all the marrow of life, to live so sturdily and Spartan-like as to put to rout all that was not life, to cut a broad swath and shave close, to drive life into a corner, and reduce it to its lowest terms.

"McKenna?"

A voice from a million years ago, and a voice from her whole life. McKenna didn't raise her head, not right away. She wanted to hear it again.

Her mother's voice, speaking as if she weren't mad about everything McKenna had put her through, but only so glad to see her alive and well that she formed her name as a question, afraid to be sure. "McKenna?"

In one motion, McKenna lifted her head and stood. Sam's machines beeped. Her parents were in the doorway, staring as if she were some alien being and not their own daughter. Staring like they weren't sure they had permission to cross the threshold, and also weren't sure, once they mustered up the courage, whether they wanted to hug her or throttle her.

McKenna took two steps. Her parents took four. They were there, in front of her. They'd come all this way and would have come a million miles farther. To bring her home.

"I'm sorry," McKenna said. "I'm so sorry."

"Oh, McKenna," her mother breathed, and she started to cry.

Not surprisingly, her parents decided against the throttle in favor of the hug. McKenna never imagined it would feel so good just to have their arms around her.

Quinn didn't know the name of the restaurant, she barely knew the name of the town. She sat across the table from McKenna, drinking in the sight of her. McKenna had requested Italian food. They would have agreed to pretty much anything McKenna asked for. Any anger over the duplicity, the bad decisions, was all eclipsed by the fundamental fact of their daughter being healthy and well.

"It's a good thing we never knew you were lost," Jerry said. They had barely touched their pasta, while McKenna had already devoured her salad, most of a basket of garlic bread, and half her enormous plate of stuffed shells. "I don't think we could have survived it."

McKenna nodded. Although she was freshly showered, her loose hair clean and shiny, her clothes were as dingy and stained as a homeless person's.

"I'm really sorry," McKenna said. "I'm sorry for lying to you. The only thing I can say is, the thought of not doing it—of not hiking the trail—was so terrible. It was something I *had* to do, and I just couldn't let anyone or anything get in my way. You know?"

Her mom refused to nod at this. At the same time, she had to admit to being impressed.

Jerry, though, couldn't let the moment slide without lecturing. "I'm not even going to go into that whole piece of it, lying to us. But I do want you to think about the danger you put yourself in. The first rule of hiking, especially if you're going alone, is to make sure someone knows where you are. That little trick you pulled with Courtney could have gotten you killed."

"Dad," McKenna said. "You don't think I know the danger I put myself in? I was *living* it. And believe me. I never want to go through that again. I never want to go through anything close to that again. When I say I'm sorry, I mean it. But there's a lot more to this than sorry. As far as life lessons go."

Something so deep had changed about her daughter, thought Quinn. The McKenna she'd waved good-bye to in the driveway last June had been a brave girl. The person sitting in front of her now was an accomplished woman. Someone to be listened to. Someone to be respected.

"That boy," she said. "You saved his life." There were a million more questions Quinn wanted to ask about that boy— where he'd come from, who he was. But instead of asking, she'd wait for McKenna to tell her.

McKenna nodded as she took another bite.

"I'm proud of you, honey." Quinn raised her hand to signal the waiter so she could order more garlic bread. The food here was surprisingly good. "And I can't wait to get you home."

McKenna put down her fork. She might be a new woman, but there was a familiar look rising in her eyes. The exact kind of determination and refusal to be afraid that had characterized her since toddlerhood. Quinn knew exactly what McKenna was about to say, and she tried to channel her daughter's bravery so she could absorb it and accept it, because she already knew: she didn't have any choice in the matter.

"I'm not going home," McKenna said. "I'm going back to the trail. I have to finish."

24

A few hours later, McKenna sat in the hotel's business center. Her parents had booked her a room adjoining theirs. She'd waited until they'd kissed and hugged her good night before coming down here to check months' worth of e-mail and Facebook messages. After dinner, her parents had told her the news about Buddy, and her eyes were still red from crying. She thought how empty the house must be without him. It must have been so hard for Lucy to go through, and without McKenna there, too. She understood why her parents hadn't brought Lucy along on this trip, but she longed to put her arms around her little sister.

Was there anything harder in the world than letting go of someone you loved?

Scrolling through the long row of e-mails, McKenna found an unfamiliar sender, with the subject line *Bridge Photo*. In a few seconds an image of a very different time and place filled the screen. McKenna and Sam, standing together on the footbridge that led them out of West Virginia.

Her eyes naturally fell on Sam, his face and smile. The light was perfect, clear and bright, without shadows. McKenna could already imagine the picture, framed in her room at home, a place where she'd always have it to look at.

She tore her eyes away from Sam's face and looked at her own. The freckly girl, smiling and happy. In love. McKenna was still in love as she looked at the picture now, as much as ever. If she lived to be a hundred years old, she couldn't imagine ever looking at this photo and not feeling the rising warmth, an imperative kind of leaning toward him, toward Sam. She almost wanted to say it aloud right there with the hotel clerk at his desk just ten feet away.

I love you, Sam.

But she didn't.

The tears that had gathered for Buddy had company. Sam lay in a hospital bed, thinking he had nowhere to go. But he did have somewhere to go.

After McKenna had told her parents she wasn't coming home yet (it had astonished her that they'd barely protested at all), she also told them she wasn't going to Ithaca after Christmas. Because she knew someone interested in birds who would be a great help, and who could start sooner than Christmas. As long as Al Hill didn't mind working with someone on crutches.

McKenna could tell from her dad's eyes how proud he was of her for giving up this job. For everything.

Some things just don't play like you think they will. That girl in the picture, shiny and innocent and in love: McKenna had a thing or two to tell her about standing her ground and trusting her own mind. Still, she knew that girl would understand. McKenna had to finish what she'd started. And then she had to go home and wait tables again until it was time to start school next fall.

And Sam: he had to find his own way out of the woods. She could give him a head start, but that was all.

She knew what she had to do, and it would be even harder than saving them both had been.

In the morning, McKenna and her mom did some clothes shopping, and replaced her broken iPhone. Then they drove to the hospital. So far her parents hadn't asked many questions about Sam, more or less accepting her terse explanation: "A friend I met on the trail." Exactly true, yet not even close to the half of it.

"I'll wait down here," her mom said in the hospital lobby, digging her phone out of her purse and settling into a chair.

McKenna stopped outside Sam's room. She could see that he wasn't hooked up to a drip anymore. There was a tray next to him, the remains of his breakfast waiting to be taken away. An official-looking woman was sitting in the chair by his bed, showing him papers from a clipboard. McKenna watched Sam, who seemed to be only half listening. He nodded and signed in a few places the person pointed to. Despite the healthy growth across his jaw—the closest to a beard McKenna had seen him with—he looked oddly childlike sitting there, his hospital gown coming untied behind his neck, nodding obediently as the woman spoke.

After a few minutes, the woman got up, patted Sam on the shoulder, and left, brushing by McKenna as if she didn't notice her.

McKenna walked into the room. It was the first time she'd seen him conscious and awake and sitting up, since she'd left him in the hut. Her determination did not falter. But her throat went tight at the way his narrow eyes widened at the sight of her.

This, McKenna thought, is love. Two people laying eyes on each other, everything inside them widening with happiness.

"Hey," Sam said. She'd expected his voice to come out hoarse, weak, but he sounded so normal, so exactly like himself. "Mack. Am I glad to see you. They won't let me have coffee."

McKenna smiled. Then she sat on the bed next to him and he put his arms around her. She hugged him back, her face pressed against his neck, holding him tightly but carefully. After a full minute, she sat back and took his hand. There was still a piece of gauze, a round spot of blood at the center, where the drip needle had been.

"I'm not going to get you coffee," she said. "But I *am* glad to see you, all sitting up and rosy."

"Rosy," Sam said, grinning. "First time anybody's ever called me that. What happened to your eye?"

McKenna touched her eyelid. She hadn't realized the swelling was still visible. "Bug bite," she said. "It's a lot better than it was. Who was that?"

"Someone from hospital billing. I had to sign up for Medicaid. They'll pay for all this. The luxury accommodations." He waved his other hand at the room, which was actually pretty nice. Private, with a flat-screen TV and a big window, the mountains that had held them hostage just visible in the distance.

"That's great," McKenna said. It hadn't even occurred to her to wonder how Sam would pay for all this. What a sheltered life she had led, protected from the world and all its details.

"There are advantages to being dirt-poor," Sam said.

"No, there aren't," McKenna said flatly. "We both know there aren't."

Sam's smile vanished. She could tell he hadn't expected her to get serious so soon. She wondered what he *did* expect, where he thought they would go from here. She picked up the bag from REI and placed it on the bed.

"Remember I was going to tell you how sorry I am about your mom when we were in a hospital room and you had a cast on your ankle?"

Sam nodded.

"Well, I am," McKenna said. "I'm so sorry, Sam. For your loss, for your mom. For everything you had to go through. You deserved better."

"Thanks," Sam said. His voice was hard to read. His face was deadpan.

"We got you some clean clothes," she said. "Jeans, T-shirts, sweats. A new pair of sneakers. I think I got the right sizes."

He looked at the bag and blinked. McKenna remembered all the times she'd tried to buy him things on the trail and he'd refused. *Too bad,* she thought now. *You're just going to have to sit back and accept help.*

"That's okay," he said after a minute. "I mean, that's really nice, but I'm good."

"Oh, really? Are you going to leave the hospital in that gown?"

The clothes Sam had been wearing when they found him were completely wrecked—McKenna guessed the hospital staff had already tossed them, and as far as she knew, they had never recovered his pack. And his sneakers were 80 percent duct tape by now.

Sam shrugged. He reached out and touched the handle of the bag. "Thanks," he said eventually.

"You can thank my mom," McKenna said.

"Yeah? Am I going to meet her?"

"Do you want to?"

She wasn't sure why their voices sounded like they were arguing. Maybe Sam could sense it, the thing she'd planned to say.

"Hey," McKenna said. "Sam. Seriously. What are you thinking? About what you're going to do? Where you're going to go?"

"I just barely woke up," Sam said.

"Well, they're not going to let you stay here forever. The drip's gone, you're rehydrated. What did they say about how much longer you'd be here?"

"I don't know," Sam said. "Couple of days."

"What then?"

"I guess I can't go back to the trail." He gestured down toward his ankle.

"No. I guess you can't."

Sam didn't look at her. He kept his eyes on the bag of clothing, not opening it to see what she'd picked out for him. Finally he said, "What are you going to do?"

"I'm going to finish. My parents are dropping me off at the trailhead tomorrow."

Sam leaned his head back on the pillow and closed his eyes. For a second McKenna thought that tears were about to snake out between his lashes. But his eyes were dry. He put his hand, the one McKenna wasn't holding, on the top of his head, cradling the top of his skull. Wide, strong knuckles, chapped and red. She leaned forward and kissed them, then sat back.

"Sam. Listen."

In a rush, she told him about her plan, him going up to Ithaca to work for Al Hill. "He's got a place for you, an apartment over his garage. It's part of the pay. It's where I was going to stay."

Sam still didn't open his eyes. "How am I supposed to get there?" he said.

"My dad will buy your plane ticket. You can pay him back when you can. You know, out of your paycheck."

"Wow," Sam said. "You've got it all figured out."

"No," she said. And then, because this didn't sound quite honest: "It's just a suggestion. Nobody's telling you what to do. We're just trying to give you options."

He opened his eyes, impossible blue. "We," he said. "That's funny. I remember when *we* meant me and you."

She was not surprised that when she drew in a breath it felt damp and shuddery.

"Listen," Sam said. "Before you say what you're about to say, just listen. Because I need to say it, and I need to say it first."

McKenna nodded, twisting her hands together. She felt two ways. She wanted to get away, out of this room, to have the hard part be over. And she wanted to stay right here, wherever Sam was, forever.

"Thank you," Sam said. "Thank you, McKenna, for saving me. And I'm sorry. I'm sorry for almost . . ." He stopped, then collected himself. "I'm sorry I almost got us killed. You were right, and I was wrong. If I'd listened to you, we wouldn't be here. In the hospital. With you about to break up with me."

It seemed so odd, the phrase *break up*. McKenna had never heard Sam speak about them in any kind of conventional terms, like *boyfriend* or *girlfriend* or *relationship*. Certainly not *break up*.

"But that's not the point," he continued, before she could contradict him. "The *break up* part, I mean. I'm not complaining. I'm grateful. Are you listening? Grateful like I can't express."

He paused. McKenna knew him well enough to know he wanted to say *I love you, Mack*. But he didn't, because he didn't want to make this even harder on her. A burst of her own love rose up. She didn't bother fighting it.

"The main thing is," she said, "you need to take this. The

job. The loan. Okay? If you . . . if you're grateful. For me, this is how you can say thank you."

"It doesn't feel like saying thank you. It feels like taking more. Letting you do more for me, when you've already done everything."

McKenna leaned forward and put her hands on the bed next to him, clasping them as if she were praying, which, in a way, she was.

"Sam," she said. "Sometimes people need a helping hand. You know? And that's okay. The reason I can go back to the trail, the reason I'm going to college next fall . . . it's because people, my parents, have been helping me my whole life. And you haven't had that. You've survived, and become you, amazing you, even while all those hands were trying to hold you back and beat you down. So please. Take these hands we're offering you. Because you deserve them, Sam."

She watched his face, trying to figure out what he was thinking. More than she'd ever wanted anything in her life, she wanted Sam to agree to this. His face looked so stony and so pale, no answer visible there.

When he did speak, his voice sounded clear, composed, and calm.

"I don't suppose you'd want to come to Ithaca for the winter," he said. "When you finish hiking. Come and live with me."

She swallowed, sharp and prickly against her throat. "They'd never let me do that," she said. "My parents, I mean. And Al wouldn't allow it, if they said no."

Afraid she'd just given him a reason to say no to the job, she hurriedly added, "Anyway, I have to work at the restaurant. I promised my dad I'd make money to help pay him back for the hike. And then in the fall I'm going to Oregon. We're only eighteen. And you have to find a way to finish high school. Go to college yourself. You're so smart, Sam."

"What about all the *I love yous*?" Sam said, his voice flat.

"They're exactly why I'm doing this," she said. Her voice came out in such a whisper, for a moment she wasn't sure he'd heard her. But then there was a gesture, almost imperceptible, a slight movement in his jaw, as if he was thinking about nodding.

"It's not like I'm saying we'll never see each other again," McKenna said. "Because I hope we do, Sam. I can't say how much I hope we do."

He started to shake his head, but changed his mind and nodded, looking at her very carefully. Then he put his hand on top of hers, his palm easily spanning the giant fist of both her hands.

McKenna gathered a little more strength. She couldn't continue much longer. Part of her was disappointed that Sam wasn't putting up more resistance to the end of the two of them. The other part knew the reason. So she went ahead and said the last of it.

"It's too soon to plan our lives around each other right now."

Sam had been determined, from the moment McKenna walked in, to not let on how weak he still felt, how shaky. He wanted to seem like himself, the guy he'd been before he'd talked her off the trail. Before he'd almost killed them both. He wanted to seem like Captain John Smith, someone who could survive, someone who could save her, instead of someone who needed saving.

Which was kind of tough when you were sitting in a hospital bed, wearing a dress that tied in the back.

And on top of that, here she sat, handing him a new life on a silver platter. Sam wasn't sure he'd ever seen an actual silver platter. Probably at Mack's house they had drawers full of them. But he couldn't let himself think that, the sort of knee-jerk and dismissive attitude that had kept her at bay for so long. All he wanted to do at this moment was pull her closer.

And here she was, calmly telling him she had her own life to live.

Sam picked up her two hands—together they only made one tiny fist—and brought them to his mouth. He kissed them. How could her hands feel so soft after everything they'd both been through?

All he wanted to do was talk her out of it. He knew it wouldn't take much. He knew she loved him, a lot. It was all over her face. It was all over everything she'd done for him— getting him a job and a place to go. Not only saving his sorry-ass life, but working to make it a lot less sorry.

Thanks to her, he'd finally have a place to go. He wished that place could be with her. But he understood if it couldn't. At least for now.

"Hey," McKenna said. "Life is long. You know? Who knows what'll happen down the road."

"Yeah," Sam said. He laughed a little, hoping he didn't sound bitter. "We'll keep in touch. We'll be Facebook friends."

"Sam."

"Or maybe I'll be the first person with a GED to get a scholarship to Reed."

"Wouldn't surprise me a bit," McKenna said. "And I would love that."

"Oregon. Plenty of hiking trails for us to wander off of."

"Or stay on."

"Right," Sam said. "Next time we'll stay on together."

After all his fantasies about taking care of her, rescuing her, she was the one who'd rescued him. So if the thing he had to do to pay her back was let her go, he could handle that. This was no time to be weak. Wasn't that what he'd always wanted, to know that she would walk away from him if she needed to? Because he loved her. Someone, somewhere, must have done something right. Because Sam knew what he had to do for someone he loved.

"Thank you, Mack," he said.

"You're welcome, Sam."

And then they kissed, their bodies not touching, the most concerted effort to keep that good-bye to nothing but lips. Only after the kiss did McKenna run her hand over his head, brushing the hair off his forehead. Sam wondered if any other face in his life would ever be as beautiful or as important.

"I love you," she said.

"I love you, too."

And still he let her walk out the door.

He waited until her light footsteps had retreated down the hallway, the gentle swing of the outer doors opening and then closing. And then he did what he hadn't done in a million years, not since his mother had died: he cried.

It felt good. It felt purging and healing and very honest. Like these tears had been coming for years, forever, for a lifetime. And now the one thing painful enough to break them loose had finally happened. One more thing he'd have to thank McKenna for if ever he had the chance to see her again.

25

On a clear, crisp day in the Smoky Mountains, after three days of showers and regular meals, McKenna returned to the Appalachian Trail. It was the first day of November, and she had her phone fully charged, and protected by an outer case. Her pack was slightly heavier than it had been, stuffed with warm clothes and a healthy supply of food. Her parents drove her in their rental car to the trailhead, and hugged her good-bye. They didn't say anything admonishing like, *Be safe*, or, *Use your head*. They just said, "Good-bye," and, "Have fun," and, "We'll see you in a few weeks—but you'll text tonight. Right?"

"Right," McKenna promised.

She headed onto the trail without turning around to see if they stood watching her go. She just walked. One foot in front of the other. The mountains stood silent in the distance. Not cruel or uncaring. Just there.

She walked past the spot where she had seen Walden. Just over there were the two trees where Sam and then she had crashed off the trail. All these days later there was nothing re-markable to mark the spot; fallen leaves covered any footprints they might have left, and there were no broken branches. Mc-Kenna didn't stop to contemplate. She just walked straight past, noting the white blaze on the birch tree just four steps beyond.

She walked. Feeling so much stronger than that day not so long ago when she had tried to scale Katahdin. And at the same time knowing that she was drawing from the same well of strength she'd had then, deep inside her, and that the well would flourish always, as long as she was smart enough to listen to the inner voice of reason that came with it.

She was lucky.

Dangling from the front of her pack were her whistle and pepper spray. Also the good brass compass, which Walden had taught her how to use. From now on at any given moment, she would know what direction she was headed in, no battery charge or cell tower necessary.

Fifteen miles, an excellent pace, especially for the first day back. McKenna felt the usual euphoric relief at slipping off her pack. She set up her tent, then pulled on her new fleece sweats and old wool cap, her old fleece jacket. She had a down jacket, too, in case it got bitterly cold over the next weeks. But for now, even with the setting sun and altitude, she was fine without it.

While the water on her stove boiled, she unpacked a bag of freeze-dried pad thai and some baby carrots. Before she ripped into either, she took out her phone and texted her parents, telling them she was okay, and how many miles she'd walked, and where she was camping. She'd promised to do so every night. Fair was fair.

Tomorrow they'd be driving Sam to the airport. *Take good care of Sam,* she typed, though she knew they would. The thought of Sam with her parents raised a little lump in her throat, and also a few tears.

There wasn't much time, though, to cry. Because just then there was a rustle in the woods, and a panting burst of fur, and who should be standing in front of her, wagging and drooling, but Hank. McKenna threw her arms around him.

"Hank!" she said. "Thank you. Thank you for saving our lives."

He wagged his tail some more and licked her face, then sat beside her to share her carrots.

The water boiled. McKenna dumped in the dried noodles. The sun had set and McKenna shivered a little, scooting closer to Hank.

"Listen up," she said. "You're going to sleep in my tent tonight. Got it? And you're not going to run off."

Hank thumped his tail, happy at the sound of her voice, and at his portion of pad thai, a full half, served in his own bowl.

It was good to be alone. And at the same time, it was nice to have company. In the tent Hank settled in at her feet. McKenna hunkered down in her sleeping bag, condensation from her breath already gathering on the red ceiling above. Her shoulders ached. Her legs ached. Her body ached. Everything within her was gathering itself up, settling in to rest so she could wake in the morning and start all over again.

There was no question. By this time McKenna knew without a doubt: she would be the one in four who started out on a thru hike and actually made it.

Hank slept in McKenna's tent every night. He walked beside her all the way to Georgia, right up to the very last mile marker on the Appalachian Trail. McKenna had to hike up Springer Mountain to reach it, and there at the top she signed the first trail registry of her journey, at the southern terminus.

"I made it," McKenna wrote as she spoke the words aloud to Hank. "I hiked every single mile of the Appalachian Trail."

In the registry, she added the date she'd started, and then checked her phone for the date she'd ended. Then she walked back down the mountain. Hank followed. He was even there when she came back from getting the very last stamp in her passport book at the Hiker Hostel in Dahlonega, sitting patiently like a dog who was not only tame, but trained.

"I made it, Hank," she said again. "Can you believe it?"

She'd already texted her parents and told them she'd be renting a car instead of using her plane ticket to come home. Which still meant getting to the car rental place. Somewhere along the way she'd have to find a vet where she could get Hank his shots. She'd have to get both of them a cheeseburger—she was starving—not to mention a hot shower (or in Hank's case, a bath). And probably she should buy a leash and a collar. They were back in civilization now.

But before all that: McKenna sat down on the ground and put her arm around the dog. Her parents would be so happy to get the news that her hike was over. She had done it, she had arrived safely, and she was stronger than she'd ever been in her life.

The adrenaline she felt at the thought of it all was nearly enough to make her shoulder her pack back on and head to the trail to walk—all the way back to Maine.

But for now, the walking was done. She'd been strong enough to succeed, to live. She was an official thru hiker. Now she just needed to find out if she was strong enough to survive and thrive out in the real world.

"I'm pretty sure I am, Hank," McKenna said.

The dog cocked his head. And McKenna heard a voice in her own head, clear as anything she'd heard in her life. A wry voice, full of good humor, a dose of bravado, and—most notably—love. *You know you are, Mack,* it said.

McKenna pushed herself to her weary feet, picked up her pack, and headed off to face the rest of her life.

AUTHOR'S NOTE

McKenna's route on the Appalachian Trail is fictional. If this book has inspired you to hike any portion of the AT, please use an official guidebook such as *The Appalachian Trail Thru-Hiker's Companion* by Robert Sylvester, or *The A.T. Guide* (Northbound or Southbound) by David "Awol" Miller. Further information about planning your hike can be found at the Appalachian Trail Conservancy website, www.appalachiantrail.org.

Wishing you safe and happy travels!

ACKNOWLEDGMENTS

Thanks to Peter Steinberg for arranging this opportunity. Working with Pete Harris and Claire Abramowitz was more fun than anyone should be allowed to have, and I am so grateful that they trusted me with this story. Thank you, Shauna Rossano, for your grace and patience, you are the smartest and loveliest of editors. And thanks to Jen Besser, Chandra Wohleber, and everyone at Penguin Young Readers Group.